W9-BGB-234

TRESPASS

TRESPASS

PHILLIP FINCH

Franklin Watts 1987  *New York / Toronto*

Library of Congress Cataloging-in-Publication Data

Finch, Phillip.
Trespass.

I. Title.
PS3556.I456T74   1987   813'.54   87-10683
ISBN 0-531-15044-5

To Jane Kelso
Who needed no map

TRESPASS

PART I
DEPARTURES

1

For almost eight months the notebook lay in a kitchen drawer, in among some screwdrivers and pliers, rubber bands, a leaking tube of Krazy Glue, and several Christmas tree bulbs of questionable integrity. Inglorious repose for so potent a talisman.

It is a spiral-bound pad, roughly three inches by five, about a hundred pages thick. Fifty-nine cents at any drug store. In penciled block letters on the front cover: GROUP JOURNAL. I don't know who wrote the words. Charles, maybe. Or Hollenbeck; it is exactly the dutiful, compulsive sort of gesture which Hollenbeck would have performed.

The first time I saw the notebook its covers were fresh and unmarked, the pages blank. There were nine of us then, most of us strangers to the others. We had met a couple of hours earlier, at the airport in Billings, Montana. Now we were near Red Lodge, in a meadow that was a front lawn to the fortress of the mountains. We were slightly bewildered, dazzled by the uncompromised color and light and air. Gary Currey walked up and handed the notebook to me, and said, On these trips we keep an informal log—everybody takes turns.

He wanted me to make the first entry that night, then give it to someone else the next morning. Write what happens, he said, Whatever seems important. He said, After it's all over we photocopy it in Billings, everybody gets one. Makes a nice keepsake.

I did what he asked, and passed it on, and it came around to me again. At the end it was in the back pocket of my wool pants, and I found it several weeks later when I was unpacking. No way could I open it then. Touching it was all I could manage, and then just long enough to take it into the kitchen. I shoved it quickly into the drawer and interred it with the junk.

Yesterday afternoon I went rummaging for a few loose nails and it was there. I looked down on it, the wire spirals mashed, the cover turning up at the corners, edges water-stained. I thought of where it had been, what had happened around it. Like the black lump of a meteor that somehow has survived a journey across unimaginable space and time to be turned up one spring by a farmer's plow.

I lifted it out of the drawer with the respect due such a relic. Outside there was plenty of commotion and warm sunlight. This was important. Fifty years from now, I will still need warmth and light and life around me before I open the journal.

On my front porch is an old swing. I took the notebook there. For a while I only held it. Around me kids kicked a soccer ball in the street, dogs yapped, leaves scraped as wind ruffled the trees. The noise and the movement, the profusion of life, gave me courage to open the book. I went to the last entry, in what I knew was my own hand, though distorted by fear and fatigue.

Day Ten
Monday, September 15
We didn't come into these mountains expecting death. Blistered feet, yes, and aching backs. We expected to hurt, no more. But here we are. One dead. At least one more close to dying. Amend that: we are all close.

We don't seem shocked at what has happened. These are the mountains, and we have learned fast that here you are always close to something awful or magnificent. On the brink in every way. There is no place like a mountain for getting down to essentials, for handing you the consequences of your own mistakes.

I tell this to Ellie, who says, Don't fart around, put it this way: you can't bullshit a mountain.

My fingers clench the nub of a pencil. When I'm finished I'll have to pry them straight. It is so cold. Outside the wind bucks and whines. It yanks up a flap of the tarp, knifing through with a swirl of snow crystals. I reach to shelter the guttering candle and Ellie grabs the plastic and pulls it tight. The flame wobbles, ripples, then rights itself.

Can't dwell on how high the snow must be outside, how deep we will stand in it tomorrow. If we can stand at all tomorrow. Can't think of the endless miles, the tall rock walls. Makes us seem too inconsequential, the fires inside us even dimmer and feebler than they are.

Have to keep those fires going. Convincing ourselves that we deserve to live. Or am I the only one with that problem?

Instead I think of places where at this moment people are standing on sidewalks. Eating dinner. Screwing beneath clean sheets. People who have no idea of cold dark hell in the mountains and three dying humans pressing together, balled up like baby mice in a nest.

The candle is down to a frozen puddle of wax, near the end of the wick. Last one. The flame lurches and spits. I give it two minutes.

Ellie watches it and says, I'll see you in the morning, Ray. As if trying to convince us both.

The flame leaps and writhes.

We are so cold.

We are so scared.

We are so alone.

Forgive the histrionics. Maybe a hero faces his demise with equanimity. We were just ordinary souls in deep trouble, unaccustomed to having death so near, quailing in its presence.

There was Hollenbeck and Travis and me, and Poague,

and Charles and Donnie, and Eleanor, and Gary and Andrea. Somewhere among us was the truth of what happened in the mountains. I'm trying hard to get at it. I was there for much of it, so I can say what I saw, what I felt: but that's just my truth, after all. I've talked to the others who are left, heard what they have to say. That's their truth, or what they choose to reveal of it. Some of it died with the dead, and I must deduce from their acts what they thought and felt.

In the end we're left with speculation. But isn't that the way so often? Motives and intentions are always obscure, and we must divine reality from enigmatic words and gestures. Playing tennis in foggy darkness, reacting to sounds and the occasional swirl of mist across the net, a hopeless guessing game.

This much I know. In the mountains there was only one truth, and it was clear. It allowed no doubt. Mountain truth sliced clean to the heart, and if I were a braver man I would go up there again for another chance to see the world and people the way they really are.

2

I say that we were ordinary. But then I remember Paul Travis. You don't mill his sort with a punch press. He had been handcrafted, a one-of-a-kind item.

Obviously Travis started with rare raw material, killer good looks so extravagant he had to be a freakish mutation. He had straight sandy hair that fell across his face, a slab of a stomach, wide strong shoulders with back and legs following in proportion.

But looking special is only a start. Travis must have grown up believing that he was special. He must have remained convinced of it despite all of life's attempts to kick him in the shins. Which life does to everybody: takes its cuts, tries to whittle you down. Any one of a thousand possible stumbles would have turned Travis ordinary, but he had avoided them all. He was a golden genetic mistake compounded by a million-to-one long shot.

The man defied tarnish. Travis's existence could have been a TV beer ad, shot in that buttery glow and unreal crystallization of image. Travis the athlete, eyes intent with competition, a drop of sweat poised picaresquely in the cleft of his jaw. Travis the professional, sleeves of his pinpoint Oxford neatly rolled up, gesturing to make a point to his colleagues. Travis the adventurer, snap-rolling his Pitts biplane in a coppery evening sky. Travis the lover, slow-dancing in the darkness with a woman who wears pearls and a black sheath the way others wear corduroy.

Travis really did these things, really did turn life into just such a collection of stylized set pieces. Travis, charmed and charming. Confident and sure. Convincing. A guy like Paul Travis could move plenty of beer.

––––––

First Hollenbeck and I were pals. We were in the same office, working for a company called Modern Data Concepts. Which is to say that we were working for Jonas Poague. Then Travis joined the firm and for some reason sought out Hollenbeck and me. He was impossible to resist. I became his friend, but we rarely tested the friendship with needs or demands. He seemed to want little from me beyond affable companionship. From him I expected nothing except the thrill of the exotic.

MDC occupies two floors of a twenty-story office building in Bethesda, Maryland, a suburb of Washington, D.C. Bethesda used to be a crossroads village until a boom in office construction during the early 1980s left it with snarled rush hours and a toothed skyline of glass and concrete and steel. Many of the new buildings' tenants, including MDC, are consulting firms whose primary client is the U.S. government; MDC designs computer systems to manage the information that is both the nourishment and the effluent of the governmental hydra.

Travis, Hollenbeck, and I were systems analysts, a job far less impressive than it sounds. We did not engineer computers, or write programs. We knew as much about computer hardware as the average car salesman knows about cars. Which is damn little. But he knows how to write a bill of sale, and how to stack the options. That is what we did, on a slightly elevated level. Computer systems analysts are to the electronic workplace what an interior decorator is to the home. They make decisions for people with more money than good sense.

I mention all this so you'll know that the job demands little in the way of knowledge or carefully acquired skill. Most of it is talk and persuasion.

There were twelve systems analysts at MDC. We occupied identical cubicles, each a hundred and thirty feet square, formed by partitions about five feet high. One morning in late June, Poague's secretary came out of the front office suite, down the aisle outside our cubicles, and stopped momentarily at three of them in turn. Travis's, Hollenbeck's, mine. At each she left a typed memo: "My office. 11:50 today," signed JP in bold slashes of black ink.

Clipped to the memo was a foldout brochure. It was the first I ever heard of the Beartooth Mountains.

———

SpiriTrek Wilderness Enterprises
Montana Mountaineering Adventure

GENERAL INFORMATION

SpiriTrek Adventures are a unique form of outdoor education, intended primarily for the novice. They are designed to promote leadership, confidence, and self-reliance. Knowledgeable counselors teach the skills necessary to survive and master the unfamiliar wilderness environment.

SpiriTrek Adventures aren't easy! Rather, they safely provide a distilled challenge that is frequently missing from modern daily life, a challenge that is as much mental and psychological as it is physical. A SpiriTrek Adventure may be among the most memorable events of your entire life.

COURSE SPECIFICS

SpiriTrek's Montana Mountaineering Adventure consists of a fourteen-day backpacking expedition through the Beartooth

Primitive Area in the southcentral part of the state, near Yellowstone National Park. The terrain is steep and uncompromising, varying from lodgepole forests at elevations around six thousand feet to a high plateau well above timberline, at an altitude of more than ten thousand feet. Boulder fields, glaciers, and soaring peaks are predominant features at the higher elevations.

This is a mobile course, with a different bivouac site each night. The counselors, veteran mountaineers, will teach such necessary skills as wilderness navigation, campcraft, and basic survival techniques. Activities will include a full day of rock climbing on one of the sheer granite faces common in the area, as well as an attempted ascent of one of the numerous massive peaks that reach above twelve thousand feet. Total distance covered is ninety to one hundred miles.

WHAT YOU NEED

SpiriTrek will furnish backpacks, rain gear, sleeping bags, other mountaineering equipment, and food. Clients are expected to provide all items of clothing. Severe weather is commonplace in the Beartooths, and clients must prepare to dress for all seasons. A full list of required clothing has been compiled by experienced experts, and must be followed closely. A good-fitting pair of mountain boots is essential. They should be broken in by daily wear for at least three weeks before departure.

Perhaps the most important commodities on any SpiriTrek wilderness experience are perseverance and a sense of teamwork. The members in your group of six to eight will be your constant companions for two weeks. A satisfying conclusion to the trip depends on your willingness to work with others and to extend yourself to your limits—limits that will expand every day.

Important note: The use of tobacco, alcohol, or drugs of any kind (except by prescription) is strictly prohibited.

Required clothing and equipment to be supplied by client:
1 pair mountain boots
2 pair heavy wool socks
2 pair inner socks or sock liners
1 heavy wool sweater
1 wool shirt-jacket or synthetic pile jacket
1 set of polypropylene thermal underwear
1 pair heavy wool gloves
1 wool hat
1 cotton turtleneck shirt
1 pair heavy wool pants
1 pocketknife
1 small flashlight
sunscreen
lip balm
toilet articles, personal items

Thank you for choosing this SpiriTrek Adventure.

———

A year earlier Poague had taken this trip. Apparently he was going again, and he was asking the three of us to join him. Not once did I think it was a casual invitation. Nor did Travis or Hollenbeck, I'm sure. Everything Poague did was heavily freighted with significance for us.

You should know that most of us who worked for him feared Jonas Poague. He was a difficult boss who fired people suddenly, and rarely for apparent reason. This alone would not have been so frightening. But Poague paid us generously, better than we could have expected elsewhere, better than most of us deserved. Inevitably we grew to need those bloated paychecks, or thought we did, and we feared Poague the way a junkie fears his pusher. I was certain that he knew it, too, that he understood what a hold over us his largesse afforded him. Exquisite despotism, to terrorize with generosity. I believed him capable of it.

He was in his late sixties, lean and ascetic. His stern face—

gray brush-cut hair, rimless glasses, taut skin—rebuked waste and excess. He daily wore a navy blue blazer, charcoal slacks, white shirt with bow tie. Tall and erect, he stalked the aisles at MDC, peering over shoulders, walking into conversations, intercepting memos. He was full of pointed questions that were always direct, verging on rude.

It was his place, after all. He imprinted himself on it. He detested Styrofoam cups; therefore each new employee was issued a ceramic coffee mug. His passion was classical music; hence Mozart and Mendelssohn and Chopin softly overlaid the chiming of telephones, the ticking of keyboards in the firm's offices.

Poague did have his ways, and in a more endearing man such deviance would have been amusing. But in Jonas Poague it seemed evidence of some perverse instability, an intemperate exercise of power, all the more reason to distrust him and to despise as crude bait the inflated figures that appeared on our weekly checks.

Of course we cashed them anyway.

Poague had a thing about the wilderness. During my five years with the company he had gone trekking in the Himalayas, rafting through Canyonlands Park in Utah, backpacking along the Brooks Range in Alaska, cross-country skiing in Yosemite. He would return from these outings even slimmer than normal, his gaunt face ruddy.

Supposedly he had once chosen a company comptroller on one such expedition. According to legend, he invited the three most outstanding candidates to join him on a trip to Minnesota. This was in January, and the trip consisted of two weeks of dogsledding—Poague and three CPAs mushing through the Great North Woods at forty below.

The survivor of this alleged trial had left the firm by the time I was hired. But the story persisted, and we had heard it many times, Travis and Hollenbeck and I.

The only clock in the office was a time code generated by the company's central computer. There were dozens of terminals in the place, each with a line to the main unit. They showed time of day at a keystroke. I kept the display on the screen all that June morning, and at 11:49:30 I rose from my chair and put on my suit coat.

Hollenbeck was already making his way up the aisle. Some fat men are said to move with an inborn dignity and grace. But it was not true of Hollenbeck. He walked as if slogging through ankle-deep mud, the muck grasping his feet before reluctantly letting go. Only it was not mud but his own mass that resisted movement.

A few seconds later Travis left his cubicle. We met in front of the walnut double doors that separated Poague from his hirelings. We went in, and his secretary immediately showed us through to his office.

A topographic map was spread across his desk, and Poague stood over it, leaning forward, his arms bracing him. I had never seen a topo before. This one showed no towns or roads, only blue pools and green blotches on a field of white. There were elevation figures and names of mountains and lakes. The most obvious feature was an indecipherable tangle of thin lines covering the paper, patterned like the combs and waves and whorls of a fingerprint.

"Gentlemen," he said without glancing up. "The Beartooth Mountains." He often spoke more loudly than necessary, with measured pauses and orotund pronunciation; the banal proclaimed in stentorian voice. "It is a truly magnificent place. As you may know, I was there last summer on an expedition. It was a most fulfilling fourteen days. I am returning again in September, and I want you to join me."

We murmured yes, of course, be honored, but Poague wasn't listening; he knew what our answer must be. He hadn't even asked a question.

"There are those who seek out the mountains for their grandeur," he said after a few moments. His right hand moved slowly across the map, almost caressed it. "Others are attracted to their stunning physical beauty, or to the peace of a high and lonely place that is marred by few human footprints. I appreciate all these aspects of great mountains. However, I find myself returning to them not for any of these reasons, but because mountains show us so much."

For the first time he looked up at us. I saw his pinched eyes, his narrow lips, the skin molded to his cheeks and jaw as if it had dried there in the sun.

"If you want to find out about someone," he said, "one day among the mountains is worth a year any place else."

His look passed over Travis, lingered for a moment on me, then settled on Hollenbeck.

"I urge you to prepare yourselves mentally and physically," he said. "You will be challenged and exhausted in any event. But much benefit will be lost if the activities of each day drain you totally."

His eyes dropped and he began speaking to the map again, more in the same vein about tests of character and the inner man. This was a typical meeting with Poague, respectful silence in the tabernacle while the Lord boomed cryptic inanities.

Finally I caught a drop in his voice, and I knew we were about to be dismissed.

"All expenses will be the company's," he said. "Buy what you need of clothing. It should be the best. Then submit the bills."

We filed out, and walked into the aisle without a word. It was starting already, this business of deciphering what Poague had said, reading portents in it, each of us wondering what it might mean to himself, individually.

Hollenbeck spoke first, when we reached his cubicle.

"I'm not sure I can take two weeks straight with that man," he said. A safe sentiment.

"The jackpot," Travis said. "How did we get so lucky?"

"Be grateful we didn't win second prize," I said. An old joke—they didn't catch it. "Second prize is four weeks with Poague."

The question of what the trip might mean, what Poague had in mind, never came up among us. The implications were too large.

For a few days I tried not to think about it. Then I heard the rumor; at MDC a good one was always current. For this I blamed Poague's refusal to confide or confirm. Having been denied even a glimpse of the machinery that shaped our future, we shamelessly indulged in malignant hypothesis.

The rumor was that in the fall, Poague was going to create a director of systems analysis, promoting from within. It was a job that Poague had always held, in fact if not in formal title. Systems analysis was MDC's main service. The manager of that department—our department—would instantly become the second most powerful figure in the firm. And Poague was near seventy.

This was bombshell stuff. We were no cretins, Travis and Hollenbeck and I. We concluded immediately that Poague was bringing us to Montana so he could choose his new director from among us. Though we never discussed it, I'm certain that the others heard the rumor, and that they performed the same pirouette of Poague-logic that I did. It made sense, if you knew the man. It was how he did things.

I should add at once that I never considered myself a good choice for the position. As an analyst, I was only mediocre: it was always an empty task to me, and I could not spur myself to care about it. What qualified me to manage a job done by others if I did not first excel at the job myself? On past performance, Travis would have been the runaway pick. Nobody was better. At lunch with contracting officers, stroking nervous middle-level managers, speaking in arcane acronyms at the Pentagon, he was magnificent. Untouchable.

But we were not dealing here with objective standards. I was perfectly willing to accept that in some chance remark or offhand act of mine, Poague had detected latent virtue that all others had overlooked, and now was ready to bestow on me the mantle of future greatness.

This new position was the kind of opportunity that could make a life. If it came down to the three of us in the mountains, a crapshoot for his affections, I figured I had as good a roll as anyone.

———

My father would have been appalled to learn that it had come to this: that my prospects for even modest standing among men of substance finally had been reduced to piquing the whimsy of a Jonas Poague.

We are the Furlows of Prince George County, Virginia. The family home is a former plantation house that overlooks a rose garden and the James River, at a point above Williamsburg where the water slows and broadens into an estuary. Old men in short sleeves still tip their hats from storefronts when my mother or my aunts pass by. For decades we have subscribed the two front pews in a redbrick Episcopal church with white pillars. At the age of six I was trundled off to a military boarding school in Greenville, South Carolina, where I lived the greater part of the next twelve years.

Let us trace briefly the professional history of the family's recent male offspring. Harry Furlow was a pharmacist at the beginning of this century. Of Harry's three sons, the only one who survived World War One and the killing flu of 1917 was my grandfather, Thomas Furlow, a G.P. who tended the rural folk of the Tidewater until he died at eighty-two. His only son among four children, my father, Raymond, became a cardiac surgeon with practices in Richmond and Washington, and regular appearances in all the right journals.

Of the latest generation I am the sole son; to maintain such a spectacular trajectory through the healing arts, I probably must discover a cure for cancer. It ain't about to happen.

The summer of the trip to Montana I turned thirty-eight. With bonuses, my salary that year was sixty-three thousand. I have been married and divorced once. I own a home and a mortgage, and drive a leased Thunderbird. My tangible assets include an Individual Retirement Account vested to about $13,000, and a hundred shares each of Coca-Cola, GM, and Xerox. My father would have scorned all this. Not because it was insufficient unto itself, but because it was insufficient for his son.

Whether I ever could have pleased him is a moot question, in that I seldom met even my own goals, far more modest.

At the military academy I was a resolutely lackluster scholar, soldier, and citizen. So paltry were my attainments that I ought to have been barred from the University of Virginia, a destination to which I had been ordained from birth; but the gravity of three generations of Furlow forebears, all alumni, pulled me through the thicket of the admissions board and into a pre-med curriculum.

I skated through the first three years. Fourth year, the ice broke under me. I left with my degree, and a set of marks too poor for even the most indulgent medical school. At that time I blamed my failure on beer, killer weed, and a waitress in Madison County whose enthusiasm for the carnal exceeded even my own. Now I wonder.

To my father it was a disgrace beyond redemption. He stopped hoping but he did not stop being disappointed. I could chant for you a litany of minor personal scandals, small humiliations, bad jobs badly done. It would require several paragraphs and I probably wouldn't skip more than two or three of the highlights. My father heard the list for fifteen years, every item; I always brought my defeats home with me. I was the bird dog of champion stock who bolts from pheasants to chase mice and chipmunks, returning finally to lay bloody bits of vermin at the boots of his master.

Gentleman that he was, my father took his hurts quietly. He had a proud high forehead, and the only way I knew that I had pricked him badly was a tightening around the corners of his eyes, extending across his brow. I wish I knew why I bludgeoned him with the truth this way. A perverse urge to lay waste his hopes, perhaps, my defense of last resort against his demands.

Three years ago, a few weeks short of sixty, he died: a cerebral hemorrhage just a couple of centimeters behind the rigid furrows of that forehead. I remember enough of physiology to know that the location was only a coincidence. But still.

The morning we buried him I woke and dressed and went to the church feeling some undefined expectancy. It distracted me at the funeral: later one of my sisters told me how she had admired my strength under distress. At the cemetery my sense of forthcoming was so strong that I can remember little but waiting; as if lightning had rent the sky and I was holding my breath until the thunderclap.

It was a drenched October day. Rain dripped off the eaves of the open-walled canvas tent. The minister said his words, and two of the undertaker's men cranked the casket down into the hole, and it was over. I kept an arm around my mother as we walked out to the limousine, around puddles, over slippery grass that yielded spongily underfoot. We got into the limousine and it carried us through the cemetery, through the gates, onto the highway outside. I realized what I had been waiting for, and knew that it was never going to happen. Realized that nothing was changed, nothing would. He was still in me, damn him. He was going to be in me forever.

This spring I bought a copy of the topo map that Poague had spread before him in his office. The label read: Alpine quadrangle, Montana-Wyoming, U.S. Geological Survey fifteen-minute series. Took it home and unrolled it and studied its kinked and swirling countour lines. Tried to identify the eminences that had awed and punished us. And thought, God, the suffering—that ought to be here somewhere.

3

MDC had a corporate member-
ship at a health and racquet club three blocks from the office.
The club is full of ferns and blond wood and mauve carpets,
but a serious sweat is possible if you're dedicated. Piggybacking
on the corporate account cost us about half of a normal
membership, so Hollenbeck and Travis and I all joined.

At least once a week we played cutthroat racquetball, a
vicious game. It bears a short explanation. There are three
players, all competing against each other, and only one winner;
thus, cooperation is fleeting and tenuous. About the only
strategy is to hit it to the weaker opponent as often as possible.
Good players can do this, pick their spots, so vulnerabilities get
exposed and exploited quickly.

The court gets small when three men are running and
swinging on it, smashing ninety-mile-per-hour returns. We
raised plenty of welts and bruises. I always knew that the game
is wicked sport. Recently I have realized that it is also
industrial-quality metaphor, if that's your taste.

Travis usually won our games, and he always looked good,
even in the rare close defeat. He had a way of creating open

space through which he moved in a shuffling glide, balanced, snapping off hard shots that skimmed above the floor, He was good enough to pick on the weaker player, but so much more skilled than both Hollenbeck and me that it didn't matter.

Between the two of us, I was better than Hollenbeck. I got to more shots because I was quicker and more willing to skin my knees. But in cutthroat racquetball, as in much else, there is very little point in second place.

————

Life is tough on fat boys. No, I take that back. Life doesn't give a damn one way or the other. We the people are tough on fat boys. It starts when they're barely old enough to walk, never quite as steady as the rest of us at that age. By the time we're in kindergarten we have all learned that the fat kid can be pushed off his feet, that if we steal his candy or crayons we can forever stay a few steps ahead of his waddling pursuit.

And it shouldn't be true, but usually is, that out of a dozen or fifty or a hundred boys, the fat boy is the one whose eyes are most likely to well up under provocation. That's all we need to see, tears on chubby trembling cheeks. That's blood in the water for us circling sharks.

I've never seen the family album, but I would bet a bundle that Hollenbeck was born a fat boy, grew up that way, and never changed.

He was five-eight, and that June he was at least forty pounds overweight. I had seen him heavier.

That summer I figured I would make some advance payments on the inevitable debt of physical misery that would come due in Montana. I tried to plod four miles a day on the indoor jogging track, twenty laps to the mile, eighty enormously boring circuits of which the greatest challenge was keeping count. In the infield of the track was an array of exercise machines, and often as I tramped around the banked turns Hollenbeck would be there, wracking himself on the stationary bicycle or a rowing machine, his chest heaving under a soggy gray sweat suit.

He was worried about the trip. Worried about making

himself look like a fool, about feeling Poague's scorn, about being slower and weaker than anyone else. I could guess all these, and he surely had plenty more worries besides. The worries made him work hard, but not until the last few days did they make him stop eating. I don't think he lost an ounce before September.

Two weeks before we left, I went to dinner at his house. We did this about once a month. Hollenbeck and his wife fed me, and I rented a movie for the VCR.

George and Anne Marie owned a split-level in a new development north of Bethesda, outside the city of Rockville. It was a place neither humble nor arrogant, populated mainly by couples in their thirties and forties. Among them no big winners, but no deadbeats either. Plenty of respectable Chevys and Toyotas in the driveways. The neighborhood was as irreproachable and free of hubris as a wool overcoat.

Anne Marie brought out pizza and beer, and we ate in the furnished basement downstairs while we watched the movie. I passed on the third slice and the second bottle of St. Pauli Girl. Hollenbeck had four of each. I watched him and realized that he was hardly aware of the movie. He nestled happily in an overstuffed chair. His eyes ceased darting and his shoulders dropped to rest. The tension that he carried through the day sloughed off him as he bit through the stringy cheese and chewed and licked the sauce off his upper lip. He was a genuinely joyful glutton.

After the movie we talked about the Redskins for a while. Anne Marie sat a few feet from Hollenbeck, bent over a square of bargello needlework. She was a small, pretty woman with black hair that she wore cut close, above the neckline. Whenever Hollenbeck was present she seemed maternally alert, watchful. Even now a sliver of her seemed to warily monitor what happened around her husband.

Hollenbeck said he had something to show me. He got up and left the room. Anne Marie watched him as he went away. She looked just a moment at me, and went back to her needlework.

He returned with a large canvas duffel and opened it on the

floor in front of us. It was full of new clothing, gear for the trip. He urged me to take it out and look at it. I dutifully fingered the fabric and examined the labels.

"What do you think?" he said.

"I don't know, George. It looks good to me. I think we've been spending Poague's money in the same overpriced outdoors store."

"Look at these."

He held out a huge pair of hiking boots, slick and dark, and tacky to the touch.

"It's snow wax," he said when I rubbed my fingers. "The guy at the store said it was good to waterproof them. You melt the wax and then smear it on. I've put on five or six coats."

The boots must have weighed nearly five pounds each, primitive instruments of torture, the leather as hard and unyielding as iron.

I told him they were heavier than the ones I had bought.

"You think they're too heavy?" He sounded anxious. "I didn't know. These cost a hundred and ninety. Poague said to buy the best."

"I'm sure they're fine."

"Have you been wearing yours to break them in?"

"When I remember. They're not bad."

"I've been wearing mine every day. I go out for a walk, eight or ten blocks at least." He looked at Anne Marie, as if he needed her to approve or affirm this statement. "They are kind of heavy. I got blisters at first but I stayed with it."

I imagined Hollenbeck, his hands sticky with wax, clopping along suburban asphalt in these fantastic gunboats. It must have made me smile.

"What's the matter?" he said.

I shook my head.

"I'm a little concerned about the hiking," he said. He leaned toward me and spoke confidentially. "You know, the altitude, these mountains. It sounds rough. I know I'm not as fit as I should be."

"You'll be all right, George."

"Tell me the truth. Do you think I'm badly out of shape?"
I shrugged.

"I've been working out—you've seen me." It was a plea. "I've been very diligent. I try to get my heart rate into the target zone at least three times a week."

He was a gentle soul. But something about him grated at me now. His earnestness, the suggestion that he would be able to hustle up any mountain if only I would sanction his regimen.

"Shit, George, I know for a fact that you haven't had your heart in the target zone at any time during this decade. In two weeks you're going to be hauling yourself and seventy pounds of pack over some of the ruggedest country in North America. You're pretty sure you're not ready for it, and you want me to tell you it's going to be okay. I can't do that."

"You really think it'll be hard?"

His face showed that he was ready for the worst. I couldn't stop myself.

"Damn right I think it'll be hard. I think our lungs will burn and our legs will feel like rubber, and our hearts will gallop so hard, it'll sound like the back stretch at Pimlico. I think we'll regret every milk shake, every Big Mac, every chocolate-covered cherry we ever let slide past our tonsils. I think it'll be the worst two weeks of our lives. If we last that long."

Anne Marie had stopped her stitches, and skewered me with a look. Hollenbeck sat heavily back in his chair. His face was drained. He looked stricken.

"A seventy-pound pack," he said.

The poor guy was such an easy mark.

"Actually, I don't know for certain that they weigh seventy pounds. That's the whole point, George. I don't know any more about this than you do."

"Damn you, Furlow. I never know when you're joking."

"Almost always."

"Tell me the truth," he said. "Could you carry a seventy-pound pack? If you had to?"

"I have no idea. But I figure I'll be able to carry any pack they give me. This expedition thing is like boot camp—it's supposed to look hard, but it's not designed to make people fail. What would be the purpose?"

"I was never in boot camp. I lucked out in the draft lottery."

"So did I, or I'd be singing 'Oh Canada' right now. What I'm trying to say is, they won't ask us to do anything we can't do. If they give us seventy-pound packs, it'll be because we can carry seventy-pound packs. Even if we don't know it yet."

He was unconvinced. His movements were slow, reluctant, as he replaced the clothes in the bag, folding them in carefully, leaving space at one end where he tucked in the boots. He zipped the bag and took it away, and I was alone with Anne Marie as she hunched over the work. The fingers of her right hand made severe jabbing and pulling motions with the needle.

"All in fun," I said to the top of her head.

She showed me her face, disgust and pity.

"You could have been more kind," she said. "You didn't have to lie—I'm not saying you did. But you could have been more kind, damn you."

Myself, I am five-nine, with legs that are slightly stubby for the rest of me. Give me a six-footer's legs and I would be six feet tall. My weight fluctuates within the limits that insurance companies deem healthy. It used to be that I was on the high side of that range, but several years ago the companies raised the limits, so now I'm certifiably fit.

Not that I was, or am, prepared to go blithely humping up mountains two-and-a-half miles high. I live the modern life, which has plenty of challenges for the ego and the psyche, but almost none for the *latissimus dorsi*. Even within the standards of the insurers, I had by the age of thirty-five developed dimples on my buttocks and the insides of my thighs, puckered goo that wouldn't go away for all the games of racquetball and turns of the track.

You may think I dwell unnecessarily, excessively, on the physical. It is not my usual focus. But as the trip got closer I found myself checking out the flab, skin tone, muscle mass of myself and others. Most of all in the locker room at the club, wondering how many of these city bodies could do what I would be asking mine to do. Envying Travis the striations of his calves and abdomen, feeling anger when I looked at Hollenbeck's corpulence.

Total distance covered is ninety to one hundred miles. Even Travis must have paused with some concern when he read that. So I was worried too, okay? Only I didn't let my worries bleed through the way Hollenbeck did. Ninety to one hundred miles. It did tend to concentrate the mind.

———

It is summer now, another simmering and stultifying Washington summer, my first since the trip. As the weather grew warmer this past June, I began to have a recurring memory of cold gray granite, sleet ticking against the stone and rapping against my poncho, crusted snow crunching where I stepped. Air so lean and chill it burns the throat. Now I think that summer will never again claim me completely.

4

Charles and Donnie, Eleanor, Andrea and Gary. This is their story too, and by now you should have met them. You should know something of who they were and what they brought with them to Montana. When I saw them first in Billings they were ciphers to me, but soon I realized that Poague was right: a few days in the mountains will teach you a lot about somebody.

I keep returning to the last morning we were strangers, the hours before our lives became forever altered. Some of it they described to me. Some I got from cues as subtle as a gesture, a drop in a voice's timbre; but no less true for that. Some I heard under circumstances so solemn, any talk was testament. This is as true, as real, as I can make it. I see no percentage in falsehood.

———

Eddie Willis woke suddenly, sat up straight in bed, and knew he had done wrong. The clock beside the bed said 6:35. His son had been at the door to wake him, but Eddie had fallen asleep again.

Today of all days, he thought.

He jumped out of bed, pulled on his pants, and went into the front room to holler up his son. But the boy was already there. Charles sat on the couch, dressed in his traveling clothes, his bony hands resting on his knees. On the floor beside his feet was a three-suiter valise.

"G'morning, Papa." Charles was sixteen years old, built painfully slight for his age. His clothes hung loose on him, gave him the appearance of a thin-limbed brown marionette.

"How long since you woke me up, boy?"

"Little over half an hour."

"You should have shook me again."

"I thought I'd let you rest."

"How much longer was you going to let me sleep?"

" 'Til about a quarter of."

His flight was at eight. The trip to the airport in Raleigh would take about forty minutes.

"Cutting it kind of close, weren't you?"

"No sir. You get ready right fast when you have to."

Eddie walked to him and gripped his shoulders.

"Can you carry that suitcase?"

"Yes sir, I better. I'm going to have to carry what's in it for the next two weeks."

"Then haul it out to the pickup while I find my clothes. We have to get our butts on the road."

Eleanor Farris shut the door on a big white house on pilings, beside a canal on an island called Duck Key, about halfway along the crescent of the Florida Keys. She had spent nearly four months there alone. This was the last day of the longest summer she had ever known.

She turned up Route One with the ocean brightening on her right, the gulf still dark to her left. The highway was two lanes from Key West through Key Largo, a strip of asphalt that skipped through scrubby islands, across sandy spits, over channels and estuaries. The mainland was more than sixty miles away. She accelerated up the empty road. She had plenty of reason to be far from Duck Key before the sun got high.

————

His parents were both out of town the night before Donnie Lang left. Mother gave motivational talks to women entrepreneurs, and that night she was in Arizona, motivating. Dad was a partner in a hot ad agency in San Francisco. He pitched accounts better than anyone else in the agency, and that night he stayed over in Seattle after a full day of pitching.

That meant Donnie and the Guatemalan maid were alone in the house above Tiburon. It was across the bay from San Francisco, high up on a high brown hill. The windows of their living room staged the city, and at night the city's lights leaked white pinholes across black water.

The maid went to bed around ten that night. She said goodnight to Donnie and went to her room. For about an hour he could see television colors shifting on her bedroom curtains; she liked the Spanish cable channel. But the curtains went dark and a few minutes later he went down to the garage that was attached to the kitchen.

His sixteenth birthday present had been a Kawasaki motorcycle, a Ninja 900, a lithe rippling panther of a bike that tried to shed him every time he twisted the throttle grip. It was in the garage. The motor for the garage door opener was loud, and he knew it might wake the maid, so Donnie somehow lifted and pulled the bike up the two steps into the kitchen. Then he pushed it across the floor, out onto the patio, past the Jacuzzi, and down the path that led out into the street.

He let it roll down the street in neutral with the engine still dead. When he was a block from the house he stabbed it into gear, dumped the clutch, and ripped away down the hill.

First thing, he met his friend Trey. This was at the parking overlook at the north end of the Golden Gate. Trey had some Black Beauties, and Donnie took two without water, one more than he needed. For his money, speed gave the finest high, and he had tried most of the others.

After the pills Donnie remembered some things very clearly

about that night, others incompletely. He recalled Sausalito, cruising the main street beside Trey's Suzuki. Spotting the black Porsche in the municipal parking lot by the harbor. Trey insisted that it was a 930 and Donnie tried to tell him, no, it was just a 911 with an accessory air dam and whaletail spoiler. Donnie knew his Porsches; he had been driving a 944 Turbo in Santa Cruz when the police pulled him over. The 944 belonged to somebody named Samuel J. Skinner in San Francisco. Donnie had never met the party, but had definitely admired the automobile when he saw it parked off Blithedale Avenue in Mill Valley. The keys still in it.

The judge went for a diversion program—no trial, no record—on the condition that Donnie enroll in a wilderness leadership course. So he was going to Montana.

Out of Sausalito they took the turnoff for the Coast Highway. Donnie remembered parts of that, flattening himself on the tank, his high beams clawing up the hills and around the turns, splashing off guard barriers and knifing out into open darkness beyond the road's edge.

At around five he rode home, put the bike away, got into the shower. He had to be at the airport by seven. Leaving because some judge had the idea that two weeks of playing Eagle Scout would stop him from wanting to drive other people's Porsches.

A cab took him away while the maid still slept. Even buzzing with the pills, he still felt a little down. It was the night. Not that he hadn't wanted to cruise Sausalito and play racer hero and do whatever else he had done. But he thought, Damn, did they have to make it so easy?

———

Two climbers, at opposite ends of one slim strand of rope, on the face of a granite stub near Red Lodge. From across the valley the rock appeared sheer and seamless, the climbers clinging to it the way dust clings to a windowpane.

Andrea Simms was at the low end of the rope, and her face was about two inches from the granite. Her feet had found horizontal ripples in the rock, wide enough to catch friction with an edge of each boot. She had jammed one hand into a vertical crack. The other groped outward, above her head. The rock was nearly eighty feet high, and they had climbed higher than the tallest of the lodgepole pines that grew at the base of the cliff.

"Left. Higher. There." A man's voice from the other end of the rope: Gary Currey. Today her climbing partner. He had suggested a morning climb before they drove to Billings. During the next two weeks they would lead the last SpiriTrek Montana Mountaineering Experience of the season.

The free left hand found a knob of stone. She tightened her fingers around it.

"Now kick up. Left foot. Uh-uh, got to get it higher. There. Now the move is to that flake overhead."

She could see it, beyond arm's reach, a protruding lip of granite. Along the lip, a dusty splotch of white where Gary's chalked hand had gripped it.

"I can't reach it," she yelled into the rock.

"Sure you can. Push off with the left foot, extend. For about a fifth of a second there you feel a little loose. Hit the hold, swing up with the right foot, catch that crack where you've got your hand."

She wasn't a climber, not really. She knew knots and she could use a rope or set a chock. But she wasn't a climber.

"It won't get any closer," he said. "No matter how long you wait."

Her left leg was tightening, and she could feel sweat on her right palm.

"Tell you what, you don't like the move, there's another you could try. You could always face east and bow to Mecca. Might help, you never know."

She pulled her right hand from the crack, dipped it into the chalk bag at her hip to dry the dampness. She inhaled fully, thought *now*, grunted, and thrust upward with the left leg.

Her free right hand reached for the flake. Fingertips grazed the edge and slid away. For an instant her boot and her hand hung free. She flailed both, pawing and scraping. The hand found a fingernail hold; it bought her a few seconds. The toe of the boot slipped into a depression no wider or deeper than a tablespoon. But it held.

One short breath; the fingernail hold wouldn't last much longer. Now she surged upward again, right foot, left, right hand on the lip, then the other.

She pulled herself up and stood on the flake. It was at least an inch wide.

"You missed the move," he said.

She turned and looked up at him. He sat on an overhang, legs dangling, perhaps five yards from the top.

"I got here," she said.

"But you missed the move."

She knew that in Yosemite, Tuolomne Meadows, his kind grew like fungus on the underside of a log. Lean and muscled, cocky, perpetually unemployed. The alpine equivalent of a surf bum. She guessed he was under twenty-five, which would make her at least six years older. She was afraid to ask.

The past winter she had guided canoe trips in the Everglades for SpiriTrek. This was her first trek in Montana. Gary had guided the trip three times this summer, and had been designated senior instructor. For two weeks he was her boss.

"You coming?"

Her breath had returned.

"Climbing," she said.

In about a minute she had joined him on the ledge. From here she could see the town, down valley about six miles.

"We better shake and bake," he said. "Got to pick up the dinks."

"They're clients."

"They'll always be dinks to me."

The night before in Red Lodge, after his fifth beer, he had told her how he felt about them. All summer he had been herding them through the Beartooths, had seen their jiggling flab, heard their bitching. Had treated their blisters, watched them puzzle over topos, eaten the tasteless meals they singed on Primus stoves. To him they were hopeless flatlanders with no more business in these mountains than a jellyfish had. Dinks, now and forever.

He turned and faced the rock, and began to climb. Feet and hands moved here, here, here, finding holds in combinations Andrea could never have imagined. In a few seconds he had both hands on the edge and was lifting himself over the fringe of grass at the top.

5

On the Thursday before we left, we had decided to drive together to the airport. Hollenbeck would pick up Travis, then me. He was supposed to be at my place by eight. Eight-fifteen, Hollenbeck still wasn't there, and I let myself wonder if he could have been that hurt and angry.

We had had an argument the night before. It involved the three of us, mainly me and Hollenbeck. Angry words, hasty judgments. Mainly my doing.

Two minutes later his Volvo wagon pulled up. He came out to open the back hatch of the wagon so that I could put my bag in.

I said, "Good morning George." Trying to make it sound casual.

He said good morning without looking at me.

I sat alone in the back seat. Travis was up front reading the *Post* financial page. Hollenbeck got in and snapped his seat belt.

"Listen, you guys," I said. "I'm sorry. I didn't mean it. I was wrong."

"No big deal." This was Travis. He said it over his shoulder, gave me an easy glance, then went back to the paper.

Hollenbeck sat and gripped the wheel with both hands, and looked out past the windshield.

"George? I'm sorry."

"For what?"

"For saying what I said last night. For what happened in the restaurant."

"You didn't say anything. Nothing happened."

He seemed to be inspecting the hood for blemishes.

"Come on, George, give me a break. I'm trying to apologize."

"Don't say anything." Now he had turned to me; I couldn't remember ever seeing such intensity in him. His voice quavered and a deep pink rose from his cheeks to his temples. "Nothing happened. You have nothing to apologize for."

Travis's eyes didn't lift from the stock quotes.

"Fine," I said. "I'm just trying to do the decent thing."

"I have plenty more to worry about than that. So don't say any more."

And I didn't. None of us did. We drove to Dulles in silence.

———

We had a flight to Chicago, a layover there, another flight direct to Billings. On both we occupied a full row of first class, four abreast. Poague had a window seat, and I was beside him, and then Travis and Hollenbeck across the aisle. This arrangement was identical for both flights, set before we got to the airport. I wondered—still do—whether Poague had asked to have me beside him.

We would be seated together for nearly five hours, more time than I had ever had at once with him. I decided to play the eager minion. I wanted that job. But Poague seemed indifferent to me during much of the trip, not unfriendly but absorbed.

That day Poague changed, or began to. In Chicago I sensed a relaxation around his eyes, the edges of his lips; I'm positive this isn't something I have created with hindsight. We took our seats and the plane taxied to the end of the runway, and in a few moments we were lifting off. I looked over at Poague. He had allowed his spine and shoulders to sink completely into the upright of the chair, the headrest to receive the back of his skull. His eyes were closed. I was shocked: for the old man this was pagan abandon.

When the 737 began a slow descent he stirred and came alive, watching the land that passed beneath the wing and canting his head sideways like a caged canary to peer at what lay ahead. Below was a sere, rolling plain. He touched my forearm and pointed down. The Little Bighorn River, he said; imagine.

A few minutes later the tawny plateau fell away to steep vermillion cliffs. Tucked against the bottom of the cliffs were a smoking refinery, a river, a rail yard, houses and offices and stores. Billings.

The plane banked over the city, and a few minutes later we were stopped at the terminal. While others in the cabin stood and reached for jackets and bags and belongings, Poague sat still, composed, seemingly unaware of all externals. Never had I seen him this way, without rigidity or raspy edge. Like someone in possession of a sublime conjuring secret.

I think about him that way and recall a moment in Chicago, when we waited for the flight to Billings. In the office he was always Mister Poague to his face. He used the title unfailingly when he addressed us; it was one formality I never resented, an appeal to my upbringing, maybe. That morning Hollenbeck spoke to the old man, and called him as he always had called him. Poague corrected him at once.

On this trip, he told us, we would be expected to use first names among ourselves and with the rest of the group. It was a way of breaking down barriers. SpiriTrek insisted on it, and he thought it was a good idea.

"For the next two weeks I am not your boss," he said. "You are not colleagues of one another. We are four men who happen to have a background together, but we are all equal among ourselves and with the others.

"What is behind us is immaterial. Up there you create yourself, and nothing else counts."

———

Charles and Eleanor had arrived a few minutes earlier on a Denver connection, and they were standing with Gary to meet us. So when we came through the jetway door there were seven of us, suddenly a group, shaking hands and making introductions.

These days I inveigh against the tyranny of first impressions. But I can try a few from that moment.

Gary intimidated. In three months of gauging bodies around D.C. I had seen none, not even Travis's, as fit as his, all athletic bone and sinew, scooped buttocks, carved calves, ridged forearms. There were introductions, and as we spoke he rolled his shoulders and arched his back, while his biceps flexed and jumped. It seemed an unconscious display of arrogant beauty, and I told myself that if I had such a body I would preen too.

Eleanor. Early thirties. Reticent eyes that flashed on me and then retreated, as if she feared lingering. I have to be careful here—there's so much I could say, so much I could claim to have seen and understood. But the truth is, I noticed a major league tan, and then I noticed her legs. Dancer's legs, long and trim and straight. I followed them up from the ankles until the curve of her thighs disappeared into loose khaki shorts. No more: the rest came later.

Charles was tucked behind her, easy to miss. As frail a child as I have seen, puberty alarmingly delayed. He would have been a scrawny twelve year old. And so grave. I am not a soft touch but I wanted to embrace that kid and protect him.

Gary said there was one more client, a boy named Donald who was supposed to have been on a flight from Salt Lake and San Francisco that had arrived half an hour earlier. Andrea, the second instructor, was trying to find him.

We claimed our luggage, and changed clothes in the men's room. Out of gabardines and loafers and buttondown collars, into hiking clothes. I had never seen Poague wearing anything but business clothes. His must have been fitted to deceive, because nothing in his tailored leanness had prepared me for the pipestem limbs and sunken stomach I saw when he emerged for the first time in shorts. He nearly caught me staring. I turned my eyes aside.

Travis finished first, seeming to hurry. I didn't realize why until I walked out and found that he had taken a chair beside Eleanor in the lobby. He was talking to her, eyes holding on her as if no other sight deserved his attention. She seemed flattered; I would have been.

There was an empty seat beside her. Travis was telling her about his stunt plane, the weekend he flew at an air show in Altoona. Her left hand was out of sight, tucked behind a flight bag at her side. I watched and waited, and finally the hand came up to sweep some hair behind her ear. Ring finger, below the last joint: a band of pink skin interrupting the wash of brown.

We waited. Four times in the next half hour I heard a page: "Donald Lang, please report to your group in front of the United ticket counter in the lobby." After a while Andrea appeared, quickly introduced herself, then stepped aside with Gary. She was slightly over five feet tall, her physique almost as formidable as his, though with at least a minimal overlay of a woman's soft contours.

They stood close together, trying to keep their voices low. I made out anxious words, sensed consternation. She had checked with a passenger agent. Somebody had used the boy's ticket and had occupied his assigned seat from San Francisco to Salt Lake, from Salt Lake to Billings. A maid at the house in California hadn't heard from him.

He appeared at that moment, dragging a leather portmanteau. A dirty white dinner jacket at least three sizes too large draped from his shoulders. Baggy black trousers brushed the floor. Red canvas sneakers, a gold wire ring in his left ear, haircut a fusion of punkish spike and waxed flattop. On his face, a look of baffled innocence.

"I'm Donnie Lang," he said. "Somebody looking for me?"

We were nine.

Gary went to the parking lot while we lugged our bags out to the front sidewalk of the terminal. He came around in a van, pulling a small covered trailer where we loaded the luggage. It all seemed random to me, the standing around, hoisting of luggage, loading into the van. But when it came my turn to get in, and I looked around for Eleanor, she was already inside; Travis beside her. Travis had contrived. I didn't believe that he was smarter than I was, only surer about what he wanted and how to get it.

Out of Billings we took an Interstate southwest. Andrea turned around in the front seat and said there were some topics she wanted to cover, this would be a good time. Before she could go further, Hollenbeck spoke.

"I was thinking about the name of these mountains where we're going," he said. "And I wondered. Are there bears in the Beartooths?"

6

"You bet there're bears. Black bears and grizzly bears. Grizzlies are nasty bastards. They're bigger than black bears, but since you won't have anything to compare your first bear with, the best way to tell them apart is by a hump that the grizzly has along the back of its shoulders. The other way to be sure is that only a black bear will chase you up a tree."

I give you this lecture the way Andrea gave it to us in the van, so you'll know that we didn't lack for warning.

"Anyway, the mountains were named by men who thought they resembled the teeth of a bear. I myself have never seen the teeth or any other part of a bear, and I do not intend to. If you were trying to see a bear this would be the best time. They forage heavily in September, fattening up before hibernation. You'd eat plenty too if you knew breakfast was six months away. They've got an excuse for being tubby."

She glanced at Hollenbeck and for the first time seemed to realize his size; she looked flustered, off balance, and I decided I liked her. Up front Gary said, "Think of it this way: they're meat-eaters and they're real hungry this time of year, all right? And they've got a real nose for food."

She said, "They do have great scenting ability, probably better than a dog. So we take precautions. That brings up ground rules.

"We're easy to get along with, but some things we don't fool around with. Below timberline, we bear-bag all our food, put it in a sack and hang it between two trees, high enough that a bear can't reach it. The best way to see a bear is to leave food around. For the same reasons, we don't allow deodorant —it seems to attract them.

"Soap is out, too. It pollutes the streams and lakes. Spiri-Trek practices what's known as low-impact camping. The idea is that after we've left a campsite, somebody could come along and never know that we've been there. It doesn't always work, but we try. So, no soap. The water's too cold for bathing, any-way. After two or three days we all smell. You get used to it.

"The main thing you have to learn is that we're not nine individuals going up in the mountains. We're a group. We do things as a group. Every night after dinner, we get together for a talk. SpiriTrek is very big on group discussions. If you've got a complaint, you don't like the way somebody combs his hair, that's the time to say it. Food always seems to be a problem. Whatever extra food you brought with you, eat it tonight. What we take up there belongs to everybody, no hoarding. We all eat out of the same pot.

"There are jobs that need to be done every day. Meals have to be cooked and pots and dishes have to be cleaned. Every day, breakfast and dinner. For lunch we grab snacks on the trail. Gary and I are not porters, we're not cooks. We'll carry our share and cook our share, but no more. You come up with some kind of system—we don't care what, as long as the work gets done.

"Same goes with the shelters. No tents. We use rain flies, plastic tarps. Gary and I have one. There are two others. You set them up, you take them down. Sleeping arrangements are whatever you want—except one thing. You four company guys, I want you to spread yourselves out. We don't need to bring any cliques up there, ready-made.

"You will all be issued personal gear, besides what you've got with you now. And then there's group equipment. The tarps, the stoves, climbing rope, a first-aid kit, pots for cooking. Most of all food. It all goes with us. Between you, you have to get it parceled out. We'll work on that tomorrow.

"What else?"

Beside her Gary said, The water.

"Oh yeah. You city people, you've probably been waiting all your life to stick your face in a stream and drink some of that icy cold mountain water. But you can't. There's this bug, a parasite called *giardia*, which is deposited in streams by humans and other vile creatures who relieve themselves too close to the water supply. And I'll tell you, this thing will kick the hell out of your intestinal tract. Runaway trots like you wouldn't believe. I mean killer stuff. Now this is the truth. I had a friend who got run over by a truck when she was riding her bicycle. She got better, in six months she's on a hiking trip in the Sierras, she drinks the water, she picks up some *giardia*. And a little later, it takes a few days to kick in, a little later she's in the hospital again. She stayed nine days the first time, when she was hit by the truck. She was in two whole weeks with the *giardia*. The bug hit her harder than the truck did.

"So you can't drink the water straight. What we do is, we give you little bottles of iodine, and medicine droppers. You put three drops of iodine in every quart of water—each water bottle is a quart—and then you wait half an hour. And you can drink it then. When you taste it you'll want to bitch, but don't bother. We've heard it plenty of times, we know it tastes awful. It's a hell of a note, you come up into these beautiful mountains, you have to put poison in your water so you can drink it. Welcome to the twentieth century. But use the iodine. You get stuck up there, shitting your insides out, you'll be in real sorry shape."

Evacuations, Gary said.

"I was about to get to that. Nobody will fly a helicopter

into the Beartooths any more. The canyons are too narrow, the winds are crazy, it's just too dangerous. Most other places, if somebody gets hurt, you can send for help and sooner or later the chopper will be there to make everything right. But not up here. If anybody can't walk here, they have to be carried out. I was carried on a rope litter once, for about a mile, and it was agony. And this was just practice, I was healthy at the time. I honestly think I'd rather die than get hauled eight or ten miles with a compound fracture. So the idea is, don't get hurt. Simple.

"Look, I'm not trying to scare you. Not much anyway. Enough to get you to pay attention and take this seriously. I want you to realize that up there we're on our own. Things can happen if you don't take care of yourself.

"That's all the rules. The rest is up to you. I've seen groups go out on a trip and be miserable for two weeks. Others have a great time. It's always hard work and problems. The question is whether you let them beat you."

———

While the van rolled Andrea passed out what appeared to be nylon straps, flat ribbons of synthetic fabric about an inch wide and twenty feet long. She called it webbing, and we each got a length.

We would use it climbing, she said. She wanted to show us a couple of knots.

"A bowline," she said. "Your basic all-purpose knot for securing something to the end of a rope, among other uses. Anyone who has sailed will know this one. When we climb you'll use it to tie yourself on the belaying rope."

She went through a routine about making a loop in the rope, calling that a rabbit hole; then the end of the rope becomes a rabbit that jumps out of the hole and runs around the tree and then jumps back in the hole.

We watched her do it a couple of times and then tried it ourselves. I fumbled with it, thinking to myself that in a few days I would be standing at the bottom of some place very steep, getting ready to climb, and there would be a rope dangling from above, and this is what I would do with it to keep myself from falling.

Travis naturally had done some sailing. I could see him with Eleanor, touching her hands oh-so-casually to guide her through it.

Andrea looked at his bowline and said it was okay, could be neater, but that's usually the way it is the first time you try it with webbing. I wanted to thump her on the back and buy her a drink.

At the edge of my vision I caught movement, quick and purposeful. Charles. His bony fingers swiftly pushed and tugged at the webbing, tying the knot and upsetting it and tying it again.

"You ought to look at this one," I said to her. Charles looked up, startled. His eyes shot from the knot to me, to Andrea, back to me with a look of betrayal.

I said, "Go on, show her."

He held it up slowly.

Andrea said, "Let me see that," and she reached for it. Poague took it from him and turned the knot over in his hands once, and handed it to her.

"You tied this off," she said.

"I thought you were supposed to." There was a thick drag in his words, piney woods Carolina. "I used a half hitch. Is that right?"

"Yes. And you tied it with a double loop."

"Just to try. I know webbing doesn't usually take a double loop bowline."

"The second one I wanted to show you is a water knot. Can you do that?"

"Yes, Ma'am, a water knot is easy."

He took the webbing from her, worked his fingers over the fabric for a moment, and the bowline dissolved. Then he found the two free ends, bent and twisted them faster than I could follow, and when he pulled with both hands he had another knot.

"If it was for tying a seat harness, you'd leave one end long so you could throw on a couple of hitches," he said.

"You've been practicing," she said.

"A little."

"You must have done some climbing."

"Oh no Ma'am."

"Then how did you learn?"

We were all looking at him. He slid back, fleeing to the corner where the seat met the side of the van. Small fists clutched the webbing. His eyes panned slowly away from her face, across our eyes.

"Books," he said. "It's all in books."

———

The mountains first appeared when we were about forty minutes out of Billings, gray and white wrinkles on the horizon. They grew, and we could see ragged tops. Then some forested corrugations and bare stubs of stone rose up suddenly behind Red Lodge, and the mountains dropped from sight.

Seven miles south of the town, we turned up a dirt road. About a mile later the dirt road ended at a meadow, cut through the middle by a stream and fringed with pines. Two great half-domes of granite embraced the meadow, and the mountains were visible in the split between them.

The van stopped at the meadow's edge and Gary said, "We camp here tonight, move out first thing in the morning."

We got out and meandered in the dazed way you would imagine wandering through an oasis. The afternoon light had a clean sharpness that I had never before seen, and the air was purer, clearer than any I had ever breathed. It was how light and air should be.

Charles was beside me, oblivious of everything but the mountains that showed through a deep corridor between rumpled green buttes. Charles's face was fastened on them as if by some tropism, in the seeking way a flower will turn toward the sun. They were an unbroken picket of distant peaks, many shades of gray at their thick lower parts, white with snow at the serrated tops and streaked white along the flanks.

"Those are the Beartooths?" I said.

"They have to be."

"Hey, blood, you figured out which way we're going?" Donnie had come up from behind us.

Charles pointed west to the citadel of peaks.

"Right up there."

Donnie drew even with him and looked where he was pointing.

"No. Come off it. Up there?"

"Look around. Cliffs over here, over here, behind us. We're not climbing those. We're not going back to town. This is the only way we can go."

Donnie turned around completely.

"You're right. You're right. Oh, man. I am deep in some funky shit now, for *sure*."

I heard Andrea tell Hollenbeck that here we were above six thousand feet, that the mountains ahead of us were over twelve thousand, and that they were about fifteen miles away. Montana miles, she said; you'll see the difference. I could almost hear Hollenbeck thinking that even a Rockville mile was bad enough.

At the near edge of the meadow a massive prow of stone rose out of the earth, jutted upward, and joined its shoulder to one of the half-dome buttes. The stone showed a checking of cracks and fissures, and I could see a wide perch perhaps fifty feet above the bottom. The way up was obvious even to me, even then: it would be a hands-and-feet scramble on an incline that was steep but not daunting. I decided to see how six thousand feet felt.

The hardest part was slogging through the pile of loose rock that had collected at the base of the butte, sharp-cornered chunks that poked at my ankles. Then I followed a deep vertical seam that was bisected every few feet by generous cracks, plenty of room for fists and boots. Mechanically, it was little more difficult than climbing an extension ladder, but by the time I pushed over the ledge I was sucking air through my teeth, gulping it in my open mouth. Six thousand feet. We would be climbing past twelve.

There was room on the ledge for me to lean back, stretch my legs. I gathered my breath and took in the view. The climb had brought me above treetop level, and I could see that the meadow stream came down from the mountains, ducking in and out of copses and narrow canyons, gleaming brightly where it gushed across open ground.

Below me Gary was shouting my name, saying Goddamn it, what are you doing up there? When I started down he yelled, Stay where you are, I'll come get you.

Later when we were on the ground he said, "Don't do that again. Can you imagine the liability suit, a client shows up and an hour later he falls off a rock?"

But now he was climbing up and I had a few seconds to look around again.

I looked at the mountains. In the meadow the trees obscured their girth, but from here I could see how broad and wide and massive they were, see how their bases spread over miles, a huge footprint of outthrusting buttresses; one ridge strained almost to the edge of our meadow before it succumbed and collapsed in a heap of slag beside the stream. They were rotogravure peaks, lambent in the afternoon sun, magical.

This is the last about beautiful mountains. I don't have it in me; once we began to climb I became mired in detail and lost all sense of majesty. My memory of mountains now is the sandy texture of a boulder that scraped the skin off my palm when I stumbled and fell. Frigid water swirling around my ankles as I forded a stream. A horn of rock digging up through my foam pad, through my sleeping bag, into my spine. A tiger too is beautiful, but you wouldn't want to meet one on the wrong side of a zoo moat, where the reality of the animal is reduced to its fetid breath and the soulless objectivity of its eyes. The deeper we got into the Beartooths, the less we saw of their sweep and the less beautiful they became.

———

In the afternoon Gary left with the van. When he came back about an hour later he had a passenger, and the van was full of food and equipment.

The man with him was named Emmett Frye. He was a packer from outside Red Lodge, Gary said. We would see him again in a week, and we'd be damn glad of it: he was going to pack in our supplies for the second half of the trip.

Frye leaned against the van, shaded his eyes with the brim of his cowboy hat, said nothing. He was near forty, and he was exactly what you would expect to find at the head of a pack train: bowed legs, squinting eyes, skin cured hard and brown.

We unloaded the van, food and equipment into separate piles under one tarp. Intimidating mounds—there was so much of it, and so few of us.

In the trailer there was more, individual gear. We lined up to take our shares. First backpacks. Gary said they were the frameless kind, with internal stays that we could adjust to fit. To me it looked like one-size-fits-all. Then sleeping bags, ponchos, climbing helmets, foam sleeping pads, rain pants, gaiters of coated nylon to keep pebbles out of our boots.

Put it all in the packs, he said, and we did.

Now everything from the suitcases that you're supposed to have, pack that too; and we did. By now my pack was nearly full, and we still hadn't touched the big piles under the tarp.

Finally Gary passed out large manila envelopes, one to each of us. A couple of pencils; Write your name on the front, he said.

"Now put in your valuables and wallets." At first no one moved.

He said, "Listen, jewelry just gets lost. There's no place up there to spend money, and bears don't ask for identification. Watches too; I keep one, that's all we need."

These things, the wallet especially and what the wallet carries, are as much a part of our existence as shoes. And I believe that was the point; we would shuck off what we were, or believed ourselves to be, and find out what lay beneath. You start by relinquishing the plastic you carry at your hip or in your purse. I was queasy as I emptied my pockets into the envelope. The others seemed just as reluctant. I sealed the flap and passed the envelope to him, and felt shorn.

"Okay then. Emmett's putting the suitcases and valuables

into locked storage in Red Lodge. Get your luggage. Everything but what you're taking in the packs."

I put my suitcase in the trailer, and stood aside for the others to do the same. When it was full the trailer contained all our ties to what we knew, what defined us.

Frye got in. He turned the van around in the meadow and headed it down the dirt road. I watched it disappear and knew that for the next two weeks we truly, unquestionably, belonged to the Beartooths.

———

For livid sunsets you can't beat our grimy Eastern Seaboard, where haze and smoke and floating particulates wring color from fading light, and there are no annoying natural obstacles like twelve-thousand-foot peaks to hide the display. In the Western high country the sun just slides behind a crest, takes its warmth with it, and you are in cold shadow. Most mountain evenings, even in summer, you can immediately see your breath's condensation.

That evening in the meadow it happened around seven, just before dinner. We scurried to our packs, pulled out sweaters and hats and mittens. I don't remember being totally warm again for the next two weeks.

Dinner was tuna and noodles. We sat on fallen logs, eating from flat wire-handled aluminum dishes that Andrea called Sierra cups. They are of a size to cradle in hand, and we did that often during the trip, stripping off a glove so we could feel the food's heat radiating through the metal.

We had decided to rotate chores. Gary had given me the notebook, and on the inside back cover I listed all the names in turn, and the dates we were due to cook or wash dishes. I pulled cleaning duty after dinner. It meant scouring out the two cooking pots, and the nine spoons and Sierra cups; we all carried one of each, our complete mess kit. Poague said he would show me how to clean without soap or powder, and in the darkness we knelt beside the stream, scrubbing with icy water and a single steel wool pad.

The old man saw them first. I caught him looking, and followed the path of his gaze, and that was how I saw Travis and Eleanor.

They were standing together about forty yards away, beside the stream. Not touching. They would not touch tonight, I thought. But he had her attention.

She was leaning back against a tree. He stood before her, a couple of feet away. Her arms were crossed and there was a wariness in her posture suggesting that this would not be easy, that he would have to work. But there he was, and I read in him an eagerness, a will to do whatever it took.

"He does like the ladies," Poague said.

He was still watching them.

"And the ladies like him," I said.

He nodded slowly. From their direction I heard a man's low susurrant voice.

"I suppose you have to move fast if you want to beat him to a woman."

"Even in my dreams I don't move that fast."

He hacked a harsh dry laugh.

"Is he your friend?" Poague said. When I didn't speak for a couple of seconds he said, "It's a bad sign if you can't answer that one right away."

I still didn't speak. He rubbed the steel wool inside a pot, dipped the pot in the stream, stood, and tossed the water in a sweeping arc across the meadow, fat droplets sluicing through the night, whispering into the grass.

"I'm cold," he said. "Grab the cups and spoons."

I gathered them up and was ready to leave; he stood looking at me.

"I'm glad you're here, Raymond," he said. His eyes and the lines of his mouth were indistinct in the darkness. I realized that he was speaking quietly. Had been, since we left Dulles. "It will be difficult. Every time I do one of these I tell myself it's the last. I get so tired. But I always come back. Staying away is harder than whatever we would have to do here. Do you understand?"

"I think I do."

"You will. And you won't be sorry you came. That I guarantee."

A pregnant promise. He didn't let it hang there between

— 49 —

us, but turned and began to walk, and I followed him back to the shelters.

———

Sleeping arrangements. Gary and Andrea found room beside the pile of group equipment, under one tarp. Travis and Hollenbeck and Eleanor set out their sleeping bags under a second shelter. That left the third for me and Poague and the two boys.

We rolled out sleeping bags on a plastic groundsheet. Above us the tarp was stretched taut, the grommeted corners tied with line to tree trunks and snubs of rock that protruded from the ground. It brushed our feet and stretched just a few inches above our noses. Poague slid his bag up so that it was mostly out from under the tarp. He found his glasses, lay on top of the bag, and stared up at the sky.

Beside me Donnie said, "Hey, I don't want to tell the old geezer, but it's dark out there. You can't see nothing."

"The hell you can't," Poague said.

Charles was closest to Poague, and he caterpillared forward holding his bag around him, until he was even with the old man. Then I slid out to join them and in a few seconds Donnie did too.

The sky was magnificent. In D.C., Bethesda, any metropolis and its 'burbs, you can almost count the stars that city lights do not obscure. There is always Polaris, maybe a rising planet or two along the horizon, and a random scattering of some others that manage to penetrate the smog and the sickly wash of incandescent glow that crowns our habitat, domelike. Here we saw millions beyond reckoning, a profusion of white points wherever buttes and pine did not block the view, and a gray cloudlike expanse near the top of the sky that was not a cloud at all, but the Milky Way; I hadn't seen it since I was a child.

Even Donnie was silent.

"There's more," Poague said.

Maybe a minute later, there was. A streak of light out of the southern sky, ripping directly overhead, burning from white to orange and then chunking off red, disintegrating as we watched. It lasted maybe a second.

"Did you see that?" Donnie said. "Did you see it?"

"We saw it," Charles said.

Poague got up and hung his sleeping bag and foam pad over one shoulder.

"It's a clear night," he said.

He got up and walked into the meadow. Charles looked at us, then got up and went with him. I saw them spread out the bags so that the two of them were side by side, a couple of feet apart.

Donnie pulled himself under the tarp.

I watched the sky for a few more minutes. No more slashing bolts. I was about to sleep when I remembered the journal; I was supposed to make the first day's entry. I found the notebook, a flashlight, a pen, and I wrote sitting up, holding the flashlight between my teeth.

Day One
Saturday, September 6
We have bedded down outside Red Lodge in a meadow that defines "alpine" and "pristine." It looks like something from Heidi. The homes and lives that we left this morning seem very distant.

The mountains are inescapable. Even when they're out of sight we are aware of their presence. They look cold and very high, and we all feel some trepidation at the idea that we will be in them soon. Or perhaps that's not true of everybody. Certainly we all feel anticipation. This is not just another night, and these will not be just another two weeks.

All we have heard about the altitude is true. At six thousand feet, a stroll across the meadow will get your pulse working. At twelve thousand feet . . . I hesitate to imagine. Andrea (one of two instructors) says we will acclimate. Let's hope it happens soon.

I knew we were bound for misery. I could have guessed tempest. If I had looked closer, thought longer, I might even have seen death before us too.

PART II
CLIMBING

7

In the meadow that morning there was a stillness before dawn when birds slept, and the night animals had bedded, and the wind was still. I was awake to hear it broken by dry pine needles snapping under foot.

Gary Currey stuck his head under the tarp.

"Wake-up time. Everybody up."

During the night Donnie had pulled tight the drawstring at the hood of the bag, leaving a grapefruit-sized opening where his face now appeared. His eyes blinked and the mouth moved without making a sound.

"Let's go, I want you all up."

The tarp had sagged inward, and it was crusted with rime ice, frozen from our breath. In the meadow more ice frosted the grass and the bags of Poague and Charles.

Donnie croaked: "What the hell time is it?"

"Don't worry about that—we don't need a clock. We go by the sun." He motioned to the east, where blue light edged the ridges. "And the sun says, time to roll."

When we finished breakfast the sun was over the ridge and the meadow was bright-lit, shadows crisp. Andrea called us over to the piles of food and equipment. She had pulled away the tarp, and now we could see them fully.

There were blocks of cheese, cartons of oatmeal and granola, jars of jam, cans of tuna and sardines, boxes of crackers. And more. A week's food for nine; a packer would meet us later with the second week's supplies. Beside the food were coiled ropes, the camp stove, three aluminum quart bottles of gas for the stove. And more.

I'm not sure I can convey how daunting, how malevolent, those stacks of goods looked to us. I had seen the Beartooths. I had felt my lungs clutch for oxygen when I clambered on the rocks. I thought there was a chance that I could get myself up and down those mountains, given nothing to carry. Add a backpack, extra clothes and incidentals, and it became a less certain proposition. Throw on a share of food and equipment, and it looked impossible.

"Time to do something about this," Andrea said.

"It all goes in the packs," Gary said. "Only way to do it."

We watched the piles, like gawkers at the scene of a disaster.

"Maybe we don't need all that food." That was me, trying to be helpful.

"Every bit of it," Gary said. "You walk all day, you'll want to eat plenty. Believe me. By the seventh day, we'll be scrounging for crumbs."

"My pack's full already," Donnie bleated. "I can't carry any more, there's no room."

"Pack it tighter," Andrea said. "There's room. Everybody has room."

They all stood rooted, silent. I sensed we were being tested, that there were plenty of wrong ways to do this, and we would be allowed to make our mistakes.

"You tell us how," Hollenbeck said. He meant Gary and Andrea.

"No. This is our trip." Poague said, speaking for the first time.

"There's no single right way," Andrea said.

"There's no right way at all," Donnie said.

For some reason I looked at Travis, and saw that he had something, an idea to sell. He was looking at Poague, and I realized that he was trying to see how this would go over with the old man.

Now his eyes moved from Poague to take in the group. He spoke.

"Here's how we do it. We take turns grabbing something from the pile. Make it something heavy, the first couple of times. Take it to your packs, come back, grab something else. We keep doing that until it's all gone. It's the only fair way. We all agree?"

He waited a moment.

"Then okay," he said. "Let's do what we have to do."

He moved toward the pile.

"It's not fair."

Charles Willis was almost hidden behind Hollenbeck. His voice was boyish, shrill, but it stopped Travis.

Charles moved so that the others could see him. "If we do that, it means we'll all be carrying the same weight."

"That's the idea," Travis said. "The same for everybody."

"But we're not the same. Some of us are stronger. The strong ones ought to carry more."

He looked for support around the group. Hollenbeck glanced away. Eleanor seemed about to speak, but stopped. And Poague: Poague stood impassive. His face gave away nothing. But he watched.

Travis looked at him, found nothing there.

"This doesn't make sense," Charles said. "I weigh about a hundred-ten. If my pack weights forty pounds, that means I'm carrying almost forty percent of my body weight. If somebody else weighs two hundred, then a forty-pound pack is just twenty percent of their body weight. So it really isn't the same for everybody. See?"

I saw that there was logic to this. Some of the others must have, too. Why someone didn't speak up for the boy, I don't know. Unless we were all afraid that we'd be stuck with extra.

— 57 —

"We'll work it out," Travis said. Now he had a point to prove. "It's a good plan—if there's any wrinkles we'll iron them out in the next few days."

Charles saw that the others weren't going to argue. He retreated behind Hollenbeck. Travis picked up a sack of instant cocoa and carried it away.

"What about freeze-dried food?" Donnie said. He hefted a block of cheddar cheese and put it down. "This is crazy, man, carrying all this crap around. Freeze-dried weighs nothing."

"Not enough nourishment," Andrea said.

"And it's easier to fix. Boil water, pour it in, that's all. You know they've got freeze-dried ice cream? Freeze-dried, that's what we ought to have."

"It has no taste. In a couple of days you'll be grateful for real food."

"Costs too much, I bet," Donnie said. "That's it, right? We pay nine hundred bucks, and we're eating like, government surplus. Look at this. Dark tuna. Saltines. Granola."

Charles walked past him and pulled a large sack of brown sugar off one pile.

"Powdered milk, powdered eggs. Where'd you buy this stuff, the Army-Navy store? Beef jerky, macaroni. Jello. They eat better than this in jail, man."

Charles brushed past him with the sugar and carried it to his pack, hugging it against his chest with both arms.

———

You can stuff sweaters and sleeping bags tighter than you think. Half an hour later there was nothing in the meadow except us and our jammed packs. We stood hefting them in the grass. I thought I would be able to walk with it. For about a quarter of a mile.

Charles stood over the bulging pack. It was ponderous, solid, as it lay on its side. He leaned over, bent at the knees, and slid his right arm through one of the shoulder straps. He straightened his legs; the pack pulled at him. When he tried to get his left arm through that strap he reeled and nearly fell. He let the pack slide off his shoulder and drop.

Hollenbeck was trying his, lifting it to his shoulders, walking in a small circle while he shrugged it to one side, then another. I had been through that already, had discovered that there is no magic spot where the straps don't bind and the weight becomes less burdensome.

His face was red. He put the pack down, pulled out some clothes at the top, reached in and came out with a big sack of raisins. I had seen it in the pile, and figured it for at least five pounds. He carried it to where Travis was tightening the buckle of Eleanor's pack. His own was already loaded.

"Paul." Hollenbeck looked briefly at Eleanor, then back to Travis. "I need some help. I can't carry that pack."

"Come on, George. You haven't even tried."

"*I know.*"

"I don't like to see you give up so fast."

"Travis, please. I can't do it. Just this much. Come on. You said you'd help me. You said."

Eleanor was looking at him. And he could see that others had stopped to watch. Me. Poague. Especially Poague.

I could see Travis wondering: what would Poague expect?

"Give it to me," he told Hollenbeck.

"Thank you," Hollenbeck said. "Thank you."

"No." It was Poague. We all turned to look.

"We had a plan," Poague said. "I don't know if it's the best we could have come up with, but it's a plan. Now you want to start changing it. That's okay, too. But let's change it the right way. If you're going to help people, let's help those who really need it."

To Hollenbeck he said: "You can carry that."

"No," Hollenbeck said.

"Yes. You can do it."

I know that George didn't believe him. But he put his arms out, took the bundle from Travis, and brought them to his pack.

"Now," Poague said. "What do we do? Do we stick with what we started with? Or do we help the weaker ones?"

Travis didn't answer at first. Then he said, "It makes sense to help the people who can't carry as much." Almost a mumble.

And then he reached into Eleanor's pack and got a sack of flour, and put it in his own pack. I was standing closest to Poague, and I had watched him for five years; maybe nobody else saw his face curdle, then compose itself.

He motioned curtly to Charles.

"Give me that rope."

Charles had taken one of the two braided nylon ropes, as thick as a man's thumb. Seven, eight pounds at least.

"You don't have to," Charles said.

"Just give it to me."

He handed it to Poague.

What I did next, I swear, I didn't consider. I just did it: I took the rope out of Poague's hands.

"I can handle it," he said. The old man. His starveling's legs.

I said I could handle it, too.

"Okay, the jelly." A one-quart plastic container. Charles handed it over to him.

Then Donnie, Donnie bent down and took a cooking pot out of Charles's pack.

Charles said, "Hey," and when Eleanor started to move toward the pack he said, "That's all, that's enough."

I fitted the rope across the top of the pack, under the flap. We all cinched and tightened our packs, and Gary began to complain that we had too much ground to cover and not enough daylight.

While the rest of us shouldered our packs, Hollenbeck stood over his, testing the weight, miserably lifting it a few inches, letting it drop to the ground.

I walked over to him and said, "George, you'll be okay. You can do this."

"It's a little late for that, isn't it, Ray?"

Gary shouted, "Can we please get a move on?"

Two of us were ready, waiting. Poague and Charles were standing at the trace of trail that appeared among the trees at the western end of the meadow, and Poague was pointing beyond it, past the trees to where gray spires met the sky.

Up there you create yourself, he had said in Chicago, and it is true as far as it goes. But there are limits. Some baggage follows you wherever. I remember the moment, seeing Poague and Charles, Charles now standing straight under his pack. I remember because for the first time I realized that maybe not all of Jonas Poague's authority had been bought with cash.

8

None of this business with the packs happened in a vacuum. There had been the Friday before we left; the fight, for which I accept all due blame.

I was not in complete conscious control of myself that day and night. Even to the extent that I am ever in conscious control. I have these periods when I'm a sparking live wire in a warehouse of combustibles. One sneeze and life detonates around me.

That afternoon we had a 5:30 court reservation at the racquet club. Hollenbeck's idea, as I remember. Poague had invited the three of us, and Anne Marie, to have dinner with him and his wife at seven. But the restaurant was close by and we had time for a full match. Travis normally didn't require more than about forty minutes to dispatch us.

At about a quarter after five I gathered all the papers that cluttered my desk into a single shaggy stack and dropped the pile into a desk drawer. I had shut the drawer when Hollenbeck appeared at the entrance of my cubicle.

"I'm headed over early," he said. "Got to get in at least eight miles on the Exer-Cycle. If I'm still at it when you guys get there, start without me. I figured I had to put in at least forty miles this week, and I'm still way short."

"We'll be in Montana this time tomorrow," I said. "Nothing to be gained from wiping yourself out. You know what a boxing trainer would tell you. Don't leave your fight in the gym." He looked at me numbly. I said, "It means, don't overtrain, especially when you get close to doing what you're training for."

"I know what it means," he said. "I'm not stupid. But I owe myself eight miles."

I told him I'd see him there, and he left.

The end of my work day at MDC came when I signed off the main computer. Everybody did it, an electronic version of punching a time clock. Though systems analysts at MDC were not paid by the hour, the program allowed Poague to examine the active log at any time to see what we were doing with our time. I called up the log program. The screen demanded:

Reason for logging off?

I entered *1* from the menu of choices; it meant, Daily Duties Completed.

Date and hour you expect to log on next?

I consulted a calendar and entered: *09/22* and *08:30*

Until then, where may you be contacted?

Somewhere west of Hell-and-Gone

Log-off complete. You may now power down terminal unit.

In five years I never did totally reconcile myself to asking a machine's permission to pull its plug. I turned the damn thing off, got up, put on my sport coat, and walked away from the job.

Travis's cubicle was in the row on the other side of the aisle, at the far end, directly opposite the walnut doors to the executive suites. Travis was peering at his CRT screen.

"School's out," I said. "We've sucked at the public tit long enough for one day."

"Another minute." I saw over his shoulder that he was logging out. "George went over already. Thinks he still has a chance to turn himself into a Sherpa."

Travis tapped at his keyboard, watched the screen for a few seconds, then turned off the power.

"Just a quick call, okay?"

He was asking me to leave. So it wasn't business; otherwise he wouldn't have cared. I walked out into the aisle and strolled around for a few seconds, and then I saw that the cubicle beside his was vacent.

I would like to say that I at least grappled briefly with the idea. But I didn't figure I had time for any monumental moral struggle, high ideals ferociously battling temptation, then fitfully expiring. I just went into the empty cubicle, sat in the chair, and wheeled it close to the partition. Quietly, so that Travis wouldn't notice. I know, a rotten trick. But Travis led such an interesting personal life.

He was speaking. I needed a moment to make out the words.

"It was great," he was saying. "All of it. I only wish we'd had more time. That's the only thing that kept it from being perfect. Absolutely matchless." There was silence on his end for a few seconds. I wished I could see Travis, see whether he was keeping a straight face. Because he sounded sincere enough to convince a motorcycle cop. How do you get away with a phrase like *absolutely matchless*?

"I know you do the best you can," Travis said when he spoke again. It was about this point that I sensed something awry. "I'm not trying to pressure you. I just want you to know how I feel. It's a compliment. I want you. I crave you. I can't get enough of you."

Again a pause.

"No, I'm all packed," he said. "You're sure you can get away?" Now he seemed almost cautious. "I want to. You have to know that. Just be sure he won't miss you. A jealous husband is the last problem we need."

Shit, she was married.

I needed a few seconds to think about that, ask myself

how I felt about it. The idea shocked me. Travis boffing a married woman. I had never known him to wade in that pond.

"Sure, we can do that," he was saying. His tone had lightened. "You have an extremely inventive mind. Uh-huh. I've got a few ideas of my own."

The conversation was ending. I got up, slipped out, and was standing beside my own cubicle when Travis came out.

"Let's get out of here," Travis said. "The old bastard got his money's worth out of me today."

I felt reasonably rotten as I fell into step beside him. You act like a thief, you feel like a thief.

"Better rescue George before he does something rash," I said.

"Yeah, he looked pretty serious when he left. If we don't get there soon, he might actually break into a sweat."

We walked out of the building and into the heat. The jacket that I had put on, I immediately removed. Even so the damp shirt sucked at my back, and when we crossed the street I could see bubbles where pure tar had been used to patch the asphalt. I tried to imagine wearing a sweater and thermal underwear. The idea seemed preposterous. At the end of an East Coast summer, it is impossible to remember being cold, how it feels. Or it used to be.

We reached the club and went in, and as we pulled on gym shorts and T-shirts I watched Travis. Going after a married woman, I could deal with that. Adultery had a nasty sound, but it wasn't a hanging offense. They could have their reasons. Marriages went bad. It happened.

I decided that I was feeling the shock of discovery. Children go through it all the time. What you think to be true, isn't. Travis's philandering wasn't such a big deal (I kept telling myself) but it meant that once more I would have to revise my image of the way things are, how the world works. After you have lived for a while, you think you must finally have it right. But it's never so. Some gremlin always crawls out of the shadows to bite you in the ass.

A married woman. She had to be beautiful, I thought. If Travis was taking the trouble, putting up with all the lies and evasions and jealousy that a married woman must entail, then she had to be beautiful. That much I knew.

————

We can skip the racquetball, which ended predictably. Skip drinks and dinner, too. I keep returning to what happened as we finished dessert, when the bus boy was topping off coffee and the waiter was about to suggest after-dinner liqueurs, one last strafing run on the MDC expense account.

The restaurant was called Les Cygnes. The maître d' had seated six of us around a red leather banquette intended for no more than five, rubbing knees and elbows: an arrangement much too intimate for the stiffness that had been introduced when Poague and his wife arrived. Stiffness, and more. The feel of seismic rumblings in a multitude of buried layers. Weird eddying tensions that I didn't understand until later, and an overhanging sense of decay that you might find in a room where the fruit has sat out a couple of days too long.

The trip leered at us from a day away, and closing. I knew that Hollenbeck felt its approach; he listlessly pushed the food around on his plate.

Poague perched along a curve of the banquette seat with his wife almost invisible beside him. Her name was Noreen. She was his second, about twenty years younger than Jonas. I always believed that she would have been an ideal military spouse: dutiful, unobtrusive, conservative in dress and manner. Tonight she wore a blue seersucker shirtwaist. Her makeup was negligible. In five years of occasional meetings like this one, I had never once heard her speak spontaneously.

So we were finishing dessert. Except to pass the cream and murmur how rich the chocolate mousse, no one had spoken for the past twenty minutes. The silence was becoming obvious.

Anne Marie—talking because nobody else would—said something empty about how lucky we were to be going into the mountains, such beautiful country.

Poague turned quickly toward her and fastened her in alert eyes.

"You like the mountains?" he said. "You've spent time there?"

"Not recently," she said. But when she was a teenager she used to go to her grandparents' dairy farm in New Hampshire, and she loved those . . .

Poague's look of distaste stopped her.

"Please," he said. "Please. You must not confuse our Eastern foothills with such glorious creations as the Beartooths."

He drew himself straight in the seat and tilted back his head, jutting a pointed, defiant chin, creating a vacuum of several seconds and inevitably compelling our attention. It was a practiced, theatrical gesture, the work of someone whose studied posses and artificial stillnesses were rarely challenged.

I don't want to be harsh. But I have to put it down the way I saw it and felt it that night. To me the man was such a gargoyle.

"I mean mountains," he said sharply. "A true Western mountain is a most awesome and challenging place. Even granting the possible extremes of weather on a place like Mount Washington in your White Mountains, we have nothing here to compare with it."

This became a launching pad for a lecture I had heard from him several times, about all the cushions we have built into our modern existence. Police and courts to protect us, ambulance squads to rescue us, hospitals to heal us. Hotels and restaurants and all-night grocery stores. Saying these as if the nouns themselves offended him.

I watched Hollenbeck. His fingers worried the hem of a napkin while he pointedly, miserably, avoided Poague's glance.

All safety nets, Poague was saying. They remove from us the hour-to-hour responsibility for looking after our needs.

"In the wilderness," he said, "if one is to eat, he must provide himself with a supply of food. If one is to be warm, he must have fire and shelter and clothing. These are the principal activities of a human in the wilderness: managing nourishment and making shelter. I happen to believe that they also are the principal activities of any human creature in the modern world. Only we disguise them so well and construct so many fallback cushions against failure that even the unfit may thrive."

Poague's accusing eyes ticked over everyone at the table in turn, then flicked over to include the bus boy who lurked a few feet away, desperate to clear the table. Hollenbeck somberly picked crumbs from the tablecloth.

"That is the beauty of the wilderness: the total and utter clarity about what one must do to live another day. It exposes very neatly our shortcomings. The strong and intelligent being grows stronger, even in adversity. The weak one soon perishes. A more elegant and thorough test of a man's mettle I cannot conceive."

He pursed grim lips.

"The trip we begin tomorrow is just such a test. This is not overnight camping in the Adirondacks or skiing in the Catskills. The Beartooths are a damn challenging place. People die there if they aren't prepared."

Poague showed as acid a smile as I have ever seen.

"But we're not going to let that happen," he said. "It's not in the program."

He leaned back in the seat, and his shoulders settled almost imperceptibly. Around the table there was a silent expelling of breath. Poague briskly drained his coffee cup, then stood.

"I must leave," he said. "I have five hours' work at my desk, and I must finish it before flight time tomorrow." He turned to his wife, who had stood beside him. "Stay if you wish," he told her. But she said she was ready to drive herself home, and they walked out together with Poague's elbow hooked stiffly around hers.

We watched them until they were gone, the way you watch in the rearview mirror to make sure that the State Police cruiser really does get off at the next exit.

"You boys are going to have loads of fun camping out with that character," Anne Marie said.

Hollenbeck ran his tongue over his lips.

I reached for a glass of wine.

"To the Gold Card brigade," I said, "sallying forth into the wilderness."

"It'll be great," Travis said. "Like Jack London. The Call of the Wild."

"More like The Marx Brothers Go Hiking," Anne Marie said.

Hollenbeck got up. His face was flushed.

"I'll be back," he said. He pushed past me and left the table.

———

I followed him into the men's room by about half a minute. When I found him he was kneeling in an open toilet stall, draped over the bowl, vomiting his dinner.

He gagged up what had to be the last of it, awful bile.

I said, "You had the Norwegian salmon, right? Looks like the fish came up river to spawn." That's Furlow for you; no occasion too bleak for another lame and tasteless witticism.

"Leave me alone," Hollenbeck said. Still staring at the mess in the bowl. "You're not funny, Ray. Just go away."

I backed off a few steps. But I could still hear him spitting to clear his mouth. He flushed the toilet and went to a wash basin, and was splashing water on his face when Travis came in.

"Looking kind of rocky," Travis said.

"Feeling that way. I think my stomach is wired directly to my head. Any time I get a little shaky about things, my stomach chimes right in. It's pretty stupid, a guy can't get a little nervous without blowing his cookies."

I could feel him opening up to Travis, just as quickly as he had shut me off. They were talking like confidants. I had always assumed that their friendship was as facile and slight as mine with Travis. Of course I had never seen them alone together; but it was almost that way now, the two of them seeming to pretend that I wasn't there.

Hollenbeck wiped his face with a paper towel.

"It's this hiking bit," he said. "Actually, I was thinking

that instead of getting on the plane tomorrow, I could just tell Poague I was going to look for another job."

"You don't want to do that," Travis said.

"Oh yes I do. But I won't. Poague would cut me to pieces, and Annie would kill me. I'd rather get eaten by a grizzly bear, if that's what's going to happen."

"The trip won't be that big a deal."

"You heard him now. This is going to be some macho, man-in-the-wilderness thing. It's not my kind of gig, Paul. I wasn't made for it. And Furlow, Furlow was talking about seventy-pound packs . . ."

"Furlow doesn't know shit," Travis said. Neither of them looked at me.

"I keep thinking, at IBM, they don't make you wrestle alligators. At AT&T, they don't care whether you're into sky diving or white-water kayaking. Jonas Poague is the only boss I know who cares. It's so damn stupid. Tomorrow afternoon, I could be driving up I-95 to watch the Orioles play the Red Sox. Instead I'm going to be hiking off to play Jeremiah Johnson in some place that doesn't even have a zip code."

"It'll be a pain in the butt," Travis said. "You'll get tired out, lose a couple of pounds, come home and sleep for about three straight days. That's all. It'll work out okay."

"You think so?" Hollenbeck said. He was lapping this up. It was excruciating to watch, his eagerness.

"A month from now we'll be laughing about it. I promise. Thing you have to do is quit worrying."

Travis reached for Hollenbeck, held his neck in the crook of an arm, a brotherly act that made me feel even more unwelcome.

"Did you ever do anything like this trip before?" Hollenbeck said.

"I've been backpacking a couple of times, weekend trips along the Appalachian Trail." His arm tightened around Hollenbeck's neck. "I told you, quit worrying. I'll get you through it if I have to carry you and your seventy-pound pack the whole damn way."

Maybe I was angry, standing there watching this, being treated as if I were invisible. Maybe I'd had one glass of wine too many. I guess I was envious also. Of Hollenbeck? Travis? I knew that I shouldn't speak, but I did. The words came out hotter than I expected.

"This is such crap," I said. "He can't tell you that, George."

They both stared at me. Finally.

"He wants that promotion. Same as I do, same as you do." The first and only reference to the job, but they understood. In the mirror I caught a reflection of a jerk who looked like me, gesticulating, flapping his arms. He was a buffoon, but that didn't stop me. "You think he won't be happy to see you fall on your ass? Cuts the odds down to fifty percent. How can you expect he'll get down in the dirt with you and help you look good? What's in it for him?"

I'd have figured that the anger would come from Travis, the offended party if there was one. But he just looked at me levelly and said, "Better speak for yourself, Ray."

It was Hollenbeck who glared and talked with sharp-spined bitterness.

"That's how you are, Furlow," he said. "That's your way. Always ready with that knife. I know. But not everybody's like that."

So for the second time in about five hours I felt like a Class-A jerk. And the evening wasn't over yet.

———

I think Hollenbeck started to cry. I'm not sure; I turned and left, and they were still in there when I got back to the table.

"He'll be okay," I said to Anne Marie. "He's being taken care of."

She stopped me before I could tell her good-bye. She wanted to ask me something. She wanted to know why I thought Poague was bringing us on this trip.

"You know about the job," I said. "It's a good guess, to me. This isn't a method of promotion they recommend at Harvard Business. But Poague has his own rules."

"I worry it's more than that. Less than that, I mean. I

worry he wants George along for the entertainment value."

It took me a couple of seconds to realize what she meant.

"I was watching Poague," she said, "when he did his shtick about the terrible beauty of the mountains. He could see George going green, and he kept laying it on, watching him squirm. He knows George will do poorly up there, and he can't wait to see it. It should keep him chuckling for the next six months."

I told her that would be pretty sick.

"He is not a nice old man," she said.

In my imaginings I see Travis leaving the restaurant, walking three blocks to the new Hyatt on Wisconsin Avenue. Into the lobby, to the bank of elevators, and up.

I don't know that it was the Hyatt. But it would have been his style. Probably hers, too. Maybe these details aren't important in and of themselves. But there were details, some kind, not too different from this. That's important to remember. And this is not all fanciful nonsense, either. Some of this I know now.

He rides the elevator alone, gets off, and goes to the room she has already arranged. She has handled everything; she knows how to do these things.

Travis taps at the door. She opens it. She wears a pink satin robe tied loosely at the waist, and Travis can see her breasts shift beneath the fabric as she takes a step backward from the threshold.

Later I got a face to put on the body, but that night in my imaginings the face was in shadows, and it's just a figure and pink satin that Travis follows through the door. He shuts it without looking back. The robe falls open as she reaches for him, holding his head, fingers raking the nape of his neck.

She holds him tight, and pulls him to her. The bed is one step behind her, there to catch them as they fall.

Later she sits on the edge of the bed and watches him as he dresses, pulling on his slacks. Looking at him is almost the best part, she thinks. He really is a pretty one. Not a diligent worker in bed; she has never known a really attractive man who was. But effort is no substitute for the feel of muscle at her fingertips, a body nearly as smooth and firm as statuary. He slips into his shirt, buttons it, smooths it over his chest. She's sure—looking at him really is the best part.

He turns up his collar, picks his tie off the floor, peers out the window, down at the traffic below on Wisconsin Avenue.

"I really need that job," he says.

"You mean, you need the raise."

He's grinning crookedly when he turns back to her.

"That's part of it," he says. "Everything costs so damn much. You know my condo maintenance fee is more than I paid in rent for my first apartment out of college? Flying costs me almost sixty an hour, counting the set-aside for an engine overhaul. The lease on the goddamn Benz runs over six hundred a month. It won't be so bad when I get the job, the money starts coming in."

She wants to say, How can you know? How can you be so sure? But he seems incapable of self-doubt. Not a flattering posture, from her perspective. He's like a big kid, a high-school jock who has never grown up. Grinning his way into middle age, affable but none too bright.

He sits beside her on the bed. She kisses him on the cheek and gets up to leave.

"I'll call when you get back," she says.

"Yes," he says. "Please. I need you."

More than you know, she thinks.

He looks up from tying his laces. His face is broad and open, untroubled, radiant. She gets the urge to tousle his sandy hair. And resists it only a moment, telling herself, what the hell, this is not a night to turn down thrills.

———

Sometimes I can feel it take hold, this damn awful feeling that I'm alone in a plane which is falling to earth, being pulled by forces that pay no heed to will, spiraling down to an inevitable point of impact where things come apart very badly.

I went to a pay phone at a gas station and punched a

number. A telephone rang in a house not many miles away. Two-story Colonial, whitewashed brick, on a corner lot. In the backyard was a swing set, a tool shed, rose beds. I put up the swing set. I painted the shed. I used to weed the rose beds.

She answered.

"Hey, hi, Joan," I said.

"Hello, Ray," she said. A slight wariness. "It's a little late."

Actually it was a few minutes short of eleven, but I understood. After about nine at night, calls from a former husband to his married ex-wife begin to feel unseemly.

"I don't want to cause problems. But it would be great if we could talk. Just a couple of minutes. If he wouldn't mind."

"Suppose I minded?"

"Well, you too."

"Is this important?"

"It's just that I feel like the wheels are starting to come off the cart."

She would know what that meant. Exactly. She didn't say anything at first. I imagined the husband lurking in the room— it would be either the kitchen or the bedroom—saying with a look, maybe even mouthing the syllables, *Not him again.* She married him about a year after our divorce. A decent guy, not too smart; I always thought she might have done better.

"Tell him it's only a couple of minutes. I'm not going to steal you back over the telephone."

"He's not worried about that," she said. "Actually he's not here. He's at a conference."

"A conference? Veterinarians have conferences?"

It was the one truth I withheld from my father, that his son's ex-wife was sleeping with a man whose professional clientele consisted of Pekingese and Abyssinians.

"If you're going to be snide I'll just hang up." She was too nice to remind me that even as a vet, he knew more medicine than I did.

"So it's just you and Franny," I said. Our daughter, twelve.

"Franny's at a slumber party."

"Ah. Just you."

"You're going to want to come over, aren't you?"

"I was hoping for a few minutes on the telephone. But it would be great to see you."

I could feel her weighing affections and loyalties, figuring out risks and implications. She has always been aggressively sensible; when we married I told myself it was a quality lacking in my life, and I was probably right.

"I have Jazzercise at eight in the morning. We can't make it too late."

"And I'm leaving early for Montana. Remember? So let's not waste time. I'll be right over."

"No. Not here. I don't know why. I think it would be too strange, being alone with you here. Are you at home?"

"On my way. I'll beat you there."

"Ray," she said. "This is just to talk."

"I wouldn't presume otherwise."

"Of course you would. But not tonight, okay?"

I hung up and got in the car, and started home. I thought of her doing the same, driving through the dark to meet me, and I felt better already.

The divorce was one of those rare cases when one party can say in total truth, It was all my fault. And it was. All my fault. This was a year before I started at MDC, when I was a store manager for an office equipment company. I consider myself more intelligent than physically attractive, but twice during our marriage I was sufficiently alluring to get immersed in two pointless romances, and too dumb to get out of them when I had the chance. The second one did us in. Furlow being Furlow, you can imagine that we had plenty of other problems as well, but most divorces need to be kick-started, and I did that.

Joan was ready to forgive me even the second one, but by then promises had been made to the wrong party, and I felt obliged. My advice to the married woman is that if your husband strays, and you still want the son of a bitch back, do all in your power to convince him that he is not an honorable man. Because if he thinks he is, he almost certainly will feel bound to his most recent commitment. Which almost certainly will not have been to his wife.

I turned down the block where my bungalow sits. It's in a town called Takoma Park, which abuts the D.C. line in an area of small working-class homes. The realtor had called this a "marginal neighborhood," meaning that I would be living beside people who make a living with their hands and muscles. I told him that was terrific, because I was a marginal guy with a marginal down payment.

My front yard is a modest jungle of dogwood trees, azaleas, hydrangeas, and unidentifiable shrubs, all of which seem to prosper in unkempt neglect. I came through the front gate, passing beneath the drooping willow whose roots have heaved up the front walk concrete. She was rocking on the front porch swing, wearing jeans and a polo shirt, Nikes tucked under her.

A tall blonde, trim, very pretty.

"I didn't want to keep you waiting," I said. "Must have hit every light on East-West Highway."

She said she didn't mind, it was a nice night, that the swing reminded her of back home in Illinois. She stood up and let me hug her; I tried not to let it be awkward but it was anyway, and I think we were both relieved when I stepped back.

"Still looking sharp, kiddo."

"Thank you. These days it takes more work than it used to."

I opened the door and let her in ahead of me. She went through the house with the businesslike air of a plumber come to fix a leak, turning on the window air conditioner, flipping light switches, running water for tea in the kitchen. She asked when I needed to wake up in the morning; I told her, and she went into the bedroom, and came out a few seconds later.

"I set the alarm clock. If you don't make the plane you have no excuses."

"I appreciate that."

She knew my talent for the fatal small error. Lose a checkbook. Discard the one business card in a hundred that I actually need. Tell a dirty joke too loudly in the wrong place. Others might grandly crash and burn in a single suicidal act of irresponsibility; I specialized in the minor *faux pas* with snowballing consequences. It is a highly subtle method of self-destruction. Any moron can look at a loaded .45 and see the possibilities for disaster, but to wreak misery on self and family simply by forgetting a telephone number requires a deft feel for fate's insidious clockwork mechanism.

We sat at my kitchen table with the pot of tea between us. At first the talk was light stuff, catching up on trivialities, Franny's first known crush, a bit of coy banter. It was good to have her across from me, to watch her watching my face, to hear her laughing in the right places. She is a splendid listener. Before long we were hot on the topic of the night, my aptness for jarring loose the linchpin of life.

Of course she was convinced that there are no accidents. At least not in my hands.

We had put on water for a third pot of tea when I recalled one of my classic calamities. It is a tale of missed taxis, garbled instructions, a briefcase lost or stolen on the Metroliner; its denouement has me standing in three inches of slush outside Penn Station in New York, without a wallet, without a ticket home, and suddenly without a job. High comedy, if you didn't have to live through it.

"Guess I kind of humiliated myself," I said.

She nodded.

"Without anybody else's help. All on my own."

She turned her head away but I caught a smile's glint just the same. She was more beautiful than ever; not her face alone but what I saw through it, the gentleness and the caring and the inborn grace of spirit that I had always sensed but had rarely perceived so keenly. Instantly I conceived a fantasy of laying siege her affections, an intricate campaign by which I recapture her and our daughter and our home from the usurper. How formidable could he be, a foe whose greatest daily challenge is sarcoptic mange?

I said, "Sometimes I think I'm down to my last few chances with life."

"Come on, Ray, don't get maudlin with me. I don't buy it. Your kind seems to have an unlimited account when it comes to chances. When you're eighty you'll probably still be screwing up."

"But much more slowly."

"You know, I've been expecting your call," she said. "Expecting bad news. Did you realize you're overdue?"

"I didn't even know I was on a schedule."

"I didn't either until the other night. But I started thinking, trying to remember the catastrophes, the big ones. I got out a calendar because sometimes it's easier to remember that way, from the time of year. And I realized they've come about eighteen months apart. Ever since I've known you. What do you think of that?"

I was flattered that she had taken the trouble, abashed at the meager interval between life-altering pratfalls, offended that my pain was so easily charted.

"Regular as sunspots, huh?" was all I said.

"At least until now. You make it through the next couple of months I may have to throw out my theory. But so far you're dependable."

"Hey," I said. "That's a new adjective for me. I've never been called that before."

The kettle whistled behind her.

She looked back at the stove. And then this mother of my child, this intimate companion in nine years of life, this suddenly revived object of my desires—without humor or rancor or the slightest detectable irony this person said, "Yeah, I guess it was a poor choice of words."

9

This is hiking in the high mountains. If the weather has been wet the trail is slick and if it has been dry the trail is dusty hardpan. The pack sways from side to side and the bind of the shoulder straps, that clamping, cuts through skin and muscle to grip the clavicle.

Your calves feel as if they've been slit vertically by a knife in need of sharpening. Feet smolder inside boots, chafing against fabric and leather, rubbing raw. No breath is ever deep enough. Your spine isn't supposed to fight the pack, but it always does, and always loses.

That first morning we followed the trail up from below. Sometimes it climbed gently and sometimes it climbed steeply, and occasionally it dipped for a short stretch before rising again, but through the day it climbed. The stream ran beside it all the way, coursing faster up here, splashing over rocks and spilling into pools. The edges of the path were bordered by lodgepoles and grass, and berry bushes and scatterings of tiny ivory wildflowers. The trail ran in and out of the trees, and when it was open the white tops of the great gray parapets were visible ahead.

The trail was dry, and our boots puffed khaki-colored powder when they fell. The dust caked on leather, settled in the weave of wool socks, and coated legs bare above the socks.

I recall these details now but at the time the overwhelming single impression was of moving one leg in front of another and drawing breath and resisting the pull of the pack, the thousands of fiendish vectors it found to contradict my balance.

That pack. I battled it the whole time. Try loading the weight low, Andrea told us; or try it high, keep trying until you find what works for you. Every day I tried a different way of loading it and all I ever found were different ways for the straps to pinch, for the weight to pull me backward when I climbed or shove me forward when I descended.

A moment from midday, preserved in memory. The sun was high, drawing out sweat that dried immediately from a breeze in our faces, tracing grainy salt on brows and cheeks. Yet still the promise, the threat of cold was there in the bracing breeze that blew down from the slopes ahead. I walked near the end of the single file, could see us all. All but Gary; his bored gaze I sensed at my back. Except for Andrea and him we were all struggling with the weight and the altitude and the work.

Andrea led us up front. Behind her Charles tottered under his pack, wobbling when the trail was uneven. But he didn't complain. Poague was next. He looked puny: matchstick limbs. But the old man knew how to hike. Head up, shoulders back, his steps mechanical and unvarying. Eleanor followed him, listing to her right. Three times that morning we stopped so that she could straighten her pack. Minutes later it was tilted again, pulling her to one side. I imagined it wrenching her spine. Travis was behind her, probably less taxed than the rest of us but still feeling the effort; the first time we stopped for water he took off his socks and seemed perplexed to find identical penny-sized blisters on the spur of each heel. Behind him, Hollenbeck was gasping, noisily drawing in breath and expelling it with a rattle. The pack's hip belt cut a furrow through his waist. Directly ahead of me was Donnie. His boots were loose, laces flapping in the dust; studied insolence, infuriating. Then me, walking my dink's sloppy walk, dragging toes and the sides of my feet, scraping my way up the path. Behind me I could not even hear Gary breathe. There was only the sound of his steps, heel striking the dust first and then the forefoot rolling down to meet the ground.

You can see things in pain, through pain. I walked and hurt, and realized that I was walking because everyone else was. And they continued for the same reason. There didn't have to be any other reason; there was no other. We just kept walking.

In the afternoon we began a long climb up through the forest. Beside us the stream cascaded, spraying a fine mist. Eventually the trail leveled into the bottom of a canyon, a deep U-shaped notch that cupped the trail and the stream and a few trees. Here the stream spread wide, rippling past a sand bar and parting around keg-sized rocks.

Gary stopped us there to rest. Walk long enough, walking becomes easier than stopping; the legs keep moving involuntarily, almost a death twitch. So we halted by degrees, like a string of railcars rattling and bumping to a stop. Then we shrugged off the packs, and scattered along the bank of the stream.

Charles perched on a flat rock and lowered his bare feet into the stream. I did the same, a few feet away; the water was cold, first numbing and then painful, viselike. I pulled my feet out. Charles kept his immersed.

Donnie wandered up, walking stiffly, and sat near Charles at the edge of the water. Donnie pulled off boots and slowly peeled away socks. There were red blotches at each heel and along the sides of each foot, torn skin and livid, oozing flesh where flecks of dark grit and wool fibers had stuck.

"Gnarly," he said.

"You're not supposed to let the blisters break," Charles said.

"Shit, blood, what was I supposed to do? Tell 'em to behave?"

"You can tape the hot spots before they blister."

"Hot spots? I got hot spots everywhere. I felt 'em squishing before I knew what was happening."

He slowly put both feet in the water.

"Brutal. This whole scene is brutal, man."

He had been sullen with all the rest of us. But he seemed to assume that Charles was an ally. I knew nothing about either of them but what I had seen.

"What'd you do to end up here, bro'?"

"I got sent," Charles said.

"I hear that. Just like me, I bet. Bad case of brain fade. Me and my buddy, see, we were in this Porsche. I was driving. My buddy said he wanted to go to the beach at Santa Cruz— that's about a hundred miles away from where we live in California. Bad idea. Santa Cruz is full of cops. They got us before we ever hit the ocean. If you're going to break the law, you got to be cool."

"You were driving without a license?"

"Hey, blood, it wasn't even my car." Donnie swore at the cold and yanked his feet out of the water. "So what did you do?"

Charles looked at the water curling around his ankles.

"I wrote a story," he said quietly.

"You did what?"

"A story. I wrote a story."

"A judge sent you here for writing a story?"

"It wasn't a judge that sent me. It was school. I wrote a story in English class. It was about two people lost in the mountains. The teacher showed it to the principal, and the principal gave it to the school board, and they sent me here on an alternative education grant."

Donnie's lips had the outline of a smile, but it was empty, and his eyes were mocking.

"Oh, man, that's great. A story. That's beautiful." He stood up. He was laughing. "You're bad, all right. Charlie Too Bad, that's you."

He went off baying, damp feet padding, saying, A story, Charlie Too Bad wrote a story, too much, that Charlie Too

Bad is too much. And his laughs echoed against the high palisades of the canyon.

In the afternoon when we were all certain that we had gone as far as we could take ourselves, we reached the foot of a high steep ridge. Here the stream parted from the path as it dropped, rushing and tumbling a couple of hundred yards to one side while the trail climbed diagonally in a series of switchback turns that ended somewhere above, out of sight as I bent my neck. I told myself that in the morning we would have a hard climb to start; certain that we would stop here for the night.

You have to understand that we hadn't been told where we were going or how we were supposed to get there or how far we were expected to travel. We were following Andrea and she seemed to be doing what Gary told her to do. At the base of the ridge she slowed and looked back at Gary, and when I turned to look back at him he was pointing upward with one finger, so we never broke stride. Maybe Hollenbeck groaned. Maybe Donnie bitched. But I wasn't conscious of it if it happened. We followed Andrea up. I stopped thinking about Charles wobbling under his pack, about Eleanor's crooked pack and Poague's frail legs and Hollenbeck's flab. No room for anything but the rawness in my lungs, and my dead legs pushing forward, and the pack straps gnawing my hips and shoulders.

About fifteen minutes later we came out on a broad saddle between two knobby prominences where the trail met the stream once more. It sounds so easy. *We came out on a broad saddle*. But I have a distinct memory of looking up the last leg of the trail before it topped out, telling myself it couldn't be more than fifty strides long, and counting as I stared down at my boots to watch them crunch into grainy decomposed granite. At fifty I looked up and saw that there were still some steps to go, and they were the most difficult I have ever taken because I had known that I had fifty in me, but no more.

Then we were over a lip, on a shelf where there were huge boulders, and some trees, and patches of grass beside the stream. Ahead of me the others were already out of their packs and collapsing, and I did the same. For some time I lay there and felt the cold wind and watched scattered tufts of clouds blow across a sky so deep it was more purple than blue. When I moved I started with fingers, then toes. I felt a wet hot eruption on the ball of my right foot. All day I had managed to avoid blisters; those last sixty, seventy steps had raised one and broken it.

We ate dinner in darkness. Soggy mung beans. I crawled fully clothed into the sleeping bag, and my last sensation was the sad hollow sound the water made when it plunged off the rim and down to the side of the ridge below.

––––––––––

It was almost a week before Charles told me, told anyone, what happened to him that afternoon.

We had been at the saddle for nearly half an hour. By then we had begun to set camp. Charles went to find the latrine, just a small slit trench scratched out with a folding shovel by whoever needed it first.

Up in that direction, somebody had said to him, vaguely waving toward a stand of pines. Charles picked his way through the trees, and emerged in a small clearing dominated by a boulder the size of a house. He walked around the boulder and found Poague lying there, looking as if he had dropped on the spot.

Charles ran to him and knelt down at his head. The old man was breathing hard, spittle bubbling at one corner of his mouth. His gaze was unfocused, and for a few seconds he seemed unaware of Charles bending over him, saying Jonas, Jonas, what's the matter?

Poague finally lifted his eyes and said, Better give me a little air.

He reined in his breathing. And he looked at Charles and said, I'm all right, don't worry, I'll be okay.

But his cheeks were waxy, his lips gray and trembling.

So Charles described him. The truth, I'm sure, but even now I have trouble seeing the old man that way.

"What's wrong?" Charles said.

"Nothing. I'm fine. Nothing's wrong. And listen, you. Don't say anything to anybody about this."

I can imagine how he said it, Poague when he really wanted something, even in this condition.

"Promise me," Poague said.

"I promise. But what's wrong?"

Poague didn't speak at first. He put out his hand and Charles understood that he wanted to be helped up, so Charles stood and did what he could to pull the old man up.

Poague rose in front of him, swayed, and leaned his shoulder against the big rock to steady himself.

Almost a minute went by and Poague didn't look at him, didn't seem to be looking at anything. When Charles told the story later he remembered thinking that Poague must have forgotten the question. But finally the old man straightened, stood away from the rock, and looked directly at Charles.

"Not today, boy," he said. "Maybe later. But not today."

10

Andrea came around to wake us. Or so I was told. I never heard her. It was Poague who brought me out of leaden, dreamless sleep, touching my shoulder and telling me "Raymond, Raymond, wake up Raymond."

Since it was Poague I did. I opened my eyes.

He looked down at me and said, "Ah Lazarus," and gave me an astonishing smile both sly and unaccountably sad.

The tarp was gone already. Charles was up and dressed and folding it away. I saw an unblemished cobalt sky and a bright sunrise penumbra.

I counted back two days and thought, *Monday morning*. A weekend removed from Bethesda and racquetball and a restaurant banquette. It was as remote as childhood.

So was future. The twelve hours before I might count another day done seemed an impossible chasm: I was anchored by the inertia of here-and-now. Muscles with the resilience of wet pasteboard as I peeled away nylon swaddling. An ache in one hundred joints as I stretched to put on boots, and bent my legs under me, and stood. A flare of the outraged gall on my right sole as I tried to walk.

The ponderous present; almost an oppressive physical presence, like water at a great depth. Friday night belonged to a faraway past that now seemed vaporous and ephemeral. I longed to feel that way again, free, unburdened.

Breakfast was a mucilage of oatmeal and raisins. As we ate, Gary lectured us about lactic acid: goddamn lactic acid is the reason you're all hurting, it builds up when you exercise hard and if you don't work it out you feel sore as hell the next morning.

Poague got up and left without eating much. I saw him go to his pack and take out his toilet kit and walk down to the stream. Travis wasn't even subtle; he watched Poague, immediately shoveled the rest of the glop into his mouth, then went to his own pack, got his kit, and followed Poague.

"Tried to tell you," Gary was saying, "you have to warm down with a little stretching so you can burn off the lactic acid." He began showing some exercises, bending and twisting and reaching in a demonstration of arrogant suppleness. I put down my cup and spoon, hobbled over to my pack for a toothbrush, and went off toward where Poague and then Travis had gone.

When I saw them I stopped. Poague was standing beside the stream, unfolding a straight razor. No mirror, no soap, no hot water; nobody else among us had shaved since we arrived. He bent and scooped some water from the stream in his cupped right hand, and dashed it on his face, and he brought the razor to his cheek and began to shave. Travis was maybe ten feet away, brushing his teeth, but watching this performance. Poague ignored him.

Travis took the toothbrush from his mouth and wiped his face clean. For a moment he seemed quizzical, uncertain. Then I saw him gather himself up—an act that took place almost wholly within him, but I saw it anyway—and crook a grin that I knew well, and cock his chin just so. He said something to Poague, a few words. I was too far to hear, but

I could guess: a witty trifle, slightly obsequious though not fawning.

Poague ignored him, continued to scrape at his cheek, as if oblivious. Yet he had to be aware.

Travis waited, got no reaction, and now his posture changed again. A subtle hunch of the shoulders, a submissive dip of the head. He took a couple of steps closer to Poague; I'm tempted to say that he sidled, and maybe he did.

Again he said something to Poague. One second passed. Two. Poague deliberately dropped the hand that held the razor, and when the hand was at his side he turned his face to Travis, and then he spoke. One sentence. A pause. Travis's face was set in an expression of bafflement. Poague said some more, then turned away, and brought the razor up again.

Travis seemed about to reply. But he checked himself, took a step away and stopped to look back. Finally he came striding up in my direction. I could not remember ever seeing him so flustered. Flustered at all, for that matter. He glanced at me and brushed past.

Down beside the water, Poague moved the blade along his jaw in even, precise strokes.

———

The trail and the stream both ended about half a mile from where we had camped. We came out of woods to find a droplet-shaped lake, nearly a mile long, with a pinched eastern end from which the stream flowed. There the trail met a steep field of boulders that spilled from high bluffs down to the water's edge. A heaped spread of boulders that completely covered the ground for as far as we could see. We climbed up and began to work across them, picking a path over them and sometimes through them, following the shoreline. It was the last we ever saw of trod path or trail.

The rocks were uniformly deep gray, ranging in size and approximately in shape from steamer trunks to VW vans. Most had at least one flat face where we could plant a boot, sometimes squarely but more often at a tilt, the ankle bent, playing for the friction of rubber against granular rock. To do it right you search out footfalls two and three moves ahead. It tests the mind as much as the legs, a game of checkers played with Vibram soles on granite.

As long as we stayed level the bouldering was tolerable. We were all capable of it in some fashion. The line strung out because you need room to move, to bounce from one brief landing to another. But we stayed together, caught up in the task, and for a few minutes probably we all believed that we could manage this for as long as we needed.

Then we reached the end of the lake and we looked up the long, long ramp of boulders that strained skyward from there, a great rocky funnel.

We had to go up, no other way. And we found that the vertical game is a much different game. No more hopping from perch to perch. No more smooth swinging of the foot from one boulder to another. This is no dance. When you climb a boulderfield you pay for every inch.

Gary and Andrea stood beside us and exhorted us and chanted instructions. "Use your hands for balance but don't pull yourself up. Keep moving. Make your steps small. Don't stretch, don't reach." They said the words, but the words didn't matter. It came down to this: some of us could do it and others could not. I discovered that I could. It was almost an act of faith; your right foot finds a small scooped alcove in the stone, just where it needs to be so you'll have leverage to push up and forward with that leg, and you do, and when you have reached full extension and your left foot needs another platform it is there, just where it has to be, and even when you are stymied for a moment you find the rib of stone you must have to brace yourself; it is always there, you are never left grasping emptiness; and if the way directly up is blocked, a glance to one side or the other always reveals the lateral step, six possible steps, that will get you moving again.

I could do it. Travis and Donnie and Hollenbeck could. Hollenbeck, somehow insinuating himself upward from one chunk of stone to the next, an astonishing sight. He must have been euphoric.

So there were four of us, and Gary, and we began cheating

our way up the boulders. It feels like cheating, the way it happens, the way the puzzle allows itself to be solved.

I looked back once. The others had broken into two pairs. Andrea and Eleanor, Poague and Charles. Eleanor could not do it. I watched her try to pull herself up on a table of stone while her feet slipped and scuffed beneath her.

Nearby Poague ascended two or three boulders, not quickly but with sureness, then stopped and turned and waited for the boy. I said that to climb boulders you must believe. Charles tried. But the pack rocked him from side to side, and his child's fingers slipped, and his meager legs folded under him: you can take just so much crap before faith becomes ludicrous.

Finally he reached a resting place, and then Poague climbed another three or four boulders farther, and Charles began to follow him up again. Clearly Poague could climb these rocks as well as any of us, and I thought that what he was doing was something very close to an act of love for the boy. I'm sure now that he was capable of it. I also know that he had no choice. Poague was doing all that he could in climbing a few feet and then resting while Charles caught up. Poague had that, no more, in his arms and legs.

But we didn't know that then.

Eleanor made a noise, a grunt and defeated whine that was embarrassing to hear. I didn't want to be watching struggle any more. I wanted to flee from it, and I did; I headed up and left them to their troubles.

You have to understand. When you climb boulders there is a kind of sorcery in the way holds and niches present themselves, and you feel you must steal as much ground as you can before the magic abandons you.

I guess the jumble of boulders went on for half a mile before they topped out. In the Beartooths I lost all grasp of distance; the mountains are so big, and they can punish you so much in so little time. But I would say half a mile to the top, almost an hour to get there. Near the end of the gauntlet I passed Hollenbeck, halted and gasping. We looked at each other, said nothing, and I kept climbing.

A couple of times I stopped for breath and water, but

never looked back until the top. I moved, kept moving, until suddenly there were no more niches, no more gray stone. I stepped out into a grassy flat where the others were sprawled, exhausted; there was a touch of grimness even in Gary as he sat with the pack as his backrest, knees propped up in front of him.

Before us was one last valley. Too high for trees; it was mostly bare rock interrupted by green scrub and laced with trickling brooks, and when it ended there were cliffs and more boulders, a second field higher and wider than the one behind us, and then the crest.

The peaks that had been distant in the meadow below now disclosed detail and frightening scale. Huge chiseled facets. Chutes that dropped thousands of feet, clogged with rock litter. Long rills where snowmelt from the peaks plummeted in sparkling tendrils.

Ahead were the peaks. Behind, the rest of the group. Hollenbeck close to the top, sweating and blowing, and far behind him, crawling over the convolution of stone, four tiny motes that I recognized only by the colors of their shirts.

I looked from them across the valley, to the second carpet of boulders and up to the peaks, the awesome peaks, and I knew we were interlopers. We weren't meant to be here, and if they couldn't stop us the mountains would at least make certain that only the strongest and the most determined walked among them and walked out again.

———

Some things I will never be able to remember without anger. Knowing, the way I know now, that none of it had to happen. For we didn't die from snow or cold or stone, but from who we were. The woe we brought with us into that high country.

I recall Hollenbeck and Andrea sitting in the sparse grass at the edge of the boulders. By then we had all struggled to the top, and Hollenbeck had come to ask Andrea how far we had climbed and how far we would still have to climb, and she had brought out a map to show him.

There were only two sets of topographic maps, remember;

four maps to a set. They were plastic-coated and each sheet cost three dollars, and I guess SpiriTrek figured that at twelve bucks a set, two were plenty.

Most of us couldn't read topos anyway. So Gary and Andrea kept the maps, and kept within themselves the knowledge of what lay ahead, what would be expected of us.

We had come a little less than a mile this morning, she told Hollenbeck. You couldn't go by that alone, though. Our course wasn't perfectly straight and anyway the difference was all in the terrain; the climb we had just made was worth five miles over open trail.

"Gary wants us to get to this small lake, right below the pass." She tapped the map, and moved her finger to point toward a notch between two sharp summits. "It ought to be right in there."

"Exile Lake," Hollenbeck said. "Wonderful."

"Just a name."

Hollenbeck looked at the mountains and then the map.

"So how far is that?" he said.

"Here's the scale, down at the bottom. It's about an inch to the mile."

"That has to be four miles." His voice unsteady.

"A little less."

"We can't do that. It just took us all morning to do one mile."

"We have plenty of daylight. This morning the boulder-field slowed us down."

"We've got another one. I can see it."

"It'll be okay. As soon as we get moving, work the kinks out. That's the problem with long rest stops. Everything tightens up."

Hollenbeck stood. She was trying to show him the map, talking about contour lines, but he wouldn't listen. His shoulders were slumped.

He saw me looking at him.

"That's eleven thousand feet up there," he said to me. I could have been anyone; he just had to say it. "Two miles high. What are we doing here?"

Gary was watching all this. He had been filling a water bottle from a tiny stream nearby, and when Hollenbeck left he put away his jar of iodine, and called Andrea's name. She looked over at him and he crooked a finger and she went over to join him.

They were alone, too far for anyone to overhear. But she told me later what they'd said. I could have guessed.

"Things'll go easier if you put that map away," he said.

"He wanted to know where we were going."

"That's what they all want. If they needed to know, I'd have told them already."

"They have to get map and compass training."

"They'll get their map and compass. In a week or so, when they've started to believe that they might make it to the end of this thing."

"On the other trips I've done, we were very upfront about what was happening."

"That might work, paddling canoes in the 'Glades. But these people are dragging ass. Right now the map just scares 'em. The miles scare 'em. Don't make it any harder on the poor bastards."

"They have to know."

She remembered his answer exactly. He said, "Not when I'm along they don't." She cried when she repeated the words to me.

———

How many more descriptions do you need of torturous breath-sapping climbs? The lake was four miles distant, two thousand feet higher than the valley. Across the valley was three miles; we covered that in about ninety minutes. The last mile, and the ascent of two thousand feet, was mostly boulders, and it consumed all the afternoon and all the strength we had. A harsh cold wind blew down the slope, and by the last hour my lips were chapped and red, and I had worn a blister on my left foot, and I was moving on memory, moving on habit.

Sloped granite walls surrounded Exile Lake on three sides,

like fantastic old tombstones, cracked and leaning. The lake was a small catch pond where snowmelt drained from above. Swirling wind fretted the surface and buffeted anything that stood. Dirty swatches of snow in corners that the sun rarely reached. Not a scrap of green—too high for that. The walls were scrubbed brownish gray. The banks of the lake were brownish gray clay and brownish gray gravel, and beyond the banks were sharp-spined boulders of the same color.

Not just a name. It had the look and texture and the taste of a prison where a despot might send you to die.

The log showed Donnie and me cooking dinner that night. Poague had been carrying spaghetti noodles and dehydrated tomato sauce. I sent Donnie for the food while I took the stove and the pots behind a rock where the wind wasn't so strong.

He came back with only the spaghetti, handed the package to me, and stood there.

I said, "This stuff isn't going to taste great anyway. But it'll be real bad if we serve it like this."

He looked as if he couldn't hear me.

"The sauce," I said. "Couple of foil envelopes."

The words seemed to come to him as if I were shouting across a great distance. After a delay of a couple of seconds he gave an exaggerated nod, turned, and left.

It didn't strike me as strange. We were all disconnected, assaulted by the wind and the cold and the isolation.

When he returned he squatted beside me. I gave him a pan and told him to mix the sauce. He held the pan and the foil packets and looked down at them without moving. His hands were going blue under the nails.

"Are you all right?"

He nodded, and I began to clear the stones from a flat spot where the stove could rest, and I heard him mumble, " 'Luded out."

He was smiling a disjointed smile.

" 'Luded out," he said again. " 'Ludes. Quackers. *Quaaludes.*"

A sense of betrayal momentarily alighted within me, an

ugly vulture; then spread dark wings again and flew and was gone.

He dug in the pocket of his pants.

"You want one?"

I touched his arm before he could bring it out.

"I'll be honest, kid, this place is already too strange for me."

"Fuckin'-A, Jack, you got that straight."

"Let's make this easy." I ripped the packets, poured red powder into the pan, added a few drops of water. "You take the spoon, mix it up real good. Can you do that?"

"Hey, no problem."

I turned back to the flat spot, swept away the rocks. The stove was in the same sack that carried the pans and cups and spoons, and the three aluminum fuel bottles. I took out the stove and one of the bottles, a full one.

When I opened the filler I saw that the stove was almost empty. Donnie's spoon scratched, scratched, in the pan. I opened the fuel bottle, set its cap loose on top, and put it beside the stove, to my left side, where Donnie was.

The stove was a loathsome little monster. Hard to start, difficult to fill. Not much to it: metal tank that sat on three stubby legs, regulator valve, gas jet burner. A squat bomb.

To fill it you needed a funnel. There was supposed to be a small plastic one. I bent forward to my right, began to look through the bag.

To the left I heard a solid *chunk* of metal and hard ground. Heard a gurgle. Smelled fuel. When I looked back the aluminum bottle was on its side and Donnie was looking at it and the fuel was burping out in measured splashes, soaking the ground.

I could have moved faster. Donnie didn't move at all. He was fascinated. I lunged and grabbed the bottle and righted it.

He said, "I hit it."

I must have shouted something, because Gary came over. He looked at the open bottle in my hand, and the wet patch in the brownish-gray earth.

For three days he had been watching us through a thick pane, mocking detachment. But he was not detached any more. He was there; he was immediate.

He took the bottle from me and shook it to hear the splash inside, took the stove and shook that, and said, "Damn. Damn."

I told him there were two more bottles, and I started to get them.

"One's full," he said. "The other's empty. I checked this morning."

"Don't we get more later?"

"At resupply."

"Is there enough until then?"

I thought he was about to give a real answer. But he swallowed it and said, "We'll be all right. Just don't fart around any more. There's none to waste."

He got the funnel out of the bag and filled the stove with what remained in the open bottle. Using great concentration, it seemed to me.

"Soon as you finish cooking, shut it off." He handed the stove back to me, and looked at the bottle and the damp ground and at me and Donnie. He said, "I wish you hadn't done that."

———

After dinner Gary was again at arm's length, arch and untouchable. At the group meeting he leaned against a rock with his arms folded, and listened to Donnie complain about his blisters, Hollenbeck complain about the distance we had to cover, Eleanor complain about everyone else running off and leaving her behind.

"You guys are a hoot," he said. "You think you've got it hard—it could be so much harder. Last time I brought a group in here, a low rolled in from Wyoming, rained for four days. Up here it was sleet. Three weeks ago to the day I was sitting up here with eight other jag-offs, eating dinner in the rain and sleet. It was great. You all have it easy."

"I know why there hasn't been a storm." It was Charles. We all looked—he spoke so seldom. "It's because God's been too busy laughing at us, He hasn't had time to order one up."

———

In the morning when I watched Poague and Travis beside the stream I had tried to understand what it might mean, how much closer I might be to the job. But nothing happened. Abstracts paralyzed the mind: jobs and prospects and ambition belonged to another reality.

That evening, at dinner and afterward, Eleanor manufactured a sulk so formidable that even Travis couldn't breach it. She sat curled up, cradling herself. When he tried to speak to her, she answered in a monotone, glanced at him dully, and hid behind her own misery. At another time I might have taken a petty pleasure in this second failure of his charm. But I couldn't make myself care. Boy-girl games didn't matter.

I'm trying to convey the isolation that the mountains imposed. How thoroughly they removed us from all we had held important, and replaced those concerns with a complete set of others far less ambiguous, but much harsher and more pressing and real. You might imagine the nine of us in a lifeboat, becalmed in an empty sea, having jettisoned all our belongings. Stuck with the worst of all possible companions. Our own damn selves.

11

Next day, all day, clouds covered the sky. In the morning they were pearly, corrugated. By afternoon they would become flat and low, with a gunmetal finish. Until now there had been sun when we walked, and when we stopped for rest we would always find some place in brightness to hide from the penetrating chill. But that day for the first time there was no sun. Even when we walked we wore sweaters and wool trousers. The cold was constant, and it nudged at us, taunted us. *Oh yes this can get bad oh yes just feel how bad how cold.*

During breakfast Gary told us we had one more push to the top. Another half mile, another thousand feet higher, and we would be at the pass. Beyond that, Beartooth Plateau.

He hooked a thumb over his shoulder, toward a narrow chute between two of the high cliffs. An impossible clutter of fallen rock choked the route; and it seemed to climb straight up.

"Boys and girls," he said, "your stairway to the stars."

I hear him using the same line with every group. His

flippancy, his smug delight in our pain and fear; I will never forgive him.

Breaking a bivouac camp and getting ready to leave takes longer than you might expect. Tape feet, cushion blisters, pack and repack so that the clothes and equipment you're likely to want will be ready when you need them. You might think there's a comfort in having life reduced to simple chores, but the chores are endless and they never go as fast as you think they should. Your fingers don't move right, your mind is balky, you are cold and tired and exhausted. Hike ten hours a day, and in the other fourteen you won't have a spare minute.

That morning we got ready more quickly than before, or ever again. I think we all wanted to be away from those walls. We loaded up, shouldered the packs. For two days Gary and Andrea had swapped places after every rest stop, one at the head and the other at the end of the file, but now when I began to fall in around the middle of the line Andrea came to me and said, "Ray, Gary is leading and I want to be near the front today. Do you mind walking sweep?"

"I don't know." By now I had decided that I could survive this trip if it didn't get any tougher and I was required only to stay with the others. But I wanted nothing beyond, no uncertainties.

"It's easy. You just walk at the back, don't let anybody get behind you. We may string out some, like we did yesterday, and I don't want to lose anybody. Only as far as the pass—right up at the top here. You can't get lost. We'll probably all be in sight anyway."

There was no good reason to refuse; and I saw that she was going to insist. So I stood aside to let the others gather in front of me.

Eleanor too hung back and waited. While everyone else began to file out she looked at me and spoke to me directly, solely, for the first time since we met.

She said, "So you got stuck with slug detail. What did you do to pull this duty?"

In my mind, imagination, I answer her, "I could do much worse," and her rigid face melts; I follow her up the chute and admire the seat of her tweed knickers, the turn of her calf apparent beneath tight knee socks; when the chute gets steep I go ahead of her, show her the way up, reach down to help her along; she grasps my hand firmly and warmly and holds it a second longer than necessary.

Now let me tell you. These libidinal musings are all after the fact. I was incapable of flirtation or the urge that creates it. The work had sapped me. I did not, could not, think of sex. If I tried I could remember having performed the act, but could not remember why. I know now that there are stronger drives.

What happened was this. In a voice of defeat and self-pity she said, "So you got stuck with slug detail. What did you do to pull this duty?"

I said, "Just lucky, I guess," and she turned away from me and trudged off after the others, and I followed.

Her pack was crooked. We hadn't walked ten steps and her pack was crooked. I thought, It is not that hard. You get it on straight and tighten the straps and it stays that way, makes everything easier. Even Hollenbeck kept his pack straight.

We started up. The rock was looser here than on the boulderfields. It was rubble from the walls above, most of it with sharp edges, from thumbsized chips to pointed chunks that jutted eight, ten feet out of the rubble like a sinking sailboat tipped half out of the sea.

It was hard going for everyone else; for her, impossible. In the pools of scree—Charles's word for the smallest fragments; I looked it up—she sank in past her ankles, and slid back eighteen inches for every step she took. Her floundering irked me; maybe I saw too much of myself in her.

The others pulled away from us. I watched her boots and hands miss the obvious plants, and heard that whimpering grunt.

"I could carry something from your pack," I said. Plain expedience. By now everyone else was out of sight and I didn't want to fall too far behind. "Might make it easier. Do you mind?"

She sat on the nearest flat rock and looked at me as if this offer was overdue. I opened the top of the pack and rummaged through. Clothes, a tarp, a box of crackers. It had to be the lightest load in the group.

"There's nothing heavy in here," I said.

"Some dried apples in the side pocket, see?"

"Where'd it all go?"

"I got rid of some food. That was my granola we ate this morning. Andrea took some stuff, I don't know what."

"You ought to be able to carry this much."

"Climbing is my problem. Not the pack."

"You might at least carry it straight."

"Why should it matter?"

"It looks like hell. I don't know. Like you don't care."

"I don't. I want to get out of here, that's all."

Her eyes brimmed, and I got impatient.

"Goddamn. I don't need these problems."

"Don't goddamn me," she said. "I didn't ask you to be here." Her facing was pouting, but not belligerent—not enough resolve there for belligerence. "I didn't ask for any of this."

"You think that makes you special? Nobody wants to be here. Except maybe one or two crazies—none of us actually chose to do this. We just ended up here."

She looked at me as if I were a particularly backward child.

"I do not want to be here," she said, the syllables precise to the point of insult.

I was standing about four feet away and took a step closer, so that I was almost in her face.

"I'll tell you what, Eleanor. That makes two of us. I don't want you here either."

"Thank you very much." No more pout. But hurt, real hurt. "You asshole." She contorted her face, made a fist with her right hand, swung the fist straight back, and looped it at me. It didn't hurt—she held back at the last moment and began to open her fingers, so it was just a loosely balled hand that slapped my sweater.

There was something pathetic but still funny about all that energy, that fury, exhausted to so little result. A corner of my mouth may have lifted, because she looked at me and made another fist with her left hand and hit me as hard as she could. That one I felt.

You asshole, she kept saying, crying as she did, pummeling me, and I stood there unresisting because I knew I had it coming, and I knew it helped and I could do this for her without cost to myself, and most of all because the sentient part of me was aware of something suddenly tremulously alive in that place where I feel without thinking. A place where I had never been more than a transient.

She stopped hitting me, but kept crying; she didn't lean toward me but didn't resist either when I stepped across the last few inches that separated us, gripped her upper arms and held her lightly to my chest.

Something within me. How do I put this? This stranger to me—I saw her. I *saw* her. A light shone abruptly from within the deepest part of her, and through her translucence I could see layers of being, delicate articulations and coursings and overlappings and urgent laborings all revealed. I saw and understood her stumbles, her crooked pack, her pouting and fists and tears, what was behind all that. I understood who she was and what she was and even some of what went into making her. Not the specifics: just the truth. And I know it is so because since that moment I have discovered in her ten thousand small delights, but no shocks. No great surprises.

I love her, of course. If you can comprehend someone so completely without deep tenderness, caring . . . I don't know. I couldn't do it. I saw her, I loved her.

She moved her arms to tell me that I should let go, and I did, and stepped back to recreate that narrow gulf between us.

"Well now," she said. "That was loads of fun, wasn't it? You want to say something else nasty? We could try it again with rocks. We have plenty of rocks."

"We need to get up this hill," I said.

She looked up the incline. Directly ahead of us was about fifty yards of jagged knee-high granite shards, menacing *chevaux de frise* set in gravel. An engineer could not have arrayed them more discouragingly.

She shook her head.

"The others will start to worry," I said.

"I can't go up there."

"Look, this is going to end. But before it does we have to put up with a certain amount of shit. A certain number of miles, some tough stretches like this one. That's the only way we're getting to the end. It's like prison, but there's no parole and no pardons and no escapes. You walk in, you do your time, you walk out."

To me it sounded logical and convincing. I was sure I had won the point.

While the words came out I kept marveling at this warm light inside me. Of all times, of all places, I thought. Of all people, me. That it had happened so quickly, or had happened at all, seemed perfectly natural at the moment. Only since then have I questioned how and why. My best answer is that when you have relinquished all that does not directly pertain, you're on your way to being free. In three days we had hiked not just into the cold breast of the mountains, but to the cusp of the possible.

"So what do you say?" I held my arms out, spread wide, palms up. "We take it slow and steady, it won't be so bad."

She sniffled, looked up the chute and at me.

"No," she said. She spoke very calmly. "I've decided. I am not going to leave this spot."

———

If you don't get Ellie's story right here I'll be way too far ahead of you. Because to me she was no stranger any more, and she shouldn't be to you.

This is her side of it; I choose to believe it without even listening to any other version. It all fits. No surprises, remember? No shocks.

For six years she had lived in a house at the south end of Crandon Boulevard in Key Biscayne. The plush end. Her husband was a lawyer in Miami. Coleman Farris: if the name shimmers for you with Rolexes, hearts of palm salads at lunch, and haircuts that cost more than most people pay for a pair of shoes, then you're on the right track.

When they met she had been working at a brokerage office; she was a couple of months short of finishing her training, getting her license. But Coleman made plenty, and he didn't want her to work, so she didn't.

After six years he announced that their marriage was finished. That was in May, four months before Montana.

He suggested that she live in their weekend house on Duck Key. Of course he would love to stay there, but a two-hour commute would be impossible for him. If she insisted on staying in the big house he would take an apartment in town. But wouldn't it be much more practical for her to live in the weekend place? She had no job, after all, and she loved the Keys.

She had numbly acquiesced, and found herself living alone in that white stucco home built high on pilings, overlooking the flats of the Gulf of Mexico.

The key was an island of about a square mile. It contained a luxury resort, a small marina, and fewer than fifty homes, all built along a webwork of canals. Most of the homes were empty except during the winter. Eleanor knew none of the neighbors anyway.

In the mornings, she rose when the shadows of the louvered blinds had slid down the wall and crawled halfway across the bedroom floor. That was around 10:30. Invariably she pushed aside the sheet, swung her legs off the side of the bed, and made her way to the full-length mirror that hung on the back of the closet door. She was thirty-two years old, and had always considered herself comely enough for most purposes. Every morning she studied a slim body that was becoming burnished brown, and every morning she failed to discover the defects that her husband must have found in her.

Then she would put on a yellow bikini and go outside to the chaise on the patio.

There was always open sun. She had a radio, and a TV, and sometimes a magazine. At least once an hour she rubbed her body with coconut oil. The sun climbed and her skin grew slick with sweat and oil. When the sun was high enough she went inside and filled a gallon pitcher with lime juice and orange juice and white wine, brought it outside with a bucket of ice, and put them in the shade under the chaise. The heat and the light and the wine were anesthetic, and hours could pile up when she felt none of the hurt or confusion that always came upon her when she thought about her marriage.

In the afternoons the clear blue Gulf shallows turned opaque green, and there was a gentle wind. The sawing fronds made a noise like big raindrops pattering on pavement. Often clouds grew in the western sky, burgeoning above the horizon, and the sun would set red and orange on them, and when darkness came the clouds would be backlit by pops and lingering flashes, a distant cannonade.

At night she drank more wine and thought about Cole, and wondered what she had done wrong. She told herself that a man doesn't just kick away six years of marriage. She knew he must call soon, and she would leave Duck Key and return to Crandon Boulevard.

He never called. A few times she telephoned him; he always sounded stiff—not hostile, but disengaged, which was worse. Twice a woman answered, and both times Eleanor hung up without speaking. Every night she cried.

In July her sister Denise had come to visit from Minneapolis. At the end of their first full day together her sister promised to get her out of the white house on Duck Key if she had to use blasting powder. Denise had once been on a mountaineering trip in Montana, and she booked Eleanor on the same trek.

She said to Eleanor, It will do wonders for your self-esteem.

Eleanor thought, The only thing wrong with me is that for some reason I'm not good enough for my husband.

Eleanor didn't fight anyway. Her will seemed to have cooked away on the chaise, evaporated into tropical air. She called Coleman and told him she was going to Montana; not in weeks had she heard such pleasure in his voice as when he said, Great, I'll send you all the money you need.

Then one morning before the sun rose she was in her car, headed up Route One to the airport, with a ticket to Billings. Before she got on the plane she took off her wedding ring, put it in the coin pocket of her wallet, and replaced the wallet in her purse. And three days later she was sitting on a flat rock on the flank of a mountain, bundled in wool while the gray Montana sky festered above.

"I've decided," she said. "I am not going to leave this spot."

"Sitting here won't solve your basic problem."

"The only problem I care about is climbing up those rocks. I refuse to go any farther."

I took off my pack and said, "In that case you'd better slide over and make room."

She hadn't expected that.

"I wasn't asking you to stay," she said.

"If you don't walk, I don't walk."

"You can leave, I don't care. Why don't you go ahead?"

"That's not an option. I was told not to leave anybody behind."

"It's your decision," she said. "Not mine. So long as that's understood."

"Move over. There's space for two."

The rock was about the size of a coffee table. Space for two if you sat close. We sat side by side, at first without talking or moving. In her own way she had grasped the rules of the place, the logic of the immediate. When you can see no further than the moment, deciding to outwait a mountain isn't so absurd.

And I, I sat there and happily examined what was inside

me, seeing it all the more clearly. Like the gem it was I turned it over and over to let it catch the light, noticing all its facets. Thinking, Eleanor, I know something you don't know.

If you stop moving up there, you get cold. When there's wind, and no sun, a sweater and wool pants alone aren't enough. Before long we were digging out mittens and hats, jackets, ponchos, rain pants. We put them on and sat down on the rock again.

I resisted looking at her. A couple of times she turned to see my face—I heard the poncho rustle—but I kept my eyes away from her.

Mountain time moves like the moon across the sky. It is all stillness when you try to see it happen. The wind ripped and bucked and ruffled our raingear. I stuck my hands under my legs to keep them warm, and a few seconds later she did the same. We both looked up and watched a large bird—an eagle or some big hawk, details indistinct against the clouds— turn about in the wind, skidding against it, fighting it with long and powerful strokes of the wings, then land in a crevice high up on one wall.

"I've got those apples," she said. "We can have some if you want."

Rubbery apple shavings. With covered hands we pulled them out of a plastic bag and dipped them into our mouths; washed them down with swallows from my water bottle. After the fruit the iodine had a metallic taste.

She put away the rest of the apples. I replaced my bottle. We put our hands under our legs again. Do you understand that I felt no irritation, no impatience? Only the peace that comes from certainty. Like a quiet rolling tide that sweeps everything before it.

She studied the wall across the chute, its infinite network of cracks and faults, and she said, "It's pretty cold."

"It does get cold up here."

She fidgeted on her hands. A glance up the chute. When she turned back I was staring at her, and she returned the look, broke it off, then came right back to me. Right into my eyes this time.

"It was cruel, what you said."

"I promise, I'll make it up to you sometime."

A question passed over her face.

"Now that's an odd thing to say."

"Up here anything goes. Haven't you figured that out yet?"

You cannot be more alone than we were with the wind and the timeless cliffs around us.

"This starts to feel pretty dumb," she said.

"Your basic principle is fine. Digging in your heels if you think you're getting pushed around, that's okay. But this pile of rocks doesn't give a damn about us or what we do. You're up against that."

She tucked her hands under the crotch of her arms; maybe just to warm them, but it made her look like a disconsolate waif.

"I'm not a strong person," she said. "I get swayed. I can't believe I'm telling you this. You could make me walk up there if you tried. What am I doing, talking this way?"

"I said, up here anything goes."

"Well you could kick me in the butt and make me go up there. I'd cry and scream but I'd do it."

I let myself down off the rock.

"You're going to do it anyway, right?"

"Am I?"

"Sure you are. Just like everybody else."

"I don't know how." An hour earlier she'd have whined it.

"There is no how. You just start walking, and you keep walking until it's done."

"I guess I have to."

"You'll run out of apples and water long before this mountain gets any easier to climb."

She got down. I helped her on with her pack, then wriggled into mine. After I was ready she kept tugging and loosening the straps, and I realized that she was being careful to get it right.

When we were finished she said, "Go ahead."

"I'll be behind you."

"Ray, I'm going to be slow."

"Are you going to get there?"

"Yes," she said.

"Then if I stay right behind you we'll get there together."

Strong and noble had a good feel, even if it was only pretense, even if I knew it was actually just me and therefore couldn't last long. I did enjoy the effect.

She entered the thicket of toothed rocks and began to work her way through them. They swam loosely in the gravel. Tricky and unnerving: pressure from a foot or a grabbing hand might pry one loose. I moved to one side of the chute to stay out of the fall line. She did it right, testing and probing, never fully committing her weight to any one step. Slow, not perfect, but she got it done.

When she was out of the rough patch she turned and waited for me.

"The air," she said.

"The altitude. You can really tell the difference. You had the idea—don't take two steps in a row. Step, breathe, take another step."

"Tell me if I'm doing anything wrong."

"All I know is, you have to muck through."

Now we were sweating. We got down to wool again, took turns stuffing the gear into each other's packs.

The chute crooked right, and once we were past a bottleneck of shattered granite the way was open for a while, a smooth hard trough that was too steep to collect debris. Beyond that a short level leg and then one last cataract of broken stone that ended in the sky.

Halfway up the final stretch she started to hurry, and that stole her breath. She leaned forward on the steep slope, letting her arms take some of the weight, and dropped her head to gulp in air.

"Ellie. Easy, kiddo," I said. "No rush. You're doing great. You'll get there." Panting between phrases.

She waited for me, and raised her head and stood as I reached her.

"Real close now," I said. "One more push."

"You called me Ellie," she said.

"It seemed right. I thought people might call you that."

"A few who I'm real close to. And some others who don't know me at all."

"Maybe I fall in there somewhere."

She bit back whatever she intended to say, instead faced the rock and started up. It was about twenty feet to the top, a hands-and-feet scramble that was more precipitous than anything we had climbed so far. If the grade were any more severe you would want to use a rope, and if it were much longer you'd start to worry about the damage a mistake might cause. Twice flaky rock broke under her feet, but she held on and tested for solid ground and kept going to the top.

I waited until she was there. From below I saw her straighten, lean into the wind, stare out ahead, then peer down at me.

"Ray," she said. "You'd better come."

12

She left before I got there.
When I reached the top she was among the others, all of them
gathered in an uneven circle, almost as if in prayer, facing
some object out of my sight.

I walked over, beside her. In the middle of the circle
were Gary and Poague, Poague sitting up against a boulder,
Gary on one knee holding a gauze pad against a corner of the
old man's forehead, beside the temple. Poague had brought a
beautiful Irish sweater, dun-colored, like knit oatmeal. There
were dark blotches on it now, and dried dark smears on his
face. Gary took the pad away from an inch-long gash. At
once blood welled up in it; he pressed the gauze to the wound
again.

Poague saw that I was there.

"I fell," he said. "Right down below. I was nearly to the
top. Did you see the blood?"

I mumbled no.

"I'm surprised. It started spraying. Must have hit a vein.
This looks much worse than it is. Truly."

"Don't talk," Gary said.

A touch at my back. Andrea. She motioned me to follow, and we walked over to the edge, where I had just climbed up.

"How well do you know him?" she said.

"I've worked for him for five years. I can't say we're all that close."

"But you've seen him often."

"Almost every day. Too often, sometimes."

"Have you noticed any changes in him, the last couple of months?"

"No. He's always the same. There's nobody like him."

What she said next stunned me: "Has he always seemed this feeble?"

"Poague? Come on. I know he's not young, but the guy's in terrific shape for his age. For any age. He's been doing this kind of thing for as long as I've known him. He took this same trip last year."

"Not in this condition he didn't." She must have seen my disbelief. "He's been nearly exhausted for at least two days. I'm surprised you haven't noticed. I knew he was having trouble and I wanted to stay close to him this morning."

"We're all exhausted." I felt the need to defend myself.

"No you're not. You're just more tired than you've ever been. You think you're wrung out, but there's plenty more in you if you need it. He has nothing left."

I looked down the chute, bumped and studded.

"It happened there?"

"About ten feet from the top."

"That would be a bad fall."

"It wasn't exactly a fall. He collapsed. We were going up together. I saw it happening. Almost caught him. But he slipped away from me and slid to the ledge down there and that's where he hit his head."

I could see them now, black roses blotted on the rock.

"He wanted to get here," she said. "We were quite a ways behind—everyone else was up already. Before I could get to him he was halfway up the pitch again, so I held him by the belt and he made it over."

"Will he be okay?"

"He'll bleed for a while. If there's a concussion, it's mild. He can't go on, you know. I'll have to walk him down tomorrow."

"He won't like that."

"I think he realizes."

"I'm sorry. I never noticed. I saw that he was having trouble, but damn, who isn't?"

"If it's any consolation, your friends didn't notice anything wrong either." Then once more she stunned me. "I guess you've answered this already, but I'll ask it anyway. Have you had any reason to suspect that he might be seriously ill?"

I answered more quickly than the question deserved: "Absolutely not." That sunken stomach, his starveling's limbs.

"That's all," she said. "We're not going anywhere today. After we rig the shelters, we'll crawl into the bags for a while and stay warm. Everybody can use the rest."

She walked away and for the first time I noticed where I was, the immensity of it. I must try to describe it. The lay of the land was everything to us. Topography—daunting then —soon became a crushing physical reality.

I stood facing west. The climb up the last stretch of the chute had brought us to a bench a few hundred yards wide, sloping down to the west, where it fell away gradually at first, then more insistently. At each side of the bench, immediate north and south, was a pinnacle perhaps three hundred feet higher than the pass itself. They were twin towers and the bench seemed to hang suspended from them.

The pinnacles belonged to a line of peaks that I could follow to the horizon at both ends. The range had continuity; peak jostled peak, and where the slopes met they formed a dipping shoulder like the one where I stood. This progression marched up from the south, and continued northward through three more peaks, the farthest of them a craggy, crumbling version of a castle keep; at that point the line shifted west, unbroken, more passes and summits, ragged stitchwork.

Spread before me to the west, enclosed by the line of peaks, was Beartooth Plateau. Gary and Andrea had mentioned the name, and I had let myself expect something flat;

if not prairie-flat, at least gentler than what we had been climbing. But beyond the crest, the earth fell away to a stormy geological sea of troughs and upthrust ridges, valleys and violent buttes. In the morning we might descend from the bench for a few hours, but after that there would be more climbing over the kinks and torsions of the plateau.

For three days I had been thinking of this pass, this line of mountains, as a destination. I realized now that they were really a jumping-off point into the true high and wild. And that once we entered the plateau the peaks would become a barrier containing us, standing between us and where we wanted to return.

The circle around Gary and Poague had begun to disperse. I went over and looked. This time when Gary took the gauze away there was no fresh blood. He wet a clean bandage so Poague could clean his face.

Suddenly I became aware of a smell that had been there all along, waiting to be noticed when I was done with everything else. It was potent and acrid, something close to the odor in the cathouse at a zoo, but even more direct.

I said, "Damn, something stinks."

"Mountain goat," Poague said quickly. "They're ferocious territorial markers. He leaves no doubt. Isn't it a wonderful stench?"

"An acquired taste, maybe."

"Oh, the scent is dreadful. But what it means, Ray. That old boy walks in only the highest of the high places. He breathes only the rarest air." Damp and bloody as it was, the old man's face was radiant. "And now we're on his turf. We've made it, don't you see? We're here."

Charles pulled a tarp from his pack. It billowed and snapped when the wind opened it.

I grabbed a corner, and asked him where it should go; he pointed downslope to where some wedges of limestone poked out of the bare ground. His eyes were liquid. I thought it must be the wind.

———

We stretched two tarps together on the lee side of one lime-stone slab. Seven sleeping bags, side by side. One was empty: Poague's. Gary and Andrea had arranged their tarp over a wide notch in another chunk of limestone, and Poague was with them in their shelter for much of the day.

Among the lessons I learned on that trip: what bliss a warm sleeping bag can be. I burrowed into mine and through midday and the afternoon I floated in a nether world between sleep and full consciousness, bouyant in the warmth that suffused me from outside and from within; the wonder that had come upon me down on the slope still opening petal by petal as I watched.

The wind whistled over the upright slab, and for a time there was sleet pocking on the tarp and tapping minutely where it struck the ground beyond the overhanging sheet. It had nothing to do with me. My bones melted in the warmth and my muscles melted in it and my mind melted, too, in the languor of empty hours.

Some time in the afternoon Poague got into his bag. I looked up long enough to see that he had a bandage taped over the wound on his forehead; I thought, Glad he's feeling better, and took refuge again in the comfort of warmth and unmetered time.

It ended when Andrea looked in and announced that we had to start dinner, that Charles and Poague were on the duty list and that one of us would have to replace Poague.

Poague said something, and Andrea said, "No, Jonas, I want you to rest. They'll have to get along without us after tonight anyway. They might as well get used to it. Donnie, you're doing dishes tonight, we'll just move you up."

Charles was gone already. Donnie was slow to crawl out, yapping while he did, but eventually he too left. All the rest of us were stirring. When I opened my eyes Poague was sitting up, pensive. Eleanor got out of her bag, put on her boots and got her jacket, and left. Hollenbeck put on his boots, too, but Poague asked him to stay.

"We must talk," he said. "The four of us together."

His bag was at the end of the row. He kept it around his

legs as he moved to face us and the three of us shifted so we were sitting before him.

"You are all aware of a new job," he said. "I've known it for some time. Maybe the scuttlebutt takes longer to get to my office than to other places, but it gets there. I know you came up here with expectations. I should have told you they were unfounded, but that wouldn't have been exactly accurate, either."

He said, "I'm not certain what I intended. I haven't been as clear on that as I should have been."

Nothing he might have told us could have astonished me more. Not even the awful fact that he had carried with him up the mountain, that even now he chose to keep within himself.

"I have liked you all," he said. A choice of tense that should have alerted me; he always spoke with such precision. "It's my conceit that only individuals of value appeal to me. I have always hired and promoted those whom I like. We must have some standard, and mine hasn't failed me often. I asked you to be here because I thought you might all benefit from it and, selfishly, because I wanted you with me. I wanted to share this trip with you. It meant much to me last year. And if I were filling the position I would consider each of you."

I knew he was trying to tell us something; I wanted to grab the old man and shake the rigidity out of him and make him spill whatever it was.

Hollenbeck said, "There's no job?"

"Oh. Yes, there is."

Me: "Are we candidates?"

"I should think you are. But the choice isn't mine."

"Can you explain that?" Travis this time.

"No." Abruptly. I knew there was something more. "Tomorrow Andrea and I are returning to Red Lodge. Any who chooses can leave with us. If the thought of a promotion, or of offending me, is all that keeps you up here, then you are free to leave."

None of us spoke.

"I don't know what else to say. Except that I have examined my motives, and I know they were good. That won't mean much if you feel you've been deceived."

His features tightened. At first I thought the emperor in him was surfacing once more, but then I realized it was physical pain.

"I should rest," he said. "I'm in some discomfort. Forgive me if I have wronged you."

He slid down into the bag, pulled it around him, and turned his back on us.

Travis and I got up together, put on boots and jackets and cap, and left. Hollenbeck sat in his bag and watched us leave.

A thin layer of white, like cotton lint, covered the ground outside. The sky was low and ugly. Nearby Charles and Donnie had set up the stove behind a rock, and Gary and Andrea and Eleanor were standing around them. A natural reaction, to gather where there may be warmth. The stove was no campfire, but when it got roaring and hissing it sounded as if it ought to be warm.

There was a place beside Eleanor, and I filled it. Travis stood behind Donnie.

Charles was trying to start the stove. There was a drill that usually didn't work: pump up pressure in the tank, smear some flammable gel around the burner, and when the gel has burned off and warmed the jet, open the valve so the gas can escape. Then light it with a match.

Charles struck a match, but the wind blew it out. He shielded the second one and the third with his body, but the jet only sputtered and spat fuel.

Donnie smirked beside him.

"Charlie Too Bad, what's the matter, they didn't cover this in the books?"

His head was within reach of Travis's left hand. A blue ski cap, dirty blond hair. Travis said, "You little shitheel," and knocked off the hat and grabbed the hair. Twisted a handful of it, wrenched his head back, open-mouthed, howling. Nobody tried to stop him.

— 117 —

"You little punk, you creep, he's worth fifty of you."

Travis released him with a shove, turned on a heel, and walked away.

———

Lord, the contortions that pride put us through on that stony perch. Pride, stubbornness, maybe even greed, shaping us in their own twisted image.

After dinner we hid from the wind and sipped liquid hot Jello: it warms the gullet and kicks in a swift sugar jolt. We were scattered behind every possible shelter. This time I had contrived—Eleanor and I sat together against an outcropping large enough for only two. We said very little. It felt unforced, both the silence and our being together.

Travis and Hollenbeck came up from behind us and squatted low to stay in the wind-shadow of the rock. Travis glanced once at her and then spoke directly to me.

He said, "George and I have been talking. We've never discussed this job thing, I realize. But we've known it was there, right? And now that it's all blown up, the whole exercise starts to look pretty damn pointless, don't you agree?"

They wanted to go back with Poague and Andrea, I thought. No great deduction. I wanted to go back, too.

Sometimes I had trouble seeing past Travis's relentless gloss. But I could always read Hollenbeck, and when I looked at him now I saw that he was uncertain. George wasn't sure he wanted to end this right away. His face suddenly wasn't as chubby as usual. I remembered how he had pushed himself miraculously up the boulders, and I realized why he might want to continue.

Then it was Travis who wanted to go back. Travis and I.

"George feels we have nothing to prove. I have to agree."

Travis who wanted to go back. Travis, unwilling to admit that he was tired and that he wasn't fit to play mountain man.

I said, "Paul, what are you trying to tell me?"

"Why don't we all cash it in tomorrow and go down with the others? Just bug out." His look took in Eleanor. "The two kids are the only ones who have to stay. The rest of us are adults. We can do what we want."

If only he had been willing to step out from behind Hollenbeck's frailties. If only I had been willing to let his vanity pass.

I drained the last of the Jello, tepid in three minutes.

"You don't need me," I said. "Go ahead if you want to go."

"We ought to do it together." No surprise there; we couldn't be sure that Poague hadn't conceived all this as some ultimate test. None of us wanted to fail without the others. "You actually want to stay?"

"All the same to me," I said. "I'm doing fine."

"I'm doing fine, too. George is having a little trouble. I was thinking of him." Behind him, Hollenbeck's face was still inconclusive. He winced at a sudden blast of wind.

"George looks like he's holding up okay. Are you so anxious to get off this hill, George?"

"I guess not," Hollenbeck said.

"You can still go," I said to Travis. Waiting to see a crack in that smug confidence. "Do what you want."

"I told you, I don't care." Sounding abrupt, slightly offended.

"Then maybe none of us really wants to leave," I said.

"Obviously not."

He stood, and Hollenbeck stood, and they both started off. I watched them go and I realized that even now, the right word shouted at their backs would have us all headed east again, off the mountain. I could have us all home in time to see the football game on Sunday.

I watched them until they were gone.

"How about you? Are you leaving?"

"Not now," she said.

"What does that mean?"

"What you told me this morning. I'm not going if you're not."

She put the metal cup to her lips, but I could make out a sweet softness around her brow and at the tops of her cheeks.

She knew. It should have made me feel good. Feel ecstatic. But I was under the weight of Travis and Hollenbeck, staying because of my fool's jousting with words. And she, too. The weight of all three of them, remaining because of me. Strong and noble seemed miles and miles and many miles distant.

———

The episode later that night had an unreal feel even then, an unfamiliar conjunction of the puzzling and mystical.

I woke without knowing why. Then realized, in a series of comprehensions, a deeper cold than any so far, that wind cracking the tarps overhead, a clear sky outside. And finally, two empty bags. Poague's, immediately to my right. Travis's, halfway down the end of the row.

Everyone else was asleep. I held the bag around my shoulders and slid out from under the tarp. Something outside.

For a few seconds, only the wind. Then it slackened slightly and I heard voices, two of them, angry. The wind paused and very clearly I heard Poague say, "She tells me everything," very strong and insistent, the words coming from somewhere down the slope.

Followed a few seconds later by a resurging gust, swallowing Travis's reply.

She tells me everything. Said with strength, the last word vehement. *She tells me everything.*

And then a sound that I had never before heard, and surely never will again, an eerie cross between a cat's mewl and a baby's distressed bawl. Somewhere close to my left. I turned my head.

There was an elevated point of rocks. A late three-quarter moon sat plump over the point, and silhouetted a shaggy prominence that seemed at first to grow out of the rock. Until the prominence moved, a nervous shrug, and I made out furred shoulders, a dangling beard, a pair of horns with a scimitar's curve. Poague's mountain goat, made uneasy by the clamor below him.

The animal twitched its head, shook those horns. It pivoted and made a small clatter of rocks, and was gone.

13

Eleanor's handwriting:

Day Five
Wednesday, September 10
This morning Jonas and Andrea left. We were all sorry to see them go. Now there are seven of us instead of nine, and that will take some getting used to. After they left we set off in the opposite direction (west). I kept feeling that we had mistakenly left somebody behind, and I counted heads several times to make sure we weren't missing anyone.

This was our easiest day of hiking so far, but the worst in terms of group attitude. It seems that everyone has a gripe or a grudge against someone else. The two teenagers aren't speaking to one another. Donnie isn't talking to anyone, but is especially angry at Paul, while Paul seems p.o.'ed at Ray. In fact the three (supposedly) adult males aren't getting along at all. I am upset at Gary, who answers all questions about destinations, resupply details, etc., with his infuriating grin. And somebody, I'm sure, is upset with me for some reason.

This bickering is unhealthy, and unless it is resolved the rest of the trip will be highly unpleasant.

On the plus side, we actually walked downhill for most of the morning. The packs are lighter than ever (we keep eating food, plus Andrea and Jonas took some for their trip down). Meanwhile we seem to be getting stronger. Or we are just learning to ignore blisters, aching joints, etc., etc. At the end of the day Gary told us that we had covered at least nine miles —a record for the group so far! I don't want to get my hopes up, but maybe we have been through the worst of it.

Gary did say that tomorrow we will be doing some rock climbing. Tonight we are all practicing the knots we were supposed to have learned last Sat. It seems like years ago. This afternoon we tried to get Gary to tell us how hard the climbing would be, how high the cliff, and so on. At first he joked with us about it, but very quickly he got tired of that, and became impatient. So we don't know anything about the climbing except what he finally told us: "Don't worry, we won't do anything interesting. The lawyers won't let us."

The most memorable event of the day came in the afternoon, when we met three hikers on their way out, young fellows in their twenties. We stopped and gawked at each other for a while. They looked (and smelled) awful. After they left I looked around and realized that we are almost as bedraggled. These three were the first people we have seen since Sunday morning. They said they had been on the plateau for ten days without seeing anyone else. So wherever we're going, we can't expect to find much company.

Eleanor saw plenty that day, missed plenty more.

Obviously she sensed the hole that Andrea and Poague left in us as a group. That morning Andrea took a tarp and food, and while the rest of us were still packing she and Poague started away from the pass, back down the chute. I watched them leave and got my first real sense of foreboding; not from intuition or precognition, but simple logic. With the two of them gone we had lost more heart and guts and pure good sense than we could afford.

I've wondered how early she picked up the tension among Hollenbeck and Travis and me. I was barely aware of it myself for most of the day; it didn't boil over until late afternoon.

If hiking isn't too difficult, too taxing, it leaves plenty of room for thought. In the morning we started off down the slope, down into the plateau, and it was open country, easy walking. At first I wasn't aware of thinking, certainly wasn't aware of the particular thought that bubbled in the background. Occasionally it boiled into the consciousness, but mostly it worked away out of sight, taking form, distilling, as I trudged, particles of fact and truth settling out of the murk, finding their own level.

Until one moment it was clear. What I knew and had witnessed, and intuition, and a knowledge of the way people are, all came together at once.

I won't take much credit, though. Up there clarity is no great feat.

This happened soon after we had stopped for lunch. Already there was subtle discord among the three of us, a hangover from my word games the evening before, and my enlightenment didn't make me any more cordial. But I kept the epiphany to myself for a few hours.

We descended nearly a thousand feet from the pass and then tracked northwest, across one deep ravine and traversing the slope of another. Down to a wide clear creek—into shrubbery and grass again—and then north along the creek's banks, following Gary up past a small falls and through a narrow neck where the water catapulted, until we stood on the gravelly sides of a bowl with a dark lake in the middle.

Along the lakeside the ground was too steep for a camp. But there were bluffs halfway up the bowl, and at the tops of the bluffs a few narrow flat spots where we could spread our bags and pitch the tarps.

To get water we had to go down a talus slope and then climb back up. Travis volunteered to fill some bottles. I said I'd help. I got my iodine and went with him to the water's edge.

He filled the bottles one by one and I added the iodine. I took one from him, watched the drops bloom rusty in the water, replaced the cap and shook the bottle. He was holding another for me. I took it and said, "It's Poague's wife you've been banging."

I had no proof. But I saw the look on his face, that first unguarded reaction of guilty surprise when he turned to me, before he'd had a chance to gather himself up, compose himself behind that barrier of confidence and polish and gleam.

"You must be out of your skull," he said. "This is a joke, right?"

"Come on, Paul, you can 'fess up. It's your old buddy Ray, remember?" I know I was smiling, but inside I felt vicious. "I knew you had something going with a married woman. I couldn't understand why. It's not like you have to resort to that. In fact, I'd have said you were a man of principle in that area. But that'd be a pretty ridiculous statement under the circumstances, don't you think?"

"I think the altitude is starting to get to you." Playing it as if it were all in fun.

"But you weren't doing it to have her. It was for the job. I guess you thought she might be able to help. Tell you something. Or put a bug in Poague's ear. Pillow talk, that kind of stuff."

"That's enough."

He couldn't look at me to say it.

"What you didn't figure was that she'd tell Poague. But shit, you should've known that. Poague gets people's loyalties, one way or the other. She told Poague what was going on. It was you she held out on. She didn't let you know something was screwy with the job. What a hoot. She used you."

"Why should she do that?"

"Why not? Look at you. Look at her. I would in her place."

"No more," he said.

It might have ended there. I was spent. It was all out, all that I knew or suspected, and in the open air it seemed far less monstrous than the beast that had growled and snapped inside me all afternoon. It might have ended there, if Hollenbeck at that moment hadn't come grinding down the slope, coming toward us, every step creating a slide of pebbles.

He carried the cooking pots in his arms. Come to fill them with water. He stopped where we were and looked down at us and said, "Jeez, what's eating you guys?"

His credulous presence kicked something over in me.

"Ask our buddy," I said.

Travis said, "Come off it, Ray."

"I don't think he's going to tell you, George. So I will. Old Travis here has been playing back door games with Noreen Poague. Slap and tickle with the boss's wife."

"So what?"

"God, George, think about it. He wanted the job. He was looking for an edge. As if he needed it. Forget you and me. He was going for the big one."

"I'm not listening to this any more," Travis said. He stood and started up the grade.

"Tell him it's not true," I yelled at his back. He kept walking away. "Tell him I'm wrong."

To Hollenbeck I said, "I know I'm right. I know that's what he was up to."

"I don't care," Hollenbeck said. His face showed me something like pity.

"He was screwing Poague's wife to screw us out of that job."

"I don't care. I mean, I guess it's not right to sleep with somebody else's wife. If that's what he did. Maybe so. But he wasn't trying to hurt us."

"George, you have a terrible blind spot where Travis is concerned."

"He is my friend."

"He's a jerk."

"Now listen." Hollenbeck's voice was fierce. "He has helped me. He has always helped me. You know how I got this far up here? Because I believed. You don't get anywhere up here unless you believe, and he let me believe. He told me I could do it, and he told me that if I had trouble he'd help me. I wouldn't be here except for that. It's a hell of a lot more than I can say for you."

"George . . ."

"I don't want to hear it. He's my friend." He bent and swiftly scooped up water in the pots. "He's your friend, too, if you'd let him be."

He walked away and the water sloshed, and his huge dark gunboat boots crunched up, up, in the stones.

———

The deeper you get into the mountains, the closer you approach, the less you see of their scope and range. The less you see of the world. Your view is of vertical rock that looms like a Dickens taskmaster and conceals great portions of the sky.

The bowl that contained the lake where we stayed that night could have been a huge bomb crater. Camped halfway down its steep sides, we saw nothing of the horizon beyond, nothing of other mountains. We saw nothing of the sunset that settled over those mountains and across the horizon they formed.

Poague and Andrea did. He had found some strength that morning and by the end of the day they had reached the head of the first long boulderfield. Down that field, around the lake, and they would be back on the trail again.

She knew it might be no more than a long day's walk if Poague held up. She regretted having taken so much food— enough to feed them well for at least four days—and she wished she had checked her pack more carefully. If she had, she might not have forgotten to leave the set of maps that now sat in a side compartment of the pack. She didn't need them, and she thought that Gary might be more inclined to teach some trail navigation if he could use two sets of maps.

There in the broad valley at the head of the first boulderfield there were no close walls to block the view. Andrea and Poague could see the sunset and the clouds in front of it. Poague noticed them first, a band of tufted furrows that stretched across the south and west.

Altocumulus, he said, and Andrea looked. Her first thought was of Poague: more than ever she wanted to get him through the boulders and down the trail before the next day was through. Then she remembered us, somewhere up there, and she hoped that when things got tough tomorrow, Gary wouldn't be too much of a jerk.

14

The eleventh of September, sixth day of our journey. This part I dread remembering, this and so much of what follows. It's one thing to retrace wrong paths taken, portentous mistakes, flawed judgments; they don't seem so dreadful if you manage to deal with them separately, out of their deadly succession. But eventually you get to results. At the end of every string of actions are consequences that stand alone, clear and unambiguous.

We're reaching that point now. The end of the string. What happened. Beyond rationalizing and dissembling. Whenever I think of it I become withered inside, a desiccated gourd ready to crumble under the pressure of a breath.

Gary woke us early, hustled us through breakfast. He said he wanted seven miles before lunch. Then we'd try rock climbing.

We met sunrise when we hiked over the rim. All morning we hiked northwest, angling obliquely toward the barrier of peaks in front of us. Our packs were light, our feet cushioned with a sticky amalgam of layered tape and bandages and dried blood ooze. We clopped patiently up the one long stretch that we met, and strode across the rest; that morning was as close as we ever came to meeting the Beartooths on even terms.

Two moments worth mentioning.

We had been walking for about two hours when Donnie yelled that he was going to bust a gut if we didn't stop. Gary said, "Goddamn, we just took a break twenty minutes ago, you should have done it then."

And Donnie said, "I did it then and I have to do it again."

We stopped. Donnie got the trenching shovel and went behind a rock.

"Rest of you, don't bother taking off your packs," Gary said. "We're going to get moving in two minutes whether he's with us or not."

Charles walked up to Gary, said something to him. There was a gravity about the boy that had to be confronted. Not even Gary could avoid it forever. After a moment, grudgingly, Gary reached into an inside pocket of his poncho and brought out a map.

He unfolded it, squatted, spread it across his knees. Charles haunched beside him and peered at the map, pulled it to him. I wondered whether the boy understood the map, the arcane flowing lines that I remembered from Poague's office in June. Then thought: Of course he does. He knows everything. For maybe half a minute his head snapped between the paper and the view around us, and for those few seconds he was not at all childlike, but intent, purposeful, his eyes searching the map even as Gary took it from him, folded it, and put it back in the poncho.

One more, about half an hour later. We were walking hard, down a long, declining, grassy strip beside a stream. The grass was about ankle-high, thick, dead: the color of buckskin. It swished when we walked and made a wonderful cushion for stone-bruised heels. I was behind Gary at the front of the line. The last time I had looked back, Travis and Hollenbeck were walking side by side at the rear. Neither of them had spoken to me since the evening before, there at the lake's edge.

Now I heard heavy feet sweeping through the grass, a quickened pace. Hollenbeck drew beside me. Not even breathing hard, I thought. And I noticed that the belt didn't cut nearly so deep a groove in his midriff.

He said, "Ray, I want to talk."

"I'm not the one who's been avoiding it."

"I mean without anger. As friends."

"I always thought you were my friend, George."

"I am. We go back a long way." We tramped eight, ten steps farther before he said, "You have to apologize to Paul."

"Forget it."

"His feelings are hurt."

"Oh, hell, I don't want to hear this."

"Whatever he did isn't worth getting upset about."

"What he did was to stick a shiv in my back and in yours. I'm not going to apologize for being just the slightest bit disturbed about that."

"He didn't mean to hurt us. Even if he did do what you say he did."

"Don't tell me he's still denying it."

"I haven't asked him," Hollenbeck said.

"Don't bother. He'll tell you what you want to hear. It's what he's best at—giving you a look at what you want. That's all you get, just a look. But it's enough to keep some people impressed."

"Even if he did it," Hollenbeck said. "You have to understand why. He thought he had to have that job. He's a very proud guy."

All this time I had been speaking straight ahead, watching where I walked. Now I kept walking and turned to Hollenbeck, not so that he could hear me, but to let my voice carry back to Travis.

"He's a bullshitter," I said. "The man is all show and no go. You can be his friend if you want. But don't ask me. He's not the only one with pride."

Behind me Eleanor said, "Ray."

"You're making a big mistake," Hollenbeck said.

But I ignored him, put my head down and walked harder,

faster. He chopped his steps to slow down and I moved past him. And did I ever feel righteous, and full of myself.

———————

We didn't eat much lunch. We were stopped below a set of cliffs out of a John Ford western. Tall, straight columns, mottled with dark mineral seeps and sienna streaks. When we spread out to eat, Gary said casually, "Oh yeah, by the way, this is where you're going to pretend you're rock climbers."

So while we might have been eating we kept looking at the cliff, studying its fastness.

We were going to climb straight up the wall, but you could also walk up to the top, and down from there. The cliffs and the butte they formed were half of a broad dome. Picture the dome sliced vertically in two, one half still standing and the other strewn in pieces of slag and rubble. From the base of the cliffs the direct way to the top was to climb straight up. But if you moved to either side the wall dropped down, the dome sloping until finally its curve met the ground; from there you could jump up and follow the edge of the precipice as it rose to the apex of the arch.

Gary went up that way. He took two ropes and a bag of climbing gear. He worked up top for a while, dropped a rope over the side. Charles watched it fall and gather at the base of the cliff, and said, "Looks like about ninety feet." When Gary came down it was straight down, clipped into the rope, rappeling in a single smooth descent that was so frightening, so beautiful, I had to remind myself to start breathing again when he was unhooked and walking among us.

We dragged out helmets and webbing. To each of us he gave three carabiners, big snap hooks with locking gates. He kept talking and things began to happen, too fast to take it all in. Showing us how to use bowlines and loops to fashion a sling harness around our thighs, a water knot to secure it around our waist. Instructions on where to snap the carabiners. How to tie into the rope. Belaying. A call-and-response shout between the climber below and the belayer up top, something about giving rope and taking up slack. And climbing: don't lean into the rock, don't reach too high or step too far, let your legs do the work. So much. It flew in and bounced around my head and left me shuddering and fluttering inside when it flew away.

A check of knots and harnesses, and he was going up again, walking up the curve of the arch. At the top he clipped in to some anchor we couldn't see, snugged the rope around his waist and shouted, "Okay, somebody has to go first."

We stood, looking up at him, what little of him was visible beyond the edge of the cliff. Looking past helmets that tilted awkwardly on our heads, feeling the constriction of the harness at crotch and belly.

After a second Donnie said, "Hey I'll do it if nobody else wants to." He walked forward and tied the end of the rope to his harness. A quick hop, one foot up, then another, hands grabbing, moving, and he was gripping the cliff with toes and fingers.

You're born knowing how to climb, Gary had said, then you spend your life forgetting how. Don't think about it; just do it. Donnie did, as if he had been born to do it. No pause longer than a heartbeat. Moving, moving, and up.

He stood there, untied the rope. Shouted, exultant, "That was fresh, Jack, that was sharp, that was bitchin'."

Charles next. On the rock, clinging. Long hesitations when a hand or a boot searched for holds.

"Charlie Too Bad, you got it, no problem." Donnie, kneeling at the edge and yelling down. "That crack right there. Uh-huh. Now you got it, real easy, no problem."

They walked down together, down the curve of the dome where Gary had come up.

The rest of us stood watching the sky, a dark wind biting our cheeks, our hearts shriveling inside.

"Somebody," Gary said. "Anybody." When no one moved he said, "Ray. You're up."

I remember standing at the angle where the cliff met the earth. Ducking the rope that Gary dropped down, finding the end, tying it through the harness. Another bowline. Breath coming short, shallow.

I remembered the litany and shouted, "On belay." Hollow voice that I didn't recognize.

From above: "Belay on."

"Climbing," I yelled and heard "Climb" from far away.

The standing rock seemed to stretch and grow as I looked up. The rope was an endless strand, infinitely elastic. A few inches above my head was a horizontal crevice that could have been gouged expressly to give grip to a hand. I put both of mine on it, tightened fingers, found a protrusion with one boot, stepped up, found a nubbin with the other boot, and I was on the rock.

One arm moved upward, then a boot, and the others followed in order, obeying mental commands I couldn't hear over the roaring awareness of my sudden distance from the earth.

I moved, stopped, searched for holds and bulges, reached them and stopped again. The holds no wider than a pencil, the bulges subtle swellings. But I felt them. My fingertips alive, pulsing, understanding complexities of texture and friction and angle. Hooking over a narrow edge, brushing away the grains of dirt and scraps of moss that have settled there, sensing a fault in the rock, pressing down to break away a few flaky chips, then finally finding it whole and letting it take full weight.

And all the time the insistent suction of the earth, not just the physical pull but the desperation of having left a place where I belonged, a place that wanted me back very badly. The rope was no comfort; to dangle free was as terrifying as a fall.

I clung to stone and fled upward.

"About ten more feet. Use that big mother crack to your right." Gary, sounding close. I found the crack, big enough to hold a boot, and abandoned myself to its safety. Jammed in toes and an elbow, worked my way up, found head and shoulders rising into tweedy sky, pushed up and flopped my torso forward and reclaimed legs and feet from the cliff.

I turned over on my back and lay panting.

Gary said, "Hey, nice little undercling there about halfway up. I need that rope, huh?"

I untied the bowline, started back down. For about half its length the path down was a crumbling ledge a foot and a half wide. A boulevard.

Hollenbeck went up, then Eleanor. I imagined her being where I had been a couple of minutes earlier, feeling the tug of the earth, her fingers tucked into the same creases, boots edged along the stubs that had given me security. At the top she was more sure than I had been: palms flat on the mantle, a push upward, a kick, and she was standing. Nipping the knot loose and handing the end to Gary like a hot dog vendor giving change.

Travis stood at the bottom, tried to catch the rope, fumbled it. He picked it up and began to tie in. Pulled at the knot, untied it, tried it again but stopped before he was finished. Poked the stub end through the loop and studied it and pulled it out and tore the knot apart.

I saw this from a few feet away. Over my shoulder I looked for Donnie to tell him, Hey kid, looks like this guy broke into your stash. But Donnie wasn't there and from up top Gary yelled, "Son of a bitch, you people were supposed to have those knots down. Ray, somebody, will you please do it for him?"

Charles got there before I could. Travis fixed on the top of the cliff, never looked at Charles working the rope, yanking the knot tight.

His eyes didn't move as Charles stepped away. Travis put his hands against the rock, leaned forward. I realized that he was waiting for something to happen.

"On belay," Charles said. "You're supposed to tell him."

Travis bent his head back and forced up the words, and Gary answered.

"Climbing," Charles said, and Travis repeated it louder, and Gary spoke back.

Nothing happened.

"Right above your head," I said. Some grudging wellspring of charity; I remembered how the wall had seemed to expand in front of me. "The crack right there. And you've got places for both feet."

He put his hands up there, got one foot up; the other dug and scratched before it held. A long pause before he moved. A hand. A foot. He was going up.

His climb was different from the rest of ours. In what way, I can't say exactly. I too was slow going up. Charles also was uncertain when he felt for holds. Hollenbeck's feet as well slipped and pawed before they found a rest. So we had our problems. But we had made it to the top and Travis wasn't going to. With about forty feet left he stopped and leaned into the rock and rested his forehead against the wall.

From the top Gary said, "Hey Paul, buddy, not too far now."

Travis's head moved back and forth in small distinct movements of refusal.

"You've got a hold, left hand, I can see it. Good solid ledge."

Again the quiet shake of the head.

We saw what was happening. Charles yelled up something brave and Hollenbeck did the same, clapped his hands. The kind of pepper talk you might hear from kids in a playground ball game.

He didn't budge.

"Paul," Eleanor said. "Paul, listen. You can do it. I did it. Me. You can do it."

Donnie came out from behind a rock, carrying the shovel. Dinner last night, he was saying to nobody, must have been something wicked in dinner last night.

He looked around, took it in. Took in Travis on the rock and the rest of us watching and shouting. He kept looking at us looking up at the wall. He said, "Yelling won't get him up there." He threw down the shovel and moved straight toward the cliff.

At the bottom he slowed, didn't stop. A short leap, one hand fastening, then the other, both boots thumping into the wall and staying there. He was ten feet up before Gary could shout, "No, no, you crazy little bastard you get down now, I mean it, I mean right now."

His hands and feet kept moving, sticking where he placed

them, moving. Travis shouted some more. A single snowflake drifted across my eyes; I wished the speck away so I wouldn't miss anything. Three, four snowflakes, rocking down. A dozen agitated snowflakes as Donnie climbed even with Travis.

They were talking. Travis's head didn't move. He spoke into the rock and it swallowed his words, but I could hear Donnie telling him about the big ledge. Donnie said it was good and strong, he'd hung onto it himself, that's where you have to start.

Donnie's voice dropped. I could hear a soft, confident tone. Travis moved his head away from the wall and looked at Donnie.

I stepped back from the cliff so I could see better. A hundred snowflakes. A thousand. Donnie untethered on the rock. Travis's head tilting up, his left hand reaching for the ledge, grabbing it.

Snow patted wet against my face. Where it hit the ground it disappeared. Wet specks where it had fallen. I thought of my hands on the rock—dry rock—and thought of Donnie up there, his fingers and soles touching the slickness that the snow left.

Travis moving arms and legs. Gaining a body's length. In his motions I could read belief for the first time. He stood on the ledge, Donnie talking up to him now. Snow falling in my eyes. Falling in Donnie's eyes. He brushed it away.

Travis climbed, almost frantic to get off the cliff. At the top he put out a hand. Gary lunged for it, connected, pulled him up while Travis's feet scraped on the brow of the rock.

Travis went up and over. He sprawled across Gary and for a second all I could see of them was their boots.

Donnie was alone. He raised his right arm, touched the wall, brought the arm down, wiped the hand on his pants, put it back. Wiped his left hand. The snowflakes a thick swirling overlay. Behind it Donnie climbed, one move at a time now, tentative, tensed. My face was wet from the melting snow. White pockets were collecting in the wall's recesses. Travis rolled over and sat up, and I could see Gary reaching back, unsnapping the carabiner that fastened him to his anchor.

Donnie got to the top, lifted himself over. He stood and turned to go down the path. Gary was standing too, shouting something at Donnie. I could see Donnie in the snow, pendulous flakes, Donnie turning and saying something surly over his shoulder. Snow so thick it muffled sound from the top of the wall. Gary making an angry gesture, stepping over Travis's legs at the edge, stepping clear of Travis, stepping toward Donnie.

There was loose rock along the edge, gravel. The rock must have been slippery with the snow, and Gary must have skidded on it. Must have happened that way but from where I watched the cliff just seemed to spit him off. One moment he was moving toward Donnie, swiping a hand at the air, and an instant later his feet were out from under him and he was falling, twisting his body to keep the cliff's edge beneath him, hitting the edge and slapping off it and tumbling down.

I watched him fall and waited for the tape to stop, reality to rewind itself and properly resume. He kept falling through the snow, past the mineral stains and sienna streaks and high reaching rock.

If I followed him all the way to the ground I have excised the image from my mind. Surely the impact made a sound, but I retain no memory of that either. Yet I must have seen or heard, because I knew when he hit, the exact instant. The air became a viscous suspension through which we and noise and truth moved with excruciating effort.

Charles was closest to where he fell, and started toward the place. I wanted to get there first, wanted to spare the boy that. I tried to shout him off it, but the sudden denseness stifled my call and restrained my motions when I tried to run. When I finally got there Charles was staring down. I could see his face, aghast. I forced my eyes down to see what he was seeing.

Gary lay chest down across a waist-high, sharp-peaked rock in a way I had never seen anyone lie before, a posture of violence come to pass. His head twisted impossibly to look back at me with dull eyes; his arms and legs in flagrant angles.

Eleanor was beside me, gasping, clutching my arm and crushing her face to my sleeve. Hollenbeck had Charles by the shoulders, trying to pull him away, but Charles resisted, tore free, shot an elbow into George's middle; his eyes never once leaving the spectacle on the rock.

Donnie running up, stopping short. Travis behind him, openmouthed, wide-eyed, panting. Donnie turning, head swiveling, shouting, "Help!"

He was shouting into the snow and the awful breadth of mountains, shouting Help! into the great emptiness that the mountains filled, Help! at the horizon that the mountains rumpled and mocked, shouting Please Somebody Help! into the mountains that contained us solely and completely.

PART III
DESCENT

15

For a while there we had crazy time, rapid unraveling of reason and good sense.

Charles stared, unblinking, at the broken body. Donnie wailed for help and nobody told him there was only us to hear. Eleanor removed her face from my sleeve, took out a bandana and pushed at the courses of the tears along her nose and down her cheeks; though snow fell in her face and made it wet everywhere she was very careful to dab only at the tears. Hollenbeck turned his back and looked out toward the distance. He might have been waiting for a bus. Travis kept muttering something too low for me to make out. Sanity came apart and you might argue that for as long as we were in those mountains we never again got it fully restored.

That's not for me to say, since I was caught up in the unraveling as fully as anyone.

In me it was a sudden compulsion to be at the top, to see where it had happened. I climbed the path. Rising above the shouts and tears and unblinking stares. The snow was falling faster than it could melt, beginning to coat the rocky cleats and landings where I had felt so secure a few minutes earlier.

I must have taken two or three minutes to reach the hump of the arch. Snow covered everything when I got there, thick enough that I stepped unawares on the belay rope where Gary had played it out during Travis's climb. Beside it was the anchor where he had clipped himself in, a web sling attached to two pitons hammered into the rock.

I went there, sat where he had sat, got up and walked two or three steps to the spot where he had fallen. A morbid little pilgrimage, I knew. But it seemed important. I knelt and felt the edge that he had tried to catch after he slipped. I imagined his arms touching it and then being dragged away as he fell. The last instant when he might have believed he could save himself. My hands caressed in wonderment the last piece of earth he had touched while he was still whole and alive.

I looked over the edge. His body sprawled directly below, the others keeping their antic vigil around it. I imagined his plunge down that space, the earth hurtling up to meet him, what he must have seen. His plunge through the space that yawned in front of me.

Too much, too far. I was leaning forward so abruptly that I felt once more the pull that I had resisted while I climbed the wall. Now urging me again as I leaned forward, the edge of the rock a fulcrum for my weight. A matter of balance, maybe not so much the inner ear as the soul.

I jerked myself back, a spasm of the spine, and fell rearward on the solidness before the edge.

When I stood the footing tipped and pitched beneath me, yawing so badly I got down on all fours. The dome was coming alive, a quiescent beast stirred by our presence, our arrogance. It had shrugged Gary dead and now it was trying to do the same to me.

I wanted off. Had to get down that path, now snow-coated, now impossibly narrow. I tried to walk down as I had a few minutes earlier, but the beast twitched and I fell and clutched the earth. I sat and felt it settle beneath me. So I went down that way, on hands and bottom, sliding my seat and bracing myself with rigid arms, going slowly and with great deliberation.

Getting down and off took me longer than going up. Finally I could stand and walk to the others, and as I walked could look up at the curve of the dome and find impossible the idea that I or any of us or anyone at all had stood up there.

Eleanor met me before I got to the others. Her face was wet but she wasn't crying any more. The bandana was balled in her right hand. With much effort her eyes held on me.

"He's dead," she said.

I nodded.

"It's snowing," she said.

Again nodded.

She looked down at the bandana, started to bring it to her face, but put it on my cheeks instead and brushed away the snowmelt that must have beaded there. Then she shook it out and folded it and tied it tight where the neck of her sweater met skin. Highly rational. It would keep the snow from falling in.

She summoned strength, pursed lips and relaxed them, and spoke.

"Ray, we have to do something," she said. "He's dead and it's snowing like hell."

Her calmness held off the collapsing sky.

"I guess we have to bury him," I said.

"I guess so. We should put up shelter and get out of the weather too."

"I don't want to stay here tonight."

"No. Some place else. But we have to get started."

I clasped her to me and felt her substance. When I let go the sky was lifted all the way back.

"It won't take all of us to get him in the ground," I said. "Me and one more. You take the rest and make a camp and get some food started."

That was something tangible; holding on to it kept me steady. We had started back toward the others when Travis came up and stopped us.

He said, "Listen, I've tried to tell everybody else. This is not my fault. He was past me when he went over. I don't know what happened, he was near the edge and he went over. But he was past me, understand? He was clear of me. I had nothing to do with it."

I caught the tone and the rhythm of his muttering from a few minutes earlier.

"Paul, nobody's accusing you."

"I want it known, that's all."

I realized this wasn't aimless raving. It was important to him. He really did want it known. So he was within reason after all: his own reasons, maybe, but that was enough.

He opened his mouth and began to speak again. No words came out—none that I could hear. I was captivated by a fantastic sudden vision. Travis's skin wasn't skin at all but a very thin and fragile membrane that was filled to bursting with some kind of jelly. If he instead of Gary had fallen he would have been all over the place when he hit. As it was he was coming apart, this semiliquid gluten dripping out where his seams were weak.

"I could have made it, you know," he said. I didn't want him to move, even to speak: he would only tear, and his insides spill out. "The little punk didn't have to help me. A grandstand play. I was just resting. I was going to make it on my own."

As I watched he became muscle and bone again, as solid as flesh ever is.

"I don't think it matters," I said. I wondered which state was the illusion.

"No. It's the truth."

"I believe you. Nobody's blaming you. Here, you want to help us? We have to get things squared away here."

He followed us over to the others; I watched sidelong and saw that he was avoiding the body, the sight of it.

I remembered my sling harness. It felt silly; I took it off, folded it, and put it away. The others were coming back on center. Donnie, silent, sitting near the peaked rock and holding his face in his hands. Hollenbeck, pulling out his poncho and draping it over the body.

I said, "Don't bother. Donnie and I are going to start a grave. Everybody else can find a camp site and get it going."

Hollenbeck said, "There were some trees about a mile back. They'll give us a place to tie the tarps."

I remembered a patch of dwarf pine, trunks no wider than my ankles.

"Just the way we came," I said. "Not far back, right? Make sure that's the place. We'll have to find it when we're done. Donnie and I. We don't want to have to hunt for it."

"Let's go now," Eleanor said. Charles didn't move. Eleanor said his name, and he flinched slightly. Hollenbeck pulled the poncho away and Charles seemed to see the body for the first time. He recoiled, turned, and immediately dry-retched.

Eleanor skirted the body and went to Charles. She held him, wouldn't let him turn back to look, led him away.

They got their packs, the four of them. While Travis and Charles waited, Eleanor came over and Hollenbeck followed her.

"Is this right?" she said to me. She meant leaving. I let Hollenbeck answer.

"The snow scares me," he said. "I don't like walking around in it. I want to get out of it."

"It scares me too," she said. It felt like black wrath coming down on us. Clinging and suffocating. It was wet, the kind that's good to play with in your backyard. But here rolling it up and flinging it was the last thing you would imagine. It would be like tweaking Satan.

I said, "You know what we have to do. He'd be ragging us right now to get those tarps up."

She said, "Hurry, okay?" I watched the four of them walk off into the snow.

Donnie and I and Gary's body. Us and the wall and the low afternoon light filtering dimly through the clouds. For digging we had just the one shovel. Its spade head was little broader than my hand, and the foot-long wooden shaft belonged on a bathroom plunger.

Where we stood was rock bits on pulverized rock, the shattered half of the dome. But beyond the hard scatter some stunted grass bristled through the snow. It looked like good digging ground, and for a while it was. Donnie and I took turns, one working and sweating while the other stood and shivered as sweat evaporated. Donnie was a couple of minutes into his second turn when he complained once more about what last night's dinner was doing to his stomach, so when he went off I was working again, turning up moist loam that clung to the grass roots.

He returned when I was trying to estimate the dimensions of the pit. It had to be long enough but I didn't want to dig more than necessary. I started to heel-and-toe six feet but Donnie stretched out in the fresh scar of earth. He lay there with the snow blotting his face, just long enough for me to see that I was a few inches short. Then I made him get up fast.

I thought of Gary. When my turn came to rest I went over to the peaked rock. I didn't want him to be alone. That I was keeping company inanimate meat did not occur to me, though I suppose I would have acknowledged it under enough pressure. Rather my reasoning went something like: I know he doesn't care for us, and maybe he'd rather be by himself, but he should have somebody with him at a time like this.

This is the sort of dangerous shunt your mind may take up there, where matters are usually so clear. I can only conclude that clarity and craziness share the same deep wellspring.

We worked and felt the sun dropping. We scooped and dug, taking out fresh snow with every spadeful of dirt.

We were about two feet down when Donnie hit the hard stuff. Slush for a couple of inches, mud laced with ice crystals, then ground that was frozen hard. He called me over. I took the shovel and scraped away some of the icy mud. What lay below was so hard it would accept only the tip of the spade when I jabbed it in.

Donnie asked what it was, and I told him it must be permafrost. I had heard about it in the Arctic. Never in the real world—if the Beartooths qualify. Never in any place I had ever expected to walk.

I put my hand down and pressed against the firmness. Gary's resting place on frozen earth. It was almost marble. Even through my glove I could feel the utter unyielding cold that chills earth forever. Cold was everywhere up here, in the air, the rock, in the night, even hiding beneath the soil.

"Is it deep enough?" Donnie said.

"It has to be." I thought I could make out a soft smear of brightness, not far above the hills to the west. We had maybe an hour before sunset.

We walked reluctantly to the peaked rock and the body that had lain all afternoon where it fell. Without a word I went to the head and Donnie to the feet.

I said, "Don't freak on me now."

"I won't. This isn't really him, right, Ray? He's gone. Wherever he is, huh? He's not here."

"That's right. This is just something we have to carry over to that hole. A heavy package that we have to get over there."

Donnie held him around his calves and I slid both hands under the neck of his poncho and held the fabric. I had never touched a dead man before. My knuckles grazed the back of his shoulders, those magnificently muscled shoulders.

Donnie counted three and we lifted. He was heavy.

With quiet terror Donnie said, "Ray, he's frozen all the way through."

"That's part of it."

"Oh. Yeah."

We crabbed across the snow and broken stone.

I said, "Yell if you get tired. We can rest."

"No. No stopping."

Across the snow and stone. Once Donnie slipped and grunted fearfully, went to his knees. But he kept his burden from dropping, straightened up, and we continued on.

We got him there and turned him over, face up. I don't know why. But it seemed we should. I never even questioned it. The hole had looked enormous, but he filled it up. I felt ashamed, seeing that, feeling that we ought to have done better.

Donnie took the shovel, I used my hands, and we scooped in the loose dirt. Covering his face was worst. His eyes were open and his mouth was parted. I should have closed them all but I was afraid I'd have to fight the rigor. So his blind open eyes watched me as I filled my hands with earth and let it drop out gradually, as softly as I could, over his paraffin cheeks and his lips the color of worn denim. I did three cupped handfuls, probably should have done it all that way, but I could see that smear of light closing on the earth's edge.

Finally we had a rounded hummock of fresh loose earth. We tried to pat it firm. I made Donnie empty his pack, fill it with stones, array the stones over the bulge. I lugged over some bigger ones. We did this until it was covered. I don't know the point of all this effort except that when we were finished it looked like a real grave, not something done in haste, and that seemed important. The light was dimming when we stood and looked at our work.

"We did him okay," I said.

He said, "Ray. Let's get the fuck out of here, all right?"

He was filling his pack when I saw Gary's, leaning against a rock, topped with a dollop of snow five or six inches high. Gary's was different from ours: bigger, with more pockets, somehow more serious and more formidable. With most of the food gone, ours were flabby, almost empty. But this pack still bulged, the way ours had a few days earlier.

I swept off the snow. The pack had heft when I lifted it. At least thirty pounds. Fierce crampons strapped to the back. An ice axe, even more fierce, secured by a pair of loops. A headlamp and battery in one side pocket. Folded maps in the next. I thought, Thank God; maps. Of course. Maps.

Donnie was looking at me.

"Anything in there we can use?"

"At this point we can use everything." I swung the pack across one shoulder, up on my back. Donnie stuffed what was left from my own pack into his, and we started to leave. The light definitely plunging.

We walked south toward where the others had gone. Before the snow swallowed it up I looked back at the halved dome, and thought about how the beast had stirred under my boots, the humpbacked monster that now slept again, and about all the other restive beasts that waited between us and where we belonged.

16

We walked into deep night. Hollenbeck had figured the pines about a mile away. It seemed right to me. A straight walk, no climbing. Maybe half an hour at a decent pace. There should have been that much residual daylight, and Donnie and I were hurrying.

But we walked into deep night. Donnie got out his flashlight and I put on the headlamp. He helped me fasten it over my cap and under the poncho hood, and when he was finished he said, "Ray, do you know where we are?"

I said I thought so, but I wasn't sure.

"The damn snow," I said.

Snow changes things. I'm talking about the physical look of the world, how it obscures the cues by which we realize our surroundings: eliminating color, softening abrupt edges, filling depressions, adding and subtracting until all is evenness. Under enough snow a tree is a truck is a house.

I should have known this. I could remember two or three snowstorms in D.C. that deserved the name. They had transformed the place. For a few hours, until the sun came out and the gobs of white dropped off branches and roofs and telephone lines, I could only pretend to recognize the street where I lived. In wilderness its effect is even deeper and faster, because the cues are subtler, more easily disguised. The thrust of this cropping of schist, the radius of that bend in the stream, so easily confused with hundreds of other croppings and bends. Or maybe it's all a matter of what you're used to.

"I don't remember walking downhill like this," he said. "I mean uphill. I think it was more level than this."

"This is level."

"Uh-uh. I don't think so. I think we've been going down a little for the last ten minutes or so."

We couldn't see. Too much snow, and night was near fullness.

The cold bit my nose. I could feel it in the extreme joints of my fingers, trying to force its way up. My toes didn't exist any more.

"I don't understand how we could have gone wrong," I said. Arguing against the sense of something askew that had been rising in me for the last few minutes. Arguing out of pride, I guess; Donnie had been following my lead.

"I don't know either. But this doesn't feel right."

"I thought we were headed in the direction."

"I did too. But we should have hit the trees by now."

"Maybe they're farther than we thought," I said.

"Maybe."

"I don't remember any turns or anything like that, do you? I don't think we missed anything."

"I don't think so."

"Then they ought to be out here somewhere."

He squinted in the headlamp's glare when I turned to him. He looked so young. A child, following my lead into deep night.

"We have to do something," he said.

"Let's walk the way we've been going for a few more minutes. I think we must be close."

We walked on and night huddled around us. In the incandescence wind-driven flakes gleamed and smeared our vision. We could make out where our next two steps would fall. Enough, maybe, to keep us from walking off a cliff. We couldn't even be sure of walking a straight line.

I stopped. My futility was as obvious as the darkness.

"This is stupid," I said. "I have no idea where we are. I'm sorry."

I believed that I was apologizing for our demise. No possible way could we survive fourteen hours of night and wind and snow. Already I could feel my warmth surrendering beachheads to the chill.

He said, "We have our tracks, Ray." Sounding matter-of-fact. "They won't get us there. But at least we won't be as lost as we are now, huh?"

It seemed important. Not that in returning to the dome we would be any closer to finding the others, or any less close to freezing, dying, in the night. Yet somehow the difference was crucial: to know where we were when we froze and died.

The snow was at least eight inches deep, so the freshest tracks were clear. We followed them and for a time there was solace in these marks of our human presence, evidence of our vitality. But wind eroded them and new snow filled them up. Before long we could see the wells that our steps had left, but no more the tread of our soles. Then snow drifting into the holes and rounding their edges. Then no holes, only shallow impressions, and the hinted memory of impressions, until we reached an exposed swell that the wind scoured down to bare rock. No steps there, and none that we could find beyond.

We began to wander, trying to pick up the outline of a boot, aimless, seeking direction. The falling snow seemed to pulse, raging and relenting and raging again. I could see Donnie's light to my right, faint when the snow burst down, more clear when it paused.

A shout. His voice. Saying, "Ray, c'mere."

I looked to my right. The snow gushed, a solid cascade of huge flakes. No light.

"Ray. Hey, man."

I went toward the words. No light.

"Ray. Ray. Come *on*."

I called back to him.

"Over here. This way." The wind picked up his voice, carried it around, dropped it some place different. No light.

He shouted and I shouted. Gaps appeared in the fluttering white curtain. His light, poking randomly, disappeared, then found me, and held full in my face. I churned toward him.

"I lost you," he said.

"Let's not do that again for a while, huh?"

"But look. I saw a light."

Where he pointed I could make out only hotly streaking snow. I turned off the headlamp and he averted his flash, to make dull gray snow and darkness.

"It was there, Ray."

We watched. The curtain convulsed and broke. Behind it a spot of brightness bounced with a plodding rhythm.

We ran toward it, shouting and shaking our own lights. The bouncing spot rested on us and Hollenbeck walked into our glare.

I gasped, "George."

"Oh. There you are," Hollenbeck said. "Paul was getting worried. He sent me to look for you." He turned his head, as if taking in the snow and the night for the first time. "It's rotten out here."

"We noticed," Donnie said.

"We may have gotten a little off the track," I said.

"Well, anyway," Hollenbeck said. "You made it. That's what matters."

He was turning to go back the way he had come.

"We're not anywhere yet," I said.

"Sure you are." He was walking away. I ran to catch him and Donnie was right behind. That was salvation we saw leaving us.

He covered maybe twenty steps up a slight distention of the earth. At the top he stopped, waited for us.

Ahead, close enough to fall in the beam of my headlamp, stood several bowed and beaten dwarf pines, bending under the weight of snow. Tucked within them, two blue tarps strung up to form a single tent, the ends pinched closed.

With perplexity in his voice he said, "How close did you want to be?"

17

It had been Travis's idea to look for us. And I believed that Travis had been wrong.

Don't think me ungrateful. I knew that if Hollenbeck hadn't been out there, we might have walked past the trees without seeing them. Probably had. I knew how close we had been to a miserable death. When I crawled into the shelter and joined the others I felt only gratitude and relief. Not until later did I question the decision, the impulse, that had saved us.

The tent was about chest level at its highest. Inside it had about the area of a station wagon. One flashlight for illumination; it stood upright, wedged between Eleanor and Charles at their hips. They and Travis sat up, sleeping bags pulled around their shoulders.

Charles said, "Hey, Ray, Donnie," his voice and his expression subdued. Eleanor was drained, but her face took on light when she saw us. And Travis . . .

"You're here!" Travis said. "Can you believe this snow?" He skinned the sleeping bag down to his waist, leaned forward and thumped each of us on the shoulder, a comradely gesture, a peculiarly male gesture of bond and bravado.

"I've been feeling real guilty," he said. "Letting you two get stuck with such a rotten job. I had no idea it would take so long. Maybe you needed one more hand to make it go faster, huh? I knew I should've stayed behind. Then when it got dark I started to get real worried, so I sent George out in your direction to see what he could see."

The first time, out of Hollenbeck's mouth, it had escaped me. But this time I got a quick twinge when I heard it: *I sent George out.*

I thought, Who are you to be sending George into that? To send anyone anywhere?

But his dazzle distracted me.

"Anyway, you're here," he said. "Nice navigating—I'm not sure I could have found my way back in this crap. Here, better get into your bags. It's the only way to stay warm."

We did as he said. Travis, the Travis I'd known for years, had that way about him.

"I wish I could offer you supper," he said. "But we're getting low on provisions and I thought we ought to save food and fuel in case we really need it, next couple of days."

"We were going to resupply tomorrow," I said. I hadn't thought about it.

"Uh-huh. But Gary's the only one who knew where. We're down to one full dinner of bulgur. And snack stuff; about three cups of raisins, some cocoa, box of crackers, a few inches of a hard salami, and that cheddar."

I remembered the cheese: dried, darkened, sweating rancid fat, a carved rectangle that weighed maybe ten or twelve ounces. As it ripened and hardened it had become the joke food of the trip. Suddenly I wanted some.

"This is bad," I said.

"Damn right it's bad. We're probably as deep into this country as we were going to get. Tomorrow makes one week. You've got to figure we'd have started making our way back tomorrow."

My mind worked through facts, realities. Coming out of numbness.

"A week to get here. A week back," I said. "We don't have that much food."

So softly he was almost inaudible, Charles said, "Maybe we ought to see what else we do have." He nodded toward Gary's pack.

I opened it and dumped it empty; Charles held the flash-light on what spilled out. Clothes, a sleeping bag. A metal quart bottle that Hollenbeck opened, sniffed, found full of stove fuel. A package wrapped in black plastic: two freeze-dried meals for three or four persons each. Half a dozen date-nut bars. A box of stubby candles. A third plastic tarp, smaller than the others. First aid kit; inside, the usual bandages, oint-ments, and a small plastic bottle. Donnie opened the bottle, poured a few white pills into his palm.

"Percodan," he said. To our skeptical silence he added, "Believe me."

Maps. I remembered them in the side pocket. Before I could get them Charles had them out, pinning them in the light.

"He has an idea there's a quicker way out than the way we came," Travis said. Disapproving. "But I can't see it. We've got some food, we might get hungry but we're not going to starve. I say we go back the way we know. We've been there. We know what's there. And we're in better shape now. If we bust ass it won't take us as long as it did to get here."

The crinkle of the map pages. I heard them but watched Travis. With all the other awakenings I realized that Travis had taken over. He would. Of course. The Travis that George and I had known.

"It isn't here," Charles said. "There's supposed to be another quad. Alpine quad. We're about in the middle of it. I saw it today."

"Look again. It has to be in there," I said. I kept watching Travis. Remembering the guy whom fear had seized on the rock wall, his anxious muttering. The spectacle of his soft insides bursting through.

I told myself that he had done a terrific job of putting him-self back together. Unless you knew him, and looked closely, you probably wouldn't have realized that it was a hasty, desperate task, that not all the important pieces were in place.

Eleanor took her arms out of the bag and started to search the pack's side pockets.

I watched Travis. He sensed me. He was looking at the backpack, following the movement and the searching, but his eyes shifted to me, and even in the dimness they talked to me.

So you know. Fine. Just leave me be.

"I don't think it's here," Eleanor said.

"Got to be," I said. I turned away from Travis. "He had it out this morning. He showed Charles." The image returned, a memory of the boy and Gary bending over the map. Just a fragment. Then, unsummoned, the rest.

"Oh hell," I said. "He put it in his poncho. He folded it up and stuck it inside."

"Was it still there when you buried him?" Hollenbeck said.

"I'll tell you, George, I didn't go rifling the son of a bitch's pockets, okay?"

"Too bad you didn't."

"*Hey*," Travis said. "We don't need this." Calm, fraternal, but commanding. As I say, not a bad job on such short notice. "We're in big trouble if we start tearing into each other. The only way we get out is to hold tight together, and pull ourselves through."

I said, "It's my fault. I didn't think about the map. And the last thing I wanted to do was to search his clothes."

Donnie spoke; a tremor in his voice that he didn't try to conceal: "The rest of you weren't with him all that time. We dug a hole for him. We threw dirt on him. You don't think when you're doing that. The way you get through it, you put your head in cruise control. Automatic pilot, right? Don't get on Ray's case."

"Doesn't matter anyway," Travis said. "We know the way back."

Nobody said anything at first. I felt the snow and the silence and the cold and the night outside, all of them intruding on us. The accumulated snow bellying the sides of the shelter, the cold at our faces, the night lurking at the edges of the flash-light's beam. And the silence restoring itself among us, settling in. I hoped nobody would break it for a while.

"We could use that map," Charles said. Just a whisper; but the quiet fled. "Even if we go back the way we came. Look. We didn't necessarily get here the straightest way, or the fastest. I think we've sort of been meandering, especially since we got on this side of the pass. If we had the map we might be able to save a few hours."

Travis said, "Fine. You can get the map."

I said, "I'll get it. I know where he is. If the snow isn't so deep that I can't find the place, I'll go back in the morning and dig it out."

"That's up to you."

"I mean, I'm not averse to saving a mile or two if I can."

"Fine," he said. "I'm just telling everybody this. I have no intention of dying out here. The rest of you can do what you want. But I'm saving my butt. You follow me, I'll get you out."

———

I never did talk to him about having sent George out into the storm. I was there, after all; no arguing with results. But I knew he had been wrong. Get enough of us wandering around in a blizzard and the dark, and somebody is sure to die.

Eleanor lit one of the candles. It gave light and a tinge of warmth. The frost began to melt on the inside of the tarp walls. Heating water for cocoa was Eleanor's idea, too. We had extra fuel now, she said, no point in starving completely. Travis listened and nodded, so we got cocoa.

But not until he consented; that was the point.

Afterward Charles got up to go outside. He was fully dressed in his bag; he put on his boots and poncho, and was gone. It took me longer to get ready, so I was a couple of minutes behind him when I followed him out.

The snow had nearly ended. It lay in voluptuous shapes around the bases of the trees. A few windblown flecks scintil-lated in my light.

I stopped Charles as he was returning to the shelter,

motioned him to follow me farther away, out where we wouldn't be heard.

I said, "I want to know about this route of yours."

"No route, Ray. I need the map for that. But there's a town or something, some kind of settlement, on the other side of these mountains. I don't know how far—maybe a day and a half if we're walking fast. I remember seeing it on the map this morning."

"You know where?"

He gestured toward the northeast.

"That way," he said. "Somewhere. I'll bet the packer who's supposed to supply us starts out from there. We're probably supposed to meet him between here and there."

"You think we ought to try for the town?"

"If there's nothing in the way to keep us from getting there."

"Like what?"

"I don't know. A big gorge, maybe. Or if the pass was too hairy. That would do it."

"Paul has kind of taken over."

"Nobody else tried."

"He's that way."

"Every group needs a leader," he said. "It ought to be somebody who really knows what's going on. But if you can't have that, then it's almost as good to have somebody who everyone believes in. You don't have to know much if the others think you do."

"People do believe in Paul. He's always had that going for him."

Charles didn't say anything. I felt reproached.

I said, "At least the snow stopped, huh?"

"For now."

Above, the moon was a weak milky wash through clouds.

"I had the impression that storms come and go fast in the mountains."

He said, "Most of the time they do."

Foreboding squatted out there in that cold darkness, fat and ugly as a huge toad. I had to ask: "Are we in big trouble?"

"Maybe not." He sounded steady, almost detatched. "If the snow really does stop and the sun melts what's on the ground, we'll be okay. We'll just walk out and it won't matter which way we go."

"What if that doesn't happen?"

"If the snow gets much deeper we won't be able to go back the way we came. It's too far. Nobody can walk thirty miles through two feet of snow in these mountains." Still detatched.

"Are you worried?" I said.

"I'd like to look at the map. I'd feel a lot better if I could see some stars."

———

Later we lay in our bags, waiting for the candle to burn itself out. None of us slept. Not a word among us for what might have been ten minutes, might have been an hour. Time liquid and imperceptibly flowing.

Charles moved and shifted to reach into the pack where he rested his head. He brought out the group journal, and a pencil, and held them out to Donnie.

"Your turn," he said.

"Come on, blood, we're not playing those games any more. This is real life now."

"It's been real all along."

The notebook and the pencil were inches from Donnie's face.

"You're serious. You want me to write in that thing."

I heard myself saying, Go on, go ahead, and Eleanor did the same.

"Okay," he said, "you got it," and he took them. He opened the book and flipped through to the first empty page. The pencil scratched and jumped for a few seconds. He shut the book and stuck the pencil in the spiral binding.

"Who's next?" he said.

Hollenbeck raised a hand, and Donnie tossed it over to him. George took it and put it away in his pack, and time became liquid again, without event to mark it, until the candle went out and we were really and truly alone with ourselves.

Day Six
Saturday, September 11
Today we got dumped on but good. I don't see it getting better before it gets worse.

18

While the others dozed I dressed in my bag. I didn't dwell on the idea that in a few minutes I would be defiling a grave. The fact was just there, like another boulderfield to climb or another five miles to be hiked. No question of acceptance or evasion; there are no options. You just do it.

Donnie turned over when I slid out and tied my boots.

"Ray, I'll help." Even then he looked, sounded bad.

"It's a one-man job. I won't be long."

Now Eleanor was awake.

"Let me," she said. "You shouldn't go alone."

"I won't get lost."

"I know you can find your way there and back. But you shouldn't go alone."

I got the shovel and waited for her outside, under a low cinder sky that kept dropping as the light grew behind it. Soon she came out, and we started north toward the wall.

A cold morning, crisp enough that the snow was still crystalline and granular. I recognized nothing from the evening before, nothing from my first time down this path. Overnight the wind had sculpted the fall, scooping out hollows on one side of large rocks, blowing the excess into turgid spills that reached almost to the knee, the tops of our gaiters.

I felt her beside me. It was our first moment alone since we had climbed together, the morning of Poague's collapse. That morning. For a few minutes not a word passed, but something, an awareness, filled up the space between us. I tried to think about that, and not about the toes that were going dead again, and not about what waited in the shadow of the half-dome.

She reached for me. She could have grabbed my shoulder or my elbow. Instead she took my hand. Thick mitten over thick mitten; I felt her touch anyway.

"Slow down," she said. She was breathing hard. I stopped; she still held my hand. "I can't go so fast in this stuff."

"I didn't realize I was hurrying."

"You were almost running."

"I guess I want to get this over with."

Her hand tightened. We walked again. I relaxed my fingers enough to release her if she wanted, but the grip remained, insistent, and I folded it up in mine.

The dome was closer than I had imagined. In no more than fifteen minutes it rose profiled before us, the truncation shockingly abrupt. We got closer and swung in front of it, and I could see the mottled columns again, the cracks and the stains of the wall. I remembered how they had looked from the grave site, their height and angularity. The memory guided me to the spot.

I let go of Eleanor. Where I had expected a rounded hump in the snow was a loud spray of brown dirt and rocks on tramped white. The grave an ugly rupture, a cavity; it seemed to have been blown apart. I looked at the hole and realized that sunken as it was, it couldn't possibly contain Gary.

I looked closer. In the dirt I saw one of his boots; his knit cap, nearly covered.

Eleanor found the bear paw tracks, longer and wider than

my bootprints. A furious stamping of paws at the edge of the rupture, then a single set clawing off to the west. Something dragged beside it.

They're meat-eaters and they're real hungry this time of year.

"It got him," she said. Her voice was dull. "It took him away." She looked off in the direction where the tracks went. Then at me. "If we follow the tracks we might come across the poncho."

"No. We don't want to find him." I could see us coming on torn flesh and splintered bone. What a bear might do to fresh meat. But the image stayed contained; outward, I was as level as she. "We'll do without the map."

I picked up the boot and the cap, and stirred the dirt with the shovel.

She said, "Then there's nothing else to do here."

"No. We ought to go." The cap and the boot felt futile; I tossed them back into the dirt. "Don't want to hold up the others."

We walked away. She took my arm. We could have been shoppers leaving a mall. I kept waiting for something to happen in me, pain to surface, outrage to overtake me. Nothing. I took inventory: frigid toes, a kinked back from sleeping on my side, a gray weariness when I imagined all the miles that stretched before us today. No more.

Eleanor was pulling at me. I turned to look. She had both arms around my bent elbow, her face against my sleeve, and the pulls came from the convulsions of her sobbing. She was swallowing the noise but she couldn't control the movements.

I stopped and held her. She burrowed into my chest and made choking sounds that eventually came out as words: "I hate this place. These awful, horrible mountains. I hate this place."

———

Down in Red Lodge, Poague was renting a car, getting ready to drive to Billings, fly home. He and Andrea had hiked out the afternoon before, and had hitched a ride into town. At dinner he had seemed quiet, pensive. She had thought that he must be fatigued.

Now he was almost brusque as he loaded his suitcase into the car, and turned to tell her goodbye. He thanked her, shook her hand, and was gone. All with such stiffness that after he had driven away she wondered whether she had somehow offended him.

His leaving felt wrong, she told me later. Of course he was a busy man and of course the trip really was finished for him; but it still felt wrong, she said—the abrupt way he left.

I can imagine him disconnecting that way. He had that capacity; that was the Poague I had always known. In the past I'd have called it boorishness and left it at that. Now—after what I know, after all that happened—I'm inclined to say that he didn't accept defeat well, and that he would always turn away before he would show hurt.

I've thought about him leaving, about his being home while the rest of us floundered in the mountains. The image offended me, when I first learned that he had left; though he could have changed nothing, it seemed to me that he ought to have been closer, somehow more involved, when the world came apart for us on the plateau.

I didn't know that his own was already in pieces.

———

When we told him about the map Travis said, "Well are we ready to try things my way now?"

He led. We walked most of the day, fueled by a few raisins and that chunk of cheddar, and we might have covered a respectable distance if Travis hadn't insisted on precisely following our old route.

We wasted hours and miles. I could have told him about the way snow alters the land, could have reminded him that the surroundings must appear different, coming and going, and that we hadn't been paying close attention anyway: we had never expected that we'd have to find our way back. I could have told him all these things, but he wouldn't have listened. He had that air about him.

Charles occasionally slipped a compass out of his pocket when Travis wouldn't notice. The pass was southeast from where we were, somewhere in the line of peaks rampant before us. Plow southeast by the route of least resistance and we would strike the mountains within a mile or two of the pass, then find our way up and over. It wasn't as elusive a destination as a clump of trees in night and blowing snow.

The day before we had hiked from the crater lake to the half-dome in about four hours. The return took nearly eight. Twice we wandered into territory that we didn't know, or couldn't recognize, and Travis demanded that we retrace tracks until he was sure we were set right again. We reached the bowl around mid-afternoon. Miles yet to cover before we approached the pass. Even without delays tomorrow, we would have a hard pull all day up to the summit.

What craziness this must seem to an outsider looking in. Charles knew there was a better way and I knew there was. I can't say about the others. For the first time ever I failed when I tried to fathom Hollenbeck; I had no idea whether he actually believed in Travis, or was going along, as I was, for his own reasons. But I knew the truth, and Charles knew, and we never protested.

Charles I can excuse. He was no leader. All the weight of his brains and knowledge couldn't balance off his squeaking voice and his scrawny puerile body. Somehow virility was an issue, though there's no good reason why. Strength mattered; no coup ever succeeded on ideas alone.

And I, I have since discovered any number of reasons why I didn't speak and act.

Here's a good one: clearly Travis was wound tight and would not tolerate challenge. Any opposition was at the risk of his coming undone, so I tolerated his foolishness.

And another: Travis was so convincing. In the mountains and in every other world, he had a way of drawing others to him and keeping them there. I was just Furlow, no match for his ability to make people want to believe him.

That one I can almost buy. But when I find the courage I admit the actuality. That I remained silent not because I believed that the others would never let me lead them, but because I feared that they might.

———

Emmett Frye's pack station was northwest of Red Lodge, near the summer community of Alpine. Its shacks and resort cabins show on the topo as square flyspecks: elevation six thousand, two hundred and eight feet. Thirteen miles away, and nearly six thousand feet higher, are the crest of the Beartooths and Eagle Pass, across that crest.

About three miles from the pass, just above timberline, is a small lake without a name. It is as far as pack animals can climb with any sureness; beyond, reaching up to the pass, is all upthrust slab and glaciers and unstable scree. Four times already this season Emmett had brought supplies to Gary and a group at that lake, and today he was bound there again, riding a horse and leading a single packed mule.

He started out before dawn. Earlier than usual—he knew there had been snow the night before, and that would slow him. A couple of miles up the trail, at around seven thousand feet, he found snowfall. Through the day, as the trail climbed, the snow deepened.

Around midday he reached the lake. He wasn't surprised to find nobody there. He knew the group had to come over the pass, where the fall would be heaviest.

On the way up, through timberline, he had gathered some dead branches and packed them on the mule. After he fed the animals he cleared a circular patch down to bare ground, gathered rocks for a fire ring, and started a campfire. The hikers always enjoyed that, after a week with their puny stove. On the way down from the pass the lake was visible for more than a mile, a steep and difficult descent that took most hikers more than an hour. Emmett liked to think of the hikers at the end of a long day, cresting the top and starting down, seeing the orange and yellow flicker far below, being drawn to the crackling brightness.

When the fire was blazing Emmett cleared a second patch for his tent. If he had met the group early enough, and the moon were bright, he would have tried to return that evening. But he knew from the clouds that there would be no moon, and he guessed that there would be no hikers until almost dusk, so he put up the tent and fed the fire with branches he broke over his knee, and he sat down to wait.

———

We were about an hour, two miles, past the crater lake when Donnie first complained about his stomach.

"Damn it hurts," he said. "Real bad."

Travis said forget it, we had to go at least another hour today.

We kept walking. I asked Donnie what it felt like, and he said cramps, bad cramps.

"Is it that time of month?" Travis said.

"No fooling," Donnie said. "Right here." He stroked his upper abdomen. "It hurts like hell."

Travis turned around and said he didn't want to hear any more of it, we'd been putting up with that bitching for a week, we had all had enough. He was trying to save our lives, the least we could do was shut up and get serious.

What can you do when a hero invokes his own heroism? We shut up and got serious, and we kept following Travis.

We were walking through a ravine, downstream beside a small creek. In a few minutes the ravine broadened. The creek flowed away to the southwest and about half a mile farther along we turned east and started a long climb up a ridge as hard and bare and spare as any hunk of rock I have seen.

It was a rib of granite and gneiss at least a thousand feet high, miles long and maybe a mile across, segmented by deep cracks and gullies, clear of vegetation.

We started up, climbing beside one of the gullies; it dropped off nearly a hundred feet, not sheer but steep enough that snow wouldn't cling. I stayed well clear of the edge.

Donnie was directly in front of me as we climbed. Not far from the top he stopped. He stood, holding his stomach, then folded in sections until he was sitting in the snow, bent at the waist, his head between his knees.

Eleanor and I squatted beside him. The other three were ahead of us, still walking, unaware. I called Travis's name and they came over.

Travis said, "For crying out loud."

Donnie brought his face up. It was blanched and tightened the way real pain will do.

"I can't help it," he said.

"Can you walk?" Travis said.

Eleanor cut off his answer.

"What a stupid question," she said. "Obviously if he could walk he'd be walking."

She knelt close to the boy and held him. I knew and Travis knew that she wouldn't let him be pushed further.

After a moment Travis said, "It's getting dark anyway."

Charles found a wedge-shaped nook in a granite out-cropping, as if a big slice of pie had been lifted out of the ridge. It was about three feet deep and wide enough to hold us all, though open at one end that faced westward, down toward the base of the ridge.

We cleared the snow out of it. Charles and Hollenbeck stretched one of the tarps across the top, and tied it down. The second tarp they fastened to the first, lacing the eyelets together down over the open end of the wedge.

With Donnie stretched out along one side there was room for the rest of us to sit with legs drawn up. We put our packs across the mouth of the wedge, holding down the loose end of the hanging tarp. Charles had piled snow against it on the other side, leaving room at one end for a crawlway entrance; the bank of snow blocked the wind and helped to trap our body heat inside.

Donnie said he didn't want to eat, but Eleanor told him that we were going to get warm food in him, and in all the rest of us.

A good idea, Travis said.

George cooked the last of the Jello and then boiled the bulgur. While it bubbled Eleanor sat Donnie up, leaning him against her, and she held a cup of the liquid gelatin to his lips. Soon he took it from her, drank it down, drank another cup.

It seemed to help. His face loosened. Some color returned. He looked at their shoulders resting together, and lifted an eyebrow, and said if she was going to take care of him he would have to get sick more often.

We were hungry enough that even the bulgur disappeared. We scraped out the pot and licked the cups clean.

Donnie got up, went outside, and returned a couple of minutes later.

"You feeling better?" Travis asked Donnie. The boy nodded. "Got rid of all the nasties? Probably just what you needed."

Donnie nodded again.

"That's good," Travis said. "Tomorrow we have to do some serious humping—I want everybody good and strong."

Nobody said anything. Eleanor lit a candle and we settled into a quiet neutral consciousness that I have never experienced anywhere else but on that trip, under those tarps.

Charles said that expedition climbers call it "bivouac trance."

Donnie called it "zoning out."

Floating half awake is the closest I have known elsewhere. But that state usually dissolves quickly into sleep or full awakening. We consumed hours in this suspension, clutching the sleeping bag around face and neck to seal out the cold, bodies perfectly still except for the chest's negligible rise and collapse, thinking thoughts that leave no impression on memory. If there is any thought at all.

I know it helped us save physical energy when we had none of that to waste. I suspect that it may have preserved our sanity as well.

That evening Eleanor rustled, stretched her legs, and said she was thirsty, would somebody please pass her water bottle.

Hollenbeck was closest to the pile of packs. He unzipped a side pocket of one, took out a bottle, handed it to her.

She lifted it and took a mouthful, and brought the bottle down.

She said, "Whose water is this? It isn't mine."

A demand on our consciousness; we all shifted out of the

trance. Hollenbeck was pointing toward the pack, saying, I thought this one was yours.

"From that pack over there?" Donnie said. "That's mine."

She said, "It's fresh. It doesn't have any iodine."

"Yeah. I tried it once. Couldn't take that taste."

Charles, naturally, found the handle first.

"Donnie," he said, "you've got *giardia.*"

"Uh-huh, the bug," Donnie said. "Hey, blood, I've known that, last couple of days."

19

After the candle puddled out I stayed awake for a long while. Actually I don't remember having slept at all, but I must have, because I remember waking up: an awakening as shocking and abrupt as I will ever have.

A face full of snow.

I thrashed, swatted the stuff away, and looked up. Directly above, the seam had parted where the two tarps met. An opening gaped. The tarps bent inward from the weight of fresh wet snow; clumps of it poised at the edges of the opening, ready to slide in. Flakes spiraled through the gap and settled on my cheeks, my nose.

My right hand found the flashlight that I kept nearby when I slept. I sat up on my knees, up through the gap and into the night.

The snow on the tarps was new, at least six inches deep. And growing: in the flashlight's shaft, snow surged from the sky as if there would be no end to it.

By morning we had another foot of snow, and it continued; no blizzard, but an incessant powdering that mounted with the hours. Two feet deep or more, up to mid thigh in places. There seemed no question of hiking through it.

At daybreak Travis was up and fully dressed, stalking aimlessly in the drifts outside, milling.

He stopped me when I went to get water.

He said, "I suppose everyone is very happy about this."

I groped for a response, some answer suitable to such absurdity.

"It's a good excuse to stay put," he said. "We can all sit on our cans and watch the snow come down."

"Even if we walked all day we wouldn't cover five miles in this mess."

"I could feel it last night," he said. "I'm the only one willing to do what it takes to get out of here."

"Paul, I think you're mistaken."

He gave me a look of dry pitying disdain that I felt drilling into my back when I walked away.

The only water we had found was a trickle down a crack in the rock, flowing under the snow. In one spot the rock leveled into a depression where the water pooled about an inch deep, a foot across.

I shoved aside the snow from around the pool. With Gary's axe I shattered the ice that had formed on the top and chopped away the solid ice along the sides, until I had a hole big enough to submerge a Sierra cup.

Lift out the cup, pour its few ounces into a bottle. Wait for the trickle to fill the hole. Sink the cup again, lift it out. Eight, ten immersions to top off each bottle; six bottles. I did it all with bare hands—had to keep mittens dry. The water bit my fingers when it touched them. When the last bottle was full I held them against me and churned through the snow, toward the shelter.

Travis still tramped outside, stark and silly. I had to pass within a few feet of him. He stopped, stared, as I approached.

"That's okay," he said. "I'll save your butts in spite of yourselves."

He came in a few minutes later, got into his bag, and for the rest of the day he was tense and silent, an unsettling presence among us.

———

Donnie tried to joke about the *giardia*. He was up and out of the shelter at least once every couple of hours, and every trip brought a fusillade of wisecracks. At first he had us laughing; is there a creature more naturally scatalogical than an adolescent human male?

Eventually it stopped being funny. He was ill, and we could see that he was ill. By early evening, after he had left one more time, he looked unsteady enough that Eleanor said one of us ought to make sure he didn't collapse in the snow.

Hollenbeck went out. When they came in together a couple of minutes later Donnie said, Jeez what an indignity, can't anybody have any privacy around here? But he didn't complain later when he got up to leave again and Charles went out with him.

The truth was that privacy was possible only in our thoughts. Even when we crouched, our head skimmed the ceiling of the shelter, and on the floor there was not a square foot of open space. We jostled shoulders and hips. What one of us exhaled, another breathed. We sweated in the sleeping bags, and we shared that sweat. We shared hunger, and the odors of flatulence, and the smell of damp wool, and most of all the tangible sense of dread and vulnerability that descended with the snow and gathered around us.

———

Emmett Frye says he stayed beside the lake for as long as he could, and I believe him. From what I saw of him, he didn't seem prone to panic; I could easily imagine him waiting there through the morning, letting the snow fall around him, feeding in his wood until the last of it was in the campfire and down to ashes.

He would have waited for his clients, but when he ran out of margin for waiting he also would have taken care of himself. There was snow at the pass, so he couldn't see all the way to the top. But as far as he could see there were no hikers descending, and he couldn't expect any in such weather.

Whatever was in cans or bottles, what a bear wasn't likely to smell, he took out of the packs and hid behind a rock. Gary had made camp at that exact spot each of the last three times, so Emmett was sure that if the party came this way the cache would be found.

The rest—bags of beans and sugar and macaroni and cheese—would be gone by the end of the day if he left it. There was no point in feeding grizzlies. He packed it up and started down around noon.

———

We were boiling water for a meal of freeze-dried turkey tetrazzini when the stove's jet popped twice and expired. Out of fuel. It was the last of the original three quarts. We still had Gary's bottle, so we filled the stove and finished heating the water. But those pops had the sound of emptiness and cold desolation.

One pouch made half servings for the six of us. A few ounces, enough to fill a Sierra cup. Donnie wouldn't eat his, said his stomach was upset. Besides, he said, it wouldn't stay with him long enough to do him any good.

He drank as much water as the rest of us combined. That made sense when I thought about it, the fluids he must be losing.

Through dinner and afterward, Travis kept watching him. Intensely, almost with hostility. I know Eleanor was aware of it too.

Suddenly, without preface, Travis said, "Can you walk, the way you are?"

No question that he meant Donnie.

Eleanor said, "None of us can walk in that, the way it is outside."

"I asked him. Let him answer."

"If I have to walk, I'll walk."

"It stopped you yesterday. You're worse today."

"I'll go where anybody else goes."

Eleanor said, "It's ridiculous to talk about it. We can't go anywhere."

"You want to sit here and let the snow bury us?" Travis said. "Is that it?"

I said, "There are physical limits."

Sharply and with fervor he snapped back: "You've never run into a real limit in your life. You never let yourself get that far."

He slouched and withdrew, but inside he was coiled. I could feel it, the potential within him for a kickback that I couldn't name or predict.

Later he all but told me, and I still didn't understand.

It happened that night, at some murky hour: keeping any sense of time finer than the change of days was impossible, and pointless. But the others were asleep. Hollenbeck, beside Travis, snored with a cartoon puttering.

Travis and I lay closest to the mouth of the shelter, beside the packs that held down the tarp's hanging end. There the space was wide enough that he and I could stretch out fully, head to foot. If we sat up we were facing each across the length of our bodies. That's how it happened. I heard a rustling, and raised my head and shoulders to see. Travis was already sitting, and when I moved he looked at me—or had been watching me all along, I suppose. The candle's flame wavered beside him.

Maybe my head didn't clear immediately. Or else I didn't see very well in the trembling light. But for an instant he was the Travis I had known once, across that eternity of the past eight or nine days: unshaken, controlled, so sure of himself and of everyone around him. All the pieces back in place, flawlessly finished.

I wanted to hug him and welcome him back, but he stopped me with the minute lift of one eyebrow, exactly the way he would have done if I had suddenly become sentimental after a couple of drinks too many.

He said, "Ray. You think you know. But you know only so much, and it's not enough." I was captivated by the softness of his voice. Like all the rest of him at this moment it was almost unbearably beautiful. He said, "You'll see. That's all. You'll see."

Obviously he expected me to understand, but I had no idea. Before I could ask him to explain, I saw him kissing Noreen Poague. Paralyzed on the wall. Muttering in his self-absorption.

Words would be wasted on that Travis. I set my face, turned over, and shut him out of my thoughts. Soon I was sleeping.

Since then I have wondered uncountable times what might have happened if I had asked what he meant. If I had bothered to think about him. If I had just bothered to care. You shouldn't flagellate yourself with the past, I know, but this one question I find difficult to let go.

If I had even listened.

At least I might not have been so astonished the next morning when I looked over at the empty space where his bag had been, then pushed aside the tarp to see his tracks surging up the ridge, and realized that he had left.

20

He and Hollenbeck both. The space that George had occupied beside Travis was empty, too. His bag gone. There was nobody when I looked outside. The single set of tracks baffled me until I remembered how Donnie and I had shared a set of footprints two nights earlier.

A page torn from the journal lay where Travis's pack had been. His handwriting:

Ray et al.—
Gone to get help. Sorry. Can't sit around any more.
Stay warm, don't leave. Won't be long.
Somebody had to do something.
Paul

I dressed quickly and went out to follow the tracks.

A ripened dawn. For the first time in three days the sky was clear, air colder than ever before, the kind of cold that gnaws at exposed skin. Even with the tracks, walking at anything like a normal speed or gait was impossible. The snow was above knee-high; it quadrupled resistance and effort.

Long before I reached the top of the ridge my breath was exhausted. I had to rest twice before the top.

I thought of Hollenbeck doing this, and told myself that the effort must be sapping him. No way could he go the distance. I saw him tagging after Travis like a kid after his big brother, sucked into Travis's vortex. I got angry at Hollenbeck for doing that, angrier yet at Travis for allowing it to happen.

The anger carried me up to the top of the ridge. From there I could see the tracks stitching down the other side and across a valley. There was nobody else for as far as I could see, at least two miles. A writhing white stillness, a bellowing silence. That valley gleamed the sinister gleam of a knife blade held to the throat. The horizon curled around me. I could feel it meeting behind my back, drawing itself in, constricting.

Eleanor was holding the note when I got back.

"Gone?" she said.

"Oh yeah. He's gone all right. George too."

"Can they make it?"

"Not George. Absolutely not. Paul, who knows? He's strong. He's in great shape."

She said, "Physically, maybe. For what that's worth."

I took off my boots and poncho, got into the bag. Charles shifted, and lay on his side to face us. His eyes were alert. He had been awake to hear this.

He said, "They shouldn't have done that. In a survival situation the chance of success almost always goes down if a group divides."

I remember wishing that he hadn't used the term. A survival situation. Which it was, of course; but once correctly named, some realities became almost unbearably awesome.

Eleanor said, "They're out for themselves. They can't help us if pilots won't fly helicopters up here."

"They will for Travis," I said.

Charles said he hated to be cynical about motives, but maybe we ought to check the packs, see how much food was gone.

All that we had was in Gary's pack. I went through it and

found that they had taken the third tarp, a water bottle, two date-nut bars, a pack of matches.

Now Donnie was awake. He licked dry lips with a dry tongue, and said, "Paul and George are gone?"

Charles told him yes. Gone to get help.

"Dumb bastards," he said. "Now what are we going to do?"

He spoke to Charles, who looked at Eleanor. Who looked at me. All three of them waiting for me to speak.

The answer was simple, easily reached, but I hesitated; and when I spoke, the words felt ungainly.

"Just what we would have done anyway," I said. "We're going to sit and wait."

———

Later that day I took the bottles to the small pool where I had filled them the day before. It was frozen over. I chipped at it with the ice axe, kept chipping until I hit rock. No water. The trickle had frozen.

My idea was to melt snow. But inside the shelter Charles said no, we couldn't spare the fuel. Eleanor said maybe we could just eat snow, but that sounded silly as soon as the words hit the chill air; we would never stay warm.

There was the brook through the ravine, down at the bottom of the ridge and beyond. We all knew it was there, but nobody mentioned it. I felt the distance to it, the effort in going here and getting back. And heard the last line from Travis's note: *Somebody had to do something.*

I emptied a pack and gathered the bottles in it. Eleanor said, Thank you Ray; and Charles told me to be careful I didn't slip on the rocks; and in a voice that sounded as fragile as old parchment Donnie said that he could recommend putting in iodine, it wasn't such a bad idea.

I walked out into the drifts, through burgeoning clouds of breath.

Before I reached the bottom of the ridge my boots were soaked through, socks wet with melt, toes and feet overwhelmed by cold. At the brook I slipped, plunged one foot through skim ice, ankle deep into a pool. And never felt a difference; by then my feet existed only as terminals of pain that screeched and sizzled with the weight of each stride.

I filled the bottles, put them away, started upward. Under a turtleneck shirt, sweater, jacket, poncho, hauling up against the snow, I sweated. But wind from upslope blew under the poncho and tore wet skin dry.

After maybe an hour I was back in the shelter, tossing the pack down, pulling off boots and socks, fiercely burrowing into the bag.

Donnie took one bottle and drank it empty. Five bottles full.

Eleanor started the stove and boiled a quart for cocoa that seared tongue and throat when I gulped it down. Four full. Later we cooked the second packet of freeze-dried, and through the day Donnie pulled at another bottle. Two left.

Charles said that you can dry damp clothes in a sleeping bag. Not down, only a synthetic. Body heat will do it. I stuffed boots and socks beside me and for the rest of the day we had the rankness of wet wool and leather, and the cold, and the wind that shook the loose tarp flap, and the emptiness among us where Travis and Hollenbeck had been.

Us in the shelter in the cleft of the rock, and them out there in the evermore, beyond surmise.

———

Hollenbeck caught Travis some time in the afternoon.

He says he woke that dawn and found Travis gone, found the note. He dressed without waking us and set out after him, using the tracks, thinking that he could overtake Travis and talk him back. Of course Paul was stronger, but Paul was breaking trail, and Hollenbeck had broken trail to use.

At the top of the ridge Hollenbeck could see Travis far in the valley below, at least halfway across, an almost imperceptible dark tick making almost imperceptible progress across the shimmering field. Too far for shouting. Hollenbeck shouted anyway. Travis kept walking.

Hollenbeck returned to the shelter. We all still slept. He jammed the sleeping bag into his pack and started back up the ridge. Knowing that there was no question any more of talking him back, that he was hours from catching up, that with every step he would belong less to us than to Travis. And to all that was in Travis.

By the time Hollenbeck got back to the top of the ridge Travis was out of sight across the valley. But Hollenbeck had those tracks, the certainty of being able to place his feet where Travis had placed his, knowing that the snow could be beaten, that steps had been made and were being made, and that Travis was somewhere at the end of them.

He kept going; he knew it could be done. The tracks kept pulling him along. They seemed perfectly straight, and after a while he recognized the precision of Travis's course.

Somewhere in his pack was the compass. He found it in a side pocket, took it out, examined it. He held it level, watched the needle settle, and thought, That would be north.

The needle didn't move when he rotated the compass body around it. He turned it until the N on the compass dial rested in front of the needle. It made sense. Then he could see that from where he stood the line of tracks shafted straight out through a hundred and twenty degrees. Four or five times during the day, whenever the path was open, he got out the compass and saw that the tracks' direction hadn't wavered.

In the afternoon he came over a rise. Below him the terrain dipped and rose again, and he looked across the trough to the second swell. Where there should have been tracks, the snow was unbroken. Travis hadn't been there yet. Hollenbeck plowed forward, down into the dip, and at the bottom he found Travis kneeling at a frozen stream, pushing his bottle through a rupture in snow and shattered ice.

Travis stood. When Hollenbeck approached him he said, "No lectures, George. Please."

"Did I say anything?"

"I'm doing what I have to do."

"I believe that."

"I'm not trying to save my own butt."

"I believe that too," Hollenbeck said. And he did.

"I know what they're thinking." Hollenbeck remembers

him making a vague gesture toward the west, taking us all in. Then tensing his hand in a way that oddly, specifically, represented me alone; Hollenbeck was sure of that. "I couldn't sit there feeling it. I couldn't stay, that's all."

"I understand," Hollenbeck said. "I really do."

Travis offered him the bottle. Hollenbeck came over, took the water from him.

Travis said, "What the hell are you doing here, anyway?"

Hollenbeck thought, You're my friend and you're in trouble and you need looking after. But he knew he couldn't tell that to Travis, so he said, "I wanted to come along. I couldn't stay there either."

Travis swayed slightly where he stood, as if tempest-blown. He righted himself and said, "You can follow me if you want. But this is my play, George. It won't work if I have to think about you."

If he had said that to me, even on the best of days, I'd have told him, What's the matter Paul, don't want to share the glory? But Hollenbeck said, "I can stay with you if you keep making track all the way to the end. Can you do that?"

"I'm pretty sure. It's harder than I thought. But I feel good. Now that I'm away from the others. I feel real strong."

"I'm glad," Hollenbeck said.

"I hoped I could get to the pass by this afternoon. But it's too far. We'll find a place out of the weather tonight, head up there in the morning."

Before he could catch himself Hollenbeck said, "You know where it is?

Travis was bending to fill the bottle, capping it, putting it away. He said, "Somewhere east. We'll get within a mile or so, and find it when we're close."

Hollenbeck remembered how true Travis's path had been all day.

He said, "Paul. You weren't nearly that sure about it before."

Travis said, "It's different when people are watching." He turned, crossed the stream in a couple of long strides, and started up the hill in front of him.

21

Some time that day, that night, I realized that one of us or more in the shelter might die. Let alone Travis or Hollenbeck. Life was ebbing in all of us. You can drain only so much energy before vitality contracts, and death starts to encroach and scallop the edges of life.

Not that we were dying. Not yet. But I could feel the narrowed margins. Too many miles walked without nourishment. Too many hours of fruitless sleep, the kind that consumes time but does not revive. The way to dying was evident.

That evening we ate all the food that remained; all but a couple of inches of salami. Donnie picked at his share and put it aside. The rest of us gulped ours, then his leavings. We hadn't eaten fully in almost four days, and gulping that food was like flinging it into a canyon. In a couple of minutes the food was gone but hunger was untouched.

Life was ebbing in all of us, but fastest in Donnie. Like turning down the wick of an oil lamp. Maybe we wouldn't have noticed if he hadn't burned so hot before.

Night clamped down on us. We huddled in candle's light, withdrawn into nylon and batting. After a while Donnie got up to go outside, moving slowly. He was in long johns, a poncho, unlaced boots. He crawled over to the hole.

Eleanor said, "Let one of us go with you." Charles was already dressing.

"Honest, I don't need any witnesses." His voice reminded me of dry leaves blowing off a tree, not simply the sound of desiccation, but the way it reached into me. "I've been doing this on my own for at least two or three years."

She said, "It's dark out there. Where's your light?"

"I can't find it. I think I lost it a couple of days ago."

"Wear a hat. You're going to get cold."

By now Charles was ready. He got a flashlight and they went out together.

Eleanor had been across from me, half hunched. Now she slid her bag over to mine.

She said, "Are you worried about him?"

"Mostly I'm worried that we can't do anything for him."

"I think one of us ought to stay up with him at night." The wind thumped the tarp overhead. "To make sure he doesn't go out alone. It's nasty out there."

I told her sure, we could do that. Take turns staying awake while he slept.

"I mean, it's not as if we don't have plenty of time to rest," she said. "You think I'm being silly?"

Truth was, I didn't see the point. But I knew that some time in the last few days, consciously or not, she had chosen him to care about. I liked to see that in her, liked to imagine the depth of it. In a couple of minutes the boys came back and got into their bags. Before long they were dozing, then fully sleeping. We were awake, she and I, watching this happen.

This is going to seem crazy. But we were a family there. I mean in the classic shape, a man and a woman and their children. They were our charges, and we had to be strong and smart for them; we had to be a pair for them; they bound us.

I believe she felt it. I definitely did: I knew exactly how that was supposed to go, all the moves, a great old dance that I now had a chance to do right.

The presence of death must have had something to do

with it. Forcing us down to basics. After a while Eleanor in a low calm voice began to tell me about her husband and Duck Key. From me she got the basic short version of my life from adolescence on, abridged but not so disemboweled as to be falsely flattering. It even nibbled around my father. I know the thought of dying made that easier. What else will make trivia of failure and pain?

"One of us ought to rest," she said after a while.

"Go ahead. I'm fine."

"I am tired," she said.

"Then sleep."

She shifted in the bag, lay on her side to face me.

I told her there was something I'd been meaning to ask her: about Travis.

"You were kind of interested in him at first."

"I was real interested. He makes a pretty outstanding first impression."

"And then you didn't seem interested any more. Not that it's any of my business. But I wondered why."

She answered quickly, as if she had thought about it already.

"Oh, he seemed way too clear about things," she said. "The kind of stuff I've never been real definite about. You know, about how people are and how life is going to happen. Cole's like that. It always made me nervous. How can anybody be so sure?"

"It helps if you can make people and life turn out the way you want."

She gave a sharp, short laugh.

"That has never been my particular problem," she said. "Anyway. Once I figured out that he had more answers than questions, Paul sort of lost his appeal. The cleft chin notwithstanding."

She nestled close. Her head pressed against my hip.

She said, "If you start nodding off, just wake me up."

"Don't worry about me."

The three of them slept.

Time became empty. I tried to fill it with thoughts and feelings, but it kept expanding.

When the candle guttered I bent carefully for another, and lit it off the first. My hands got cold outside the bag; I stuck them inside, tucked one against me, used the other to bunch the bag tight around my face, my collar.

Creamy warmth inside the bag. The weight of her head against my hip. Their trusting sleep. Time at a halt. Warmth inside the bag, skin melting into the fabric. Their trusting sleep. Their sleep.

You know what had to happen.

———

Travis and Hollenbeck reached a stand of woods around sunset. Hollenbeck was certain that Travis didn't plan it that way; but the trees were there when the light failed, so the two of them stopped for the night. Hollenbeck discovered a hollow under one large pine, a hole in the snow that the branches had sheltered and wind had sculpted down to bare ground. They strung the tarp over it and settled in. Below the live branches were brown limbs, wizened and stunted. Travis tore some away, broke them, and built a small, smoky fire that smelled of pitch.

Hollenbeck thought it was the most comfortable bivouac of the trip. The tarp and thick spreading branches close above; snow piled high, not an impediment now but insulation and windbreak; and the fire.

George wanted to rest. Travis insisted on talking. He went on about racquetball and Poague and MDC. To Hollenbeck it sounded like beery maundering. He didn't understand how Travis could think about anything beyond the crushing reality of the snow and the trees. But Travis didn't seem to require conversation, only an audience, so Hollenbeck shut his eyes and listened idly.

He was about to stop fighting weariness when he became aware of Travis telling him, "This thing with Ray. About Poague's wife."

Hollenbeck nudged himself awake and opened his eyes at Travis.

"I can see where he got that interpretation," Travis was saying. "The facts are basically correct. I was up for the job. My two friends and myself. Or I thought we were. And I was nailing the boss's wife. It doesn't make me look real good."

When George didn't react he went on.

"She was the one who came on to me. She's a real aggressive woman. And this was before the thing with the job. But, look, I won't lie to you. When it started to happen I did ask myself what she might be able to do for me. I did hope it would kind of give me an edge. That's the problem with crap like this. You walk too deep in it and everything gets dirty. You forget why you're there in the first place."

Hollenbeck knew his face must be stunned, blank. Travis kept waiting for a reaction, but got nothing.

"Understand?" he said. "I did what Ray said I did."

Hollenbeck said, "I thought it might be true."

"Does it bother you?"

After a few seconds Hollenbeck said, "I feel like it happened to somebody else a long time ago."

"I don't want it to change anything between us."

"You get us out of here—all of us—and nothing else will matter to anybody."

"Hey, pal. That's the whole point entirely."

Donnie was gone and the candle was out and I was asleep.

When Eleanor stirred I woke. She got her flashlight. In its light I saw Donnie's crumpled bag. I saw her reach into it. I saw from her face that the bag was cold.

She said, "Ray" in a way that was hurt, accusing, uncomprehending. My name has never sounded the same since.

Out into the night, the three of us, wincing against the snow that wind swirled off the pack, blizzard-thick. We shouted for Donnie, waded through the snow, bent into the wind. Charles thought to look into the deep gully that ran up the side of the ridge. Donnie was at the bottom, inert.

Where he had fallen was too steep to walk down. I ran a couple of hundred yards down the ridge, to where the gully was lower and gentler.

He didn't move when I got there. I felt for a pulse, found a shuddering quaver; saw a gash over one eye, felt a swelling at the back of his head, another at mid-fibia of his left leg. There were scrapes and contusions wherever skin was bare, and where the blue fabric of his long johns had torn away.

The only proper way to get him out of the gully would have been with a neck brace, a litter, a winch and cable. I held him in my arms and began to carry him. Back to where I had descended.

When I started climbing he came to and screamed a tortured scream that hurt my ears and emptied me inside. The scream died to a horrible moan so low that only I could hear. It kept passing over his lips while I climbed to the top and worked through the snow, and rose each time I slipped or jostled him, and didn't end until I had brought him into the shelter and laid him down and covered him with the cold fabric of his bag.

22

"Don't you let him die," she said.

She expected me to do something. Me.

"I don't know what to do," I said.

"You studied medicine."

"I took pre-med courses. I studied zoology and chemistry."

"Just don't let him die."

Her eyes made it a threat. Even when I looked down at him I could feel them on me, like the prod of a billy club.

We knelt beside him, the three of us. Charles at his head, Eleanor at one shoulder, I at the other. His eyes tried to follow us as we spoke, but they were slow to focus, slow to shift.

I told Charles to light the last four candles, told her to boil water so we could clean the cuts.

"Is that all you can do?"

"I'm trying to think."

I touched a shoulder and felt him shivering.

In a violent tremolo he said, "I'm real cold."

"Look. Heat that water. We'll get him to drink some."

We covered him with all the clothes we could find. I zipped my bag down and draped it over his own.

There was so much wrong with him. And we knew so little. I got out the medicine kit and opened it, looking for answers. Percodan: it would help the pain, but I didn't know what else it might do. Aspirin, yes. When the water was warm I had Charles tilt Donnie's head up so he could take two. His left eye was swollen nearly shut. Eleanor swabbed out the gash with water and iodine.

Something returned from the long ago. The summer before my junior year at UVA, a job as a lifeguard: three days of training in first aid.

I asked him, "Can you move your arms and legs?" His fingers flexed, his legs drew up tentatively under the clothes and the bags.

When he moved the left one he said, "That hurts," in a shudder.

The swelling below the knee was bigger now than before. I ripped the long johns to look. It was purpling. I touched it. He grunted, then groaned.

My hands kept finding things to do: I don't know how. Things that made sense. If the leg was broken it had to be splinted. I took a knife, cut open one of the packs, tore loose the two steel shank supports in the back. Straightened the leg, wrapped it with foam rubber from a sleeping pad, and taped the shanks to either side of his calf.

We knelt around him and watched him shiver through a third cup of tea. His pulse was no stronger, or any more regular.

I told them it was shock, and I didn't know what else we could do about it, but we had to get him warm.

Eleanor took off her poncho. I said that piling on more clothes wouldn't help, but she ignored me. She took off her boots, her gaiters, her pants. Charles understood before I did. He too was removing his clothes, putting them aside.

By now I saw. Eleanor in her long underwear, lifting the bags and the layers of clothing, moving into the space she created beside him. I told her to be careful, watch the leg, try not to put any pressure on his chest. She made a series of small shrugging motions that ended with one hand emerging, dropping a piece of dark blue fabric outside the bag. Her underwear shirt.

Like a knowing lover she folded herself around his wracking.

Charles got in on the other side. He had been watching her, and now mimicked her movements, her posture, her care.

I told myself that we didn't need so many candles any more, so I blew out all but one, and collected them. After a few seconds I realized there was nothing to see, so I extinguished the last candle and climbed into my bag.

In the darkness I could hear breathing. Theirs was measured and soothing; his, chopped and pounding at first. But while I listened it became longer, lower, more even, until it matched theirs, and I couldn't tell them apart any more.

Around dawn I fell into a brief and shallow sleep. Woke to a pinstripe of muted daylight along the edge of the tarp flap. Eleanor, dressed again, sat vigilant at Donnie's head. Charles still stretched out beside him. She looked when I moved in the bag.

"Good," she said. "We need water. There's plenty of light now."

In memory I hear undertones of sad forgiveness. But that is time's wishful warping. At the instant of reality I heard no emotion in her voice. To say that she was cold would be flattering myself. She was neutral, impenetrable, as distant and impersonal as the ticket taker at a crowded movie theater.

He rested so solidly, it couldn't have been sleep. I reached under for his wrist.

"It's not good," she said.

His pulse: arrhythmic, fitful. It boomed one beat, whispered the next.

I leaned closer to thumb back his eyelids. As if I knew what I was doing. For a second I thought she was going to push me aside; I know she didn't want me near him.

He didn't move when I touched his face.

The left pupil was open full, unnaturally large: nearly twice the size of the right. Eleanor was looking; she wanted to know what that meant.

I said, "I don't know. It isn't right."

She might have answered, *A lot of things aren't right*. But she didn't say anything, only got a near-empty bottle from under the sleeping bag, and handed it to me.

"There's no more," she said. "He'll be thirsty when he wakes up. And I ought to warm it first. So get back as soon as you can."

I thought I'd be glad to get outside, away from her blankness. But beyond the hanging tarp was the ravine. I couldn't avoid looking at it; imagining him in the dark, without a light, stumbling over the edge. Lying there unconscious while we slept. While *I* slept.

Early morning was warmer than night had been. And there were clouds, low and dirty; I had seen those clouds in the Beartooths before. But when snow is thigh high around you, you tell yourself that the stuff can't wrong you much more seriously than it already has.

I started down to the water, down a path that already had been tramped once in each direction; and I was back so quickly, she let gratitude show through for a moment before she became opaque again.

23

Travis and Hollenbeck were up and walking before daybreak. An hour later they were on a promontory, looking over several miles of the plateau's fits and heaves, across to the crest line.

They picked out the pass, the bench between twin pinnacles. Hollenbeck got out his compass and shot a bearing. One hundred twenty degrees.

This was before the snow. Half an hour later, big wet flakes descended thickly. Travis kept wading through the fall. He simply didn't stop; Hollenbeck thought his stamina was amazing. Then Hollenbeck remembered that he himself hadn't stopped either, that he was actually keeping up with Travis.

Around mid-morning they hit the last long uphill to the pass. The fresh fall was at least six inches thick by now, and Hollenbeck felt the urgency of a race—hurry or be buried. Travis picked up his stride, and Hollenbeck let himself be drawn along. He stayed pinned to Travis's back, and felt giddy about it. Hollenbeck seemed to be a spectator; the legs and the lungs that were making this happen had to belong to someone else. His own were incapable of such feats.

They pushed past the rock ledges where we had made shelter.

Travis was effervescent.

"How about this?" he said. "On the nose, huh? No futzing around this time."

"Nice job," Hollenbeck said.

"What did I say? That night at Les Cygnes? I told you I'd get you through it."

"Let's not celebrate yet." Hollenbeck thought of the boulderfields. They had to be full of snow. Couldn't make them any easier.

"Hey. From here we could roll down to the highway. Twelve hours from now we'll be in Red Lodge."

"Even without the snow we couldn't do it that fast."

"Lad, you have a truly rotten attitude. But today I refuse to let it get to me. We're on our way. Stick with me, kid, you'll be sitting down to burgers and beer before you know it."

They reached the summit, and crossed the bench to the other side. Directly below, and before them, was the long chute where we had clambered up, now lush with trackless snow that filled in all the corrugations, cloaked the harshness.

"Skis!" Travis said. "Sweet Mary Jane. Give me skis and I'd be in Red Lodge before lunch."

Poague had fallen from the stone cataract that now was at their feet, the top of the chute. Hollenbeck was telling himself that they would have to be careful on it—that backing down would be tricky—when Travis grinned at him, and whooped, and launched himself off the lip as if from a springboard at a pool. He kicked in mid-air, spread his arms, and fell out of sight.

Hollenbeck ran over to the edge. Travis lay on his back, limbs splayed, awash in new powder, motionless. Hollenbeck thought, *Stupid son of a . . .* before Travis tossed up arm-loads of showering flakes and yowled, Hot damn that's one way to get down.

He bounced up and stood, hip deep, and took several lunging steps down the slope, leaning forward, breasting the snow like a surfer paddling past breakers.

He yelled to Hollenbeck, Come on boy, take the plunge, time's a-wastin'.

The snow, falling and fallen, cushioned the shout; absorbed its clamor as it absorbed all other sound.

Hollenbeck hesitated at the top. He was looking at the snow in the chute, the deposits climbing up its sides. He thought that the chute looked pregnant: swollen, replete. Imminent.

Travis stopped, turned back, boomed to Hollenbeck, "Hey guy, you don't want to let me get too far ahead. Way I feel, you'll never catch up."

Hollenbeck came down. The slow way. Travis was a couple of hundred yards ahead, pushing. On both sides of him piles of snow climbed the chute's high walls, thick even at the top, reposing at improbable angles.

To Hollenbeck it looked discordant.

He yelled, "Hey Paul. Wait."

Travis shouted for him to get his butt in gear.

Hollenbeck noticed movement in the chute, below where he stood, above and behind Travis. A soft worrying, as if something bubbled beneath the fresh fall. It became a churning that spread wider as it chewed across the chute, up the other side, and then bore down on Travis. Building, gaining speed, raising ferocious hackles.

By the time it reached him the rolling wave was twice Travis's height and growing. Hollenbeck was astonished that it made no noise. All that weight, that force, completely silent.

Travis glanced back the instant it reached him. He existed, and then there was the wave storming, this soundless rampage that tossed and kicked snow dust in a billowing cloud, and the cloud and the wave kept boiling downhill, leaving empty the place where he had stood.

Hollenbeck started to go to the spot, wading through snow that lay now in soft disturbance, like fresh loam overturned in the wake of a harrow.

The snow was mudlike, slippery and viscous. Hollenbeck remembered that he was on the southeast side of the crest now. Even with overcast this slope would have gotten some warmth from the rising sun. He urged himself toward where he had seen Travis last. The snow began to move around him, began to flow with the deliberate firmness of wet concrete, sucking him along. He pumped his legs but found no purchase underfoot.

Above him and to his right was movement. A bushel-sized packet of fresh fall had separated from the side of the chute and was flopping down, turning over, gaining mass and momentum as it snowballed. The same thing was happening to his left, and again to his right, and again behind him, over one shoulder. The pack was coming apart again and it was taking him down with it.

Now the snow around him felt like a sluggish river. Hollenbeck forced himself to breath, think. He told himself, *If it's a river I can swim*, and that's what he began to do. A slow motion mimickry of kicking and breaststroking, pulling himself through the torpid white substance that wasn't snow any more, wasn't anything he could name.

To his right, along the side of the chute, was an island of solid pack that the movement hadn't dislodged. It was no more than a body-length away, but the flow was carrying him past it. Hollenbeck paddled and pulled. He reached for the island, dug in the fingers of his right hand, punched his mitten through the crust, and held; and then, breathless, he hauled himself up onto its firmness.

In the shelter Donnie lay before us like a festering wound. Most of the time he was unconscious, and when he was awake he passed in and out of lucidity. Even when he was inert he was all wrong: his breathing without pattern, his face contorted.

That afternoon Eleanor tried to feed him salami that she had chopped and mashed in warm water. She cradled him and spooned it past his rubbery lips. His eyes were open, heavy-lidded, but he didn't seem to notice. The spoon shook in her hand and I saw that she was crying. Looking at him, scooping up bits of meat that had shaken off the spoon, saying, All you had to do was wake me up, I told you if you get sleepy just wake me up.

He never reacted until the food caught in his throat, and he gagged, and she had to stop. She wiped his chin, lowered his head to the floor. As she was turning away he said clearly, "Cut the poor guy some slack, huh? It isn't like he pushed me. Ray, my head hurts like a son-of-a-bitch. How 'bout a couple of those Percs, what do you say?"

So he was aware. His eyes followed me as I shook out a pill. He opened his mouth and put out his tongue to take it, and swallowed. Two minutes later he was out again, eyes clamped shut, body drawn up in a posture of pain.

The wind was insistent, hectoring. Time ground slow and ponderous. Time and starvation and fatigue beat us down until we were less than we had been the day before, with the certain knowledge that a day later we would be further diminished.

You get surprised at what is worn away. Hunger. The first day of fasting is torture. After that the craving becomes just an imperfect memory. When Eleanor cut the salami I watched and thought that I ought to be hungry, ought to be interested; but I couldn't make myself want it.

Bitterness and anger go, too. They're emotional luxuries. When she reproached me there was no bile in Eleanor. Only sadness.

I went out to brush snow from the overhead tarp, and was surprised to find day draining into night.

Eleanor lit the stove, but it flamed out before the water was even tepid. Out of fuel. For a long while she stroked Donnie's head. Then asked how long before Travis and Hollenbeck got through. Never suggesting that they might fail; like sadness, hope will root wherever, survive without sustenance.

I tried to remember the sequence of days and nights that had brought us beyond the pass. It escaped me; history began the moment Gary left his feet at the edge of the cliff.

But I had the group journal, and I used it to count the days. I told her we needed two days to climb up to the pass, another to get about this far. The trip down from the pass should be faster, I said. No climbing. Even with all the snow it should be faster. If they really hustle they might get over and down in two days.

"So that would be tomorrow morning," she said.

"But nothing will happen until the weather is clear. Not even Travis will get a helicopter up in this mess." It had the feel of fantasy; any movement but our own laborings through the snow, any sound besides wind and our voices and the coursing of our blood seemed inconceivable.

I found myself holding the notebook, the pencil sheathed in its wire spirals. Maybe twenty minutes' candlelight remained.

Once more I counted the entries, and the days that had passed without an entry, and wrote.

Day Ten
Monday, September 15

During the night his bowels convulsed. I wasn't aware, but she must have been; when I woke she had stripped him, and was cleaning him with a bandana that she dipped in cold water. Her movements seemed soft even in the uncompromising glare of a flashlight. I took it in and went back to sleep.

For all I know she was up with him all night. When I woke again there was daylight around the tarp's edges, and she was kneeling beside his head.

She said, "Ray, he can't move."

I scuttled the few inches to him. His eyes were alive, tracking me. No, one eye: the left, closest to me. The right one was motionless. They both showed fear.

"He can't move his right side," she said. "He can hardly talk."

On the right half of his face the muscles were flaccid. His features were smeared, the way a careless hand might slur a bust of soft modeling clay.

I asked him if his head hurt. With half a mouth and half a tongue he said, "Hurts like hell."

"He took a bad rap on his skull. I've been afraid of that swelling. There's pressure in there, that's the problem."

"What can we do?"

"Up here nobody can do anything."

She squeezed his dead right hand and said, "Don't worry, we'll get you out."

Charles had been watching from a back corner of the shelter, squatting as far from Donnie as possible, his big eyes bigger than I had ever seen them. Now he crawled to the entrance and threw back the hanging tarp to unalloyed sunlight.

"I can see sky," he said.

A blisteringly bright morning. Donnie's morbidity was a dark well that seemed to soak up light; but beyond the tarps and past the entrance's heaped bank of snow the day was radiant. By mid-morning the fresh fall was settling into slick, sticky consolidation.

I went out, looked around, came back and dredged dark glasses from my pack. I cleared a place against an outside face of the granite that had hid us, dug and pushed the snow until I was down to bare ground. The sun was full on it. I took off my poncho and sat. On the other side of the granite, within the cleft, was stink and dimness and dying. Some stench and a crust of despair clung to me, too. But I could sense it crumbling under the bright pressure of the sun, the warmth lifting it off to penetrate shirt and sweater and skin.

It seemed a good day for flying. I tried to imagine the arrival of a helicopter. A strident thumping, the carapace of a fuselage levitating over the ridge, its blades stirring up a false blizzard as it came to earth. Then Donnie and Charles and Eleanor and I on the chopper, the side of the ridge falling away from us as the machine rose. We could see the cleft granite and the shelter and a plush upholstery of snow surrounding it, and in the distance all the hills and ravines we had tracked over and through, and beyond that the half dome with the spot on the edge that Gary had tried to grab; and it was all receding, disappearing, becoming memory as we watched. Out the other side of the ship was Red Lodge, with plains beyond town where there had been no snow, with the highway through the plains that led to Billings, to the airport, a return to some place where people survived without crawling into rocks.

I could see the whole fantastic panorama. It was the last image on my mind before I melted into the best, the deepest, the only true sleep I had slept in uncountable hours.

———

A cold shadow settled on my face. Charles stood at my feet, between me and the sun, now past its apex, descending.

"Ray. Your face is red."

No helicopter. The snow and the ridge and the rock still held us.

"You're sunburned. That looks bad."

"The least of my troubles."

No helicopter. I felt a crushing in my chest. Inhaling took a huge effort.

"Eleanor asked me to make sure you were okay."

"I'm fine."

"We need water too. I'll go if you want."

"It's my job. I know where it is."

I picked myself up and put on the poncho. The seat of my trousers was wet—snowmelt was leaking out on the ground where I sat. I remembered the frozen trickle.

The ice axe was in the shelter. I crouched and went inside. Back into the miasma.

Eleanor was at her vigil.

"They didn't make it, did they?"

"It's much too early to say." I picked up the bottles, searched for the ice axe.

"If they had, help would be here by now."

"We can't know that."

"Charles says the weather is good."

"It is. It's beautiful. You ought to get out in it for a few minutes."

"I'd rather not."

Her patience was suddenly wearisome. I got the axe and left without looking at her again.

It was a short hike to where the pool had been. A V-shaped

depression in the snow marked it. The snow was intact but I could hear dribbling beneath it, and the dribbling got louder as I trenched snow.

At the bottom, the ice had a sheen: a thin shimmering coat of water. I bashed the ice and broke it, and the water drained into the hole, and I bent to fill the first bottle.

I stood and heard my name, a sound so tenuous, so indistinct, the tiny flow at my feet almost drowned it.

Once more, louder. From higher on the ridge.

I saw a staggering bundle that flapped its arms and shouted, Ray, Ray.

It was Hollenbeck. I fought uphill to meet him. A few feet away he stumbled, fell; the waist-high snow caught him and I pulled him upright.

"Did it," he said. Breathless. "I can't believe I did it."

He seemed disappointed. As if he expected more from me than a casual hand up. But I was looking past him, up to the top of the empty ridge.

"Just me," he said. "Sorry. I'm all there is."

24

As soon as his vision adjusted to the darkness inside, Hollenbeck looked at Donnie and asked, "What happened to him?"

Eleanor said, "You know he wasn't doing too well. The night after you left we fell asleep. He went outside alone and took a bad fall. It looks like he was out there quite a while before we got him in."

She left plenty of room to distribute blame. But from the boy on the shelter floor Hollenbeck looked directly at me. He knew me, damn him; knew my ways. And knew enough to ask no more.

Instead he said, "My muscles, Lord my muscles feel like jelly." He sat up against the rock, legs stretched out in front of him, and while he kneaded his calves and his thighs, he told us all that he had done and seen, all that he knew.

———

"I pulled myself up on the solid part where it wasn't moving," he said. "Then there was some bare rock where all the snow had slid off. I climbed it back to the top. I wanted to keep going down, but there was no way. It was real hairy. I wouldn't have had a chance.

"I decided to come back here. I didn't know what else to do. For a while it was easy—just stay with the tracks. But after a while I lost them on and off. They filled up with snow. So I used the compass. Three hundred degrees is the reciprocal of one-twenty, right? And it worked. Once I got close I knew where you were supposed to be. And you were."

He kept watching Donnie. Who lay so still he might have been dead. The spectacle of waste compelled Hollenbeck as it compelled the rest of us. He said, "There's something we have to talk about. It has to do with everybody. Especially Donnie."

Hollenbeck freed his eyes long enough to look around at each of us.

"He understands," Eleanor said. "I'm pretty sure that he can hear even when he's out."

"Then we ought to talk outside."

"If it concerns him we can talk about it in front of him."

"Fine," Hollenbeck said. "Here it is. We have to get out of the mountains. We can't count on help—we don't know that they'll start looking before it's too late. There's a question of time. Without food we're not getting any stronger. This time tomorrow we'll be that much less able to do it. We have to get going. Anybody who can walk." He waited a couple of beats and said, "Ray?"

I was seeing the avalanche, imagining how it had rubbed out Travis, his brilliance there one moment, vanished the next.

I said, "It sounds right to me."

Eleanor said, "What about Donnie?"

When nobody else answered Hollenbeck said, "Donnie has to stay. The best thing we can do for him is to get the hell down and send help up here."

Now Charles and Hollenbeck began to discuss when we should leave and which route to take. Whether to wait until morning. Where we ought to try crossing the crest.

I couldn't keep up. They were talking about future, and I hadn't yet grasped a present where Paul Travis did not exist.

Between them they decided that we ought to use the good weather; let Hollenbeck rest for an hour or two, then get moving. We could walk at night, use flashlights and the moon. And we could return to the pass that Hollenbeck had left. No other choice: we might wander for days trying to find another place to cross. Maybe the snow would be more stable when we got there. Maybe we'd have to be creative. Maybe take a chance.

Their words were concrete and rational; I was glad someone could be. Eleanor didn't seem aware of anything but the boy; she was bending over him the way a mother suspends herself over her infant.

Me, I tasted fetid air on my tongue, and imagined Travis crumpled dead in the chute. From the awful present, tendrils of responsibility snaked back into the past. I didn't want to follow them too far; might find their source.

"These boots," Hollenbeck said. He was taking them off to get into a sleeping bag. "Thank God for 'em. And that snow wax. It was such a damn mess when I was putting it on."

"It worked?" I said. I remember my wet socks, frigid feet.

"Shit, look." He stuck out his legs; toes wiggled in dry wool. "Kept me going, I'll tell you."

"That's really good, George." I meant it. I could remember how overwrought those boots had seemed.

Maybe he remembered, too, because he said, "At the time you do it, you can't believe it'll ever make a difference. I felt sort of foolish, if you want to know the truth. Burning my hands, wax all over the place. It's one of those dumb tasks people say you should do. But nobody ever does except suckers. You know me. The suckers' sucker."

I took one of the boots, held it, felt its solidness. The weight and the hard-shelled leather were reassuring.

He said, "I can't believe it. For once there's a payoff—it actually made a difference. I guess it had to happen sooner or later."

———

I went out to finish filling the bottles. When I returned, Hollenbeck was out of the shelter and waiting for me.

"How bad is Donnie?" he said.

"How does he look?"

"About as bad as he could get and still be breathing."

"That's how he looks to me, too. He keeps getting worse."

"Is there any point in one of us staying with him?"

After a few seconds' thought I said, "He wouldn't be alone when he died. I don't know if that counts. The way he is now, I'm not sure he realizes we're here anyway."

"Better come in. She's decided she wants to stay with him."

I followed him inside. She seemed tiny at first, even in the midst of such confinement. Then I realized: she was not so much tiny as reduced in stature, the way a tremendous weight will bow its bearer's back. Her burden was the boy's suffering, and our misery, and the darkness and the squalor.

"I'm not leaving him," she said. "It's wrong. Even if it were right I still couldn't do it."

Hollenbeck said, "Tell her how crazy this is."

"She knows."

"We have to leave," Hollenbeck said.

"I understand," she said. "Go. You don't need me. We'll stay here, Donnie and I, while you go for help."

Charles said quietly, "Travis tried it that way already. We shouldn't split up any more. It matters. People are different together than they are apart."

"You've probably got a point," she said. "I'm still not leaving him this way."

"We can't let you stay," Hollenbeck said.

"I guess you could tie me up and try to carry me. But if you're going to do that you might as well carry him instead."

Hollenbeck's hands flew up, searched for a roost, settled uncertainly around his belt buckle.

"This is completely and utterly stupid," he said. "The kid is dying. Tell her, Ray. There's nothing left in him. You want to sit up here alone and hold hands with a corpse."

"Enough," she said.

Charles said, "I know Donnie. If he could talk, he'd be telling you to get going with us."

"Unfortunately he can't speak for himself."

Two nights earlier I had squandered whatever special influence she might once have granted me. Whether it would have been enough, I'll never know—it was gone with the ruptured bond. Now I had only insight. To watch her and know that she would meet more pressure with greater resistance.

Hollenbeck must have sensed it, too. He said, "If you knew he was up and talking, would that make a difference?"

"I don't know. Maybe."

"Then why don't we give him a chance? I'm tired. Really. I could use the rest. If we wait 'til morning, maybe we'll get this thing resolved."

Something out there had changed Hollenbeck. The miles, the snow, surviving where Travis had perished. But I could still read him.

He was thinking, *Or it'll resolve itself.*

"Whatever you want," I said.

"As long as we don't wait too long," Charles said.

Eleanor seemed to have straightened a little under the load. She said, "Do what you think is right. It's the only way. That's what I'm doing."

———

During the night I awoke. I mean just like that: awoke so immediately and completely it could not have been happenstance. A part of me must have planned it, some element that is more ruthless and more direct and more capable—above all, more capable—than the Ray Furlow who shows himself to the world.

Let me astound you with my efficiency.

All the others slept hard. I was alone with what had to be done. Why else should I have chosen the moment? I knew exactly what I had to do and how to go about it. Under my head was my backpack. In a pocket of the pack, close at hand, was the headlamp, wrapped in a T-shirt that damped the light to a firefly smudge when I turned on the switch.

Already I lay at Donnie's left side; not even Travis had ever arranged so artfully. I could touch his face as easily as touch my own. His tenuous, ragged exhaling was the loudest sound in my universe.

I propped myself up on an elbow, and studied him longer and more closely than I ever could have done if he had been conscious, or even just asleep; but this was like examining a specimen of quartz. Pain and paralysis had set his features. The soft filtered light softened them some, and when I looked past the hurt, past the bruises and the scrapes and the puffed eye, I could see a beautiful child that he had managed to keep hidden from us. Youth that made me ache. The idea of it. Youth, and innocence too. He should have had years to dissipate them both.

He didn't move when my left hand touched his throat.

Some big game hunters claim there's an instant before death when killer and quarry know each other completely, a moment of communion, total understanding. I'm not much of a hunter. But I believe this: I believe that Donnie heard me when I spoke to him in my mind. *I love you, I'm sorry, but you have to go now.*

Couldn't let her stay for him.

My left hand covered his mouth and pushed down; my right pinched his nostrils shut. He didn't fight. Eleanor was tucked against his right side. Any struggle would have awakened her. His only response was languid. He bent his left arm, raising that hand; and placed it over my own hand on his mouth; and squeezed tenderly.

I had trouble seeing through the tears. But I didn't have to see. I could feel the lungs sucking at his nose, through his teeth, his chest trying to balloon. It was as close as either of us came to violence, that reflexive urge to have air for life. But it didn't last long.

He shuddered, and his fingers relaxed completely. I felt certain that was the end. I didn't remove my hands for a while. There was no reason to: it was done now, could never be undone, and for as long as I lived I'd be alone with the deed.

25

In my heart I have snuffed him ten thousand times. It's always the same. While everyone else sleeps I wake beside him, I gaze at his face, I lovingly shut off his breath of life. When he is dead I return to sleep knowing that in ultimate judgment what I've done must prove righteous.

But from the moment when his lungs began to surge and suck, it is manufactured memory. Truth is that when I felt him in the throes I let go—he gasped—sighed—he breathed again. Truth is, I lacked the will to keep my hands and fingers locked in place until it was done.

In truth I am not nearly so confident of judgment's verdict.

You could say that at the moment of final decision I was unable to force myself to murder. You could also say that once more I failed to do what had to be done.

Either way I am left with the fact of having tried to take a life, without the redemption of actually accomplishing what had to be done. When only the executed act itself, the good that might have come from it, could possibily justify such monstrous intent.

Eventually the others began to wake. It was morning, and

Donnie remained unconscious, breathing, and Eleanor was still determined to remain with him.

Hollenbeck said, "This is stupid. Are you shooting for sainthood, is that it? Martydom?"

"Just go and leave us alone."

Even a week earlier, she might have been bullied into coming with us. But now she resisted all duress.

Time was with her; while Hollenbeck argued, Charles gathered and sorted equipment, and there was only so much of that to do. Before long he was finished, and we were ready to leave, and she remained adamant. She had outlasted him.

Charles had divided the equipment—what little we were taking—into two packs. There were our sleeping bags, the spare tarp, matches, compasses, a rope, the bag of climber's hardware. We took one water bottle, and left the others.

The crampons and ice axe were strapped outside one pack. I told Charles that we should leave the axe, that Eleanor might need it to open the small pool.

"We could need it more," he said. At the time it struck me as selfish; a day and miles later, I realized that he'd had a notion of what might be waiting.

Instead he gave her a piton from the bag of climbing gear. It was an iron blade, dull and thick. He took her outside to the pool, showed her how the piton would gouge ice if she used it right.

She said she'd make it work, thank you, don't worry.

The four of us stood in the snow. Hollenbeck put on one pack, and I had the other.

To Hollenbeck she said, "Please don't be angry." She kissed him on the cheek.

"You take care of these guys," she said to Charles, and she put her arms around him.

I stood up the ridge, at a distance of maybe ten paces. Not by accident: I wasn't sure what she would say, what final disappointment I would feel in her, and I didn't want to find out.

I raised my right hand and waved once. She answered with the same motion, smaller.

Hollenbeck went up the hill first. When he passed me he said we should take turns leading, let Charles follow; we would cover more ground that way.

I looked back once. She was at the entrance, watching us. From where I stood the shelter looked pathetically insecure. Against the immensity of snow she seemed as vulnerable and lonely as anyone had ever looked to me.

She crouched and disappeared into the hole, and I wished, for the first of many thousands of times, that I had killed him when I'd had the chance.

———

We paused for breath at top of the ridge, with the first valley spread wide in front of us.

"You actually did this, right?" I was speaking to Hollenback. "You actually walked to the pass and then walked back?"

"Uh-huh. Can you believe it?"

"It helps to know that it can be done. You may have to remind me."

Hollenbeck began laughing. *Laughing*.

"We could have a problem here," he said. "I was sort of hoping that you'd be able to remind me."

———

We walked and we kept walking. Across the valley, over the breastwork of recumbent hills on the far side, down a long and rocky drainage that funneled us toward the crest.

Words don't hurt enough. They don't infinitely expand, the way that day's minutes did, to fill themselves with misery. Truth gets telescoped beyond recognition: anything small enough for words to carry can't really belong to our trek.

But I have to try. If only out of pride. I had never before come close to feeling heroic, and probably never will again.

The snowpack was wet once more from the sun's warmth. But a beating wind blew across the flats and over the tops of the ridges, forced us to wear ponchos, and we became clammy under the coated cloth. My boots soaked through in minutes; the cold marched in with it. On other days my feet had gone numb. This time they felt as if their bones had splintered, and they roared every step.

We kept walking. You try to deny pain's existence. You try to find distraction from it. You try to look at yourself from outside, so that you're watching another someone suffer: someone else's miseries are easy to bear.

We kept walking. Legs became pulpy. The snow grabbed at boots and ankles, and we would have to shake loose. We kept walking. The far mountains, the crest, seemed to retreat before us. Yet we kept putting distance behind us, so that after a few hours we were far from where we had been, but hardly closer to where we were bound; ocean sailors floundering in mid-passage.

We kept walking. Like ocean sailors we couldn't stop and wait to gain strength; you don't make this crossing in stages. We kept walking. You try to hide from pain. We kept walking. Hide from pain, and you find yourself pushed into obscure corners of your mind, your thoughts cramped and sluggish.

We walked and we kept walking. At first we rested every hour or so, but the rest was never long enough, and when we stopped moving we stopped being able to gloss over discomfort and weariness. So during the afternoon we rested only twice; otherwise just kept walking.

Hollenbeck told us about the bivouac in the trees. He and Travis had reached it around sunset. But Travis had left before dawn that morning; our start was at least two hours later. In the afternoon clouds formed close overhead—condensation from the snow pack, Charles said—so dusk came sooner than it might have.

In the gloom Hollenbeck said we still had a way to go before we got to the trees, but it was worth pushing for. We got out the lights. The snow crusted and became brittle on the surface, grainy beneath. Full darkness. We let our lights lead us across the snow, and we kept walking.

I came apart at the oddest time. Hollenbeck was leading, so he was doing the really hard work. We were on a long descent, steep enough that almost gravity alone would pull legs forward. The snow in this stretch had been blown, and was hardly calf high. None of that mattered. My legs gave way. I was astonished to find myself leaning on my forearms in the snow, turning over, sitting, looking up at Hollenbeck and Charles.

In my thighs and calves, up as far as my buttocks, muscles suddenly relieved of weight began to go soft and dead. My head floated, and my limbs felt far removed from me, beyond my reach.

"Are you hurt?" Hollenbeck said.

I told him no, and thought, But you might as well trash me, I'm so used up.

"Come on then," he said. He put a hand down for me to grab. "Let's go."

I found the energy to shake my head.

Understand: I wasn't being petulant. My legs wouldn't carry me any more; or I thought they wouldn't.

"There's nothing left," I said.

"Ah, shit, don't give me that." His anger sounded genuine. "You were walking half a minute ago, you can damn well be walking again in another half a minute."

"I'm empty."

"You're not even close. How can you be? Damn it. I'm still standing, and I've been up and down this track once already, and while I was out here doing it you were back there nodding off." He aimed that one for the quick, and it hit.

"I guess you're just a superman, George."

"We both know better than that."

Charles said, "We're getting cold, we need to keep moving."

Hollenbeck squatted to reach my level, almost as close to me as I had been to Donnie the night before.

He said, "Ray, this is how people get into trouble in the mountains. Screw around and get cold. Now you come with us. We don't want to leave you out here."

"We won't do that," Charles said.

"The fuck we won't." His answer leaped out. It startled Charles and me, and maybe even Hollenbeck himself. But he kept on: "I'm doing all I can to get out. If I have to leave either one of you behind to do it, I will."

He shifted his weight forward from his haunches, to kneel in front of me, even closer. He gripped my shoulders.

"Here's the way it is, Ray. You're my best friend. Goddamn. I love you. Goddamn. If I lose you it'll feel like my guts fell out on the sidewalk. I'll never get over it. But I'll tell you what. I'd rather be alive without you than dead here with you."

If he would only leave me alone, I thought. Let me stretch out and sleep—I'd be okay. I would wake refreshed. I'd have their tracks to follow.

I wanted to cry but I was empty of tears. All I could do was whimper: "It's all used up. I've got nothing to do it with."

"Sure you do. You've got wanting to do it. That's plenty. I've been running on that for the last couple of days. Now. Goddamn," he said. "Let's get the ass in gear, huh?"

He stood and extended the hand again.

There was a quality about the action, the way he did it. I could call it confidence, and that's part of it, but only part. He knew that this time I would take the hand and pull myself up. He knew that once I was standing I would find a way to impel my legs forward; he didn't accept any other possibility.

I wondered how he could be so sure, when even I didn't know. While I was wondering I grasped the hand and came to my feet.

He said nothing, but in the light of my headlamp his eyes skipped once, quiet delight, flickering the way yours or mine might if we had pulled off a parlor trick requiring cleverness and guile.

He began to walk down the slope. Before I realized what I had done I was following him.

This was new in him, this sureness. I had seen it somewhere else, though, and before we had taken too many steps down the slope I realized where. Travis had had that way of informing you that he was on top of things you hadn't yet imagined.

Only one difference: when Hollenbeck told me, I believed.

———

We reached the woods, and bedded down in the same hollow that had harbored Travis and Hollenbeck. George draped the tarp over the branches the way he had before, I built a scrap fire in the old ashes, and we settled our shoulders and spines into depressions that other shoulders and spines had formed along the sides of the cavity.

While the fire still fumed Hollenbeck told us we ought to try to reach the pass by first light, give ourselves all day to get down the other side. Travis had claimed that it could be done in a day, Hollenbeck said, and maybe it was so.

I guess we slept five or six hours. Hollenbeck woke Charles and me; how long he had been up, I don't know, but he was ready.

At first his energy and alertness distracted me. Then I heard rain hitting the tarp. Rain or something sharper. Sleet. It tapped the edges of the tarp beyond the boughs of the pine.

I thought about hiking all day through freezing rain, through sodden snow.

The others didn't seem to notice. They stashed their sleeping bags, tied boots, zipped jackets. As if the pattering overhead didn't exist.

Hollenbeck said, "We put the tarp away, we'll be ready to go." One after the other we climbed out of the hollow and stood beside the tree.

We could have lost it right there. If even one of us had moaned, *Now rain, when does the crap ever end?* everything might have crumbled.

But we stood in the rain and the pellets of ice, and let them punch at us, and never once acknowledged them. Not once all day.

We folded the tarp, Hollenbeck put it in his pack, and we started out of the woods.

26

Like supplicants approaching a throne we made our way up the steep threshold of the pass, into tumbling clouds that hid the bench and the twin pinnacles flanking it. When dawn broke overhead the clouds became a milky nimbus, tattered luminescence turning and wheeling around us, ripping us with wind, spattering us with bits of ice and congealing droplets that froze where they struck our ponchos.

We dug upward, locking bent legs and pausing for breath after each step. Upward on a tilted snowfield: and beneath the snow, scree and talus that we could feel through the cover, the smaller fragments sliding and giving way when we committed our weight.

The grade became gentler, clouds less dense, footing solid. We were moving across the bench, between the pinnacles. This was my second time here, and the site seemed even more disturbing than before. Partly it was the weather's naked harshness. And there were fewer of us this time, so we were more easily swallowed. It was a place, and a moment, that you would want to put behind you.

Where the bench ended we stopped, and looked over the edge.

Below was the chute, paunchy and lush, sides precariously heaped. The latest fall had covered all sign of the avalanche, and I knew that it must have covered Travis, too, somewhere below.

The wind flogged us, drove the sleet and snow into our faces. We had to shout above it when we spoke.

"It looked like this before," Hollenbeck said. "Maybe it's not quite as bad today."

"Today is warmer," Charles said. "Wetter, too."

"Does that make a difference?" Hollenbeck said.

"It's supposed to."

"Less dangerous?"

"That depends. I'm not sure."

I said, "Just tell us if we can go down there without getting killed."

"I don't know, Ray."

"Isn't this stuff in the books?"

"Yes." He sounded hurt. "But I haven't read them all."

Hollenbeck said, "I don't need a book. I don't want to go down there. It looks too much like it did two days ago. I didn't want to go down then and I don't want to now."

I felt pressure at my back, from Eleanor at the shelter and the miles we had walked to get here, from the necessity to do something. And another sort of pressure, the physical sensation that against our will we were being shoved into the chute, down between its sheer confining walls.

See, the mountain had shaped our thinking, the cut and cast of the rock channeling our attention. If we let the flow of the land carry us along we would be swept over the bench and down the chute every time.

At the moment that I was thinking there had to be another way, Hollenbeck was saying it; and Charles was finding it.

He was looking at the pinnacles that straddled the bench, taking them in together and then individually, his eyes shuttling between them. I looked at them too, really seeing them for the first time.

The one to the south was an impossible obstacle, smooth-sided and precipitous. The other rose at the same angle, thrusting up toward the overcast, but its surface was broken and narrowly terraced in places.

Charles was looking at the one to the north. He said, "I wonder what it's like on the other side."

Hollenbeck said, "Can we get down that way?"

I said, "Getting down is easy; the trick is keeping solid ground under your feet while you're doing it."

He said, "Please Ray, not now."

But it was no joke. The fact is that as you climb a high mountain you eliminate the possibilities of where you can go next. Solid earth contracts, and empty space closes in.

Then I saw that it was not just the lay of the land, but the emptiness beyond, that kept funneling us into the chute. Because the human reaction is to stay clear of the edges, away from those places where your next step may be a thousand feet deep.

The thought buckled my knees. Charles began slogging to the north. Hollenbeck was behind him, and when my legs again had fiber in them I followed.

I joined the others where the bench narrowed and blended into the pinnacle. We faced north, the three of us. Ahead and to the left, the ground fell away hard into the low milling clouds. To our right was the pinnacle, scored and chunked. A jutting lip of granite formed a sill, now white-tufted, that joined the bench a few feet from where we stood. It hugged the face of the pinnacle, following the curve northeastward and around out of sight.

Where it met the bench, the sill was almost as broad as a sidewalk. But gradually it constricted, until it was just a few inches wide as it disappeared behind the bend of the wall.

All this we comprehended during the space between heartbeats. Simple. Where we wanted to be was somewhere beyond that curve.

"Let me," Charles said. "I know what we're looking for."

He stepped out on the sill. The pinnacle wall rose to his right; to his left, beyond the lip of the sill, was emptiness.

Before each step he swept a boot in front of him, clearing the snow. I watched a parcel of it turn end over end, break apart as it fell, and meld with the clouds swirling below.

Now he was well beyond the bench, and the sill had squeezed enough that he could no longer comfortably walk forward. He turned and faced into the wall, and began to edge along, pushing the snow out of his path with nervous scuffing kicks. The sill tapered until it was no wider than the length of his boots. Hollenbeck and I had already moved as far as we could to keep him in view, and his next sideways step took him around the curve, out of sight.

We waited. I looked at Hollenbeck. His poncho was glazed, and an ash of rime lay over his eyebrows and on the forelock of hair that bristled from under his stocking cap. He winced at a raw gust, and I thought of how it must be buffeting Charles on the far side of the pinnacle.

Where Charles had shuffled out of sight, a boot, a hand, appeared. Then the rest of him, pressed against the wall. He was looking past his right shoulder, intent on the spot where he would slide his boot next.

As the sill broadened, Charles turned about, faced us, walked the last few feet. I realized what he had done, what I had seen; the image of him silhouetted against the sky that moment when he slid out of sight. I wanted to vomit.

He ran over to us, grinning, barely contained—an adrenalin high.

Hollenbeck wanted to know how it looked, could we do it?

"I think so," Charles said. "Here."

He knelt, and swiftly scooped and packed a humpbacked loaf of snow.

"This is the mountain," he said. We got down with him so that the wind wouldn't carry away his words.

He pressed the heel of one hand into the top of the loaf— "the pass"—shaped a small peak beside the depression—"the summit right here"—with one finger slashed a deep lateral furrow—"the chute"—rubbed a thumb at the end of the furrow—"and Exile Lake at the bottom."

His finger made a crescent around the summit, the route he had just taken.

"You get about half way around, you climb down to a ridge," he said, words spilling. "That's the top of the high wall on the north side of the chute. It looked pretty easy. But you can't see far, because of the clouds.

"You know the second day, the flat part before we climbed up to the lake? Remember? I bet the ridge drops into there. If we get lucky we can walk down into that valley."

Hollenbeck said, "Great. Let's do it."

"Wait. The problem is, there are a couple of bad spots." Charles was collecting himself now. "The first one is this traverse right here. The shelf gets narrow around the other side."

"How bad?"

"It gets down to a few inches. There's room to stand. But you can't belay. And it's a long way down." There was respect in his voice. "Then when you get off the shelf, you climb down to the side of the ridge. And right there, you run into a glacier you have to cross." He pointed to a place on the sculpted snow. "There's no way around it. It didn't look wide, maybe eighty or ninety feet. But it's real steep. We can't just walk it."

I wondered out loud how else we could cross it.

"One of us uses the ice axe and the crampons to get over to the other side. You can cut steps as you go, and carry over the end of a rope. So the other two have steps and a rope to hold on to."

Hollenbeck said, "How hard is that?"

"None of this is very hard if you believe you can do it."

"I know we can."

That was Hollenbeck. I only listened, and as I listened looked over at the sill, imagined myself on its narrowness, sidling into space as Charles had done. The idea made me sway. Or feel as if I were swaying. It must have been all internal: the others would have noticed.

Hollenbeck said, "Ray, you did okay on the cliff that day, right?"

"I made it over the top." I wanted to add, But that was before I saw what could happen.

"Sure. We all did fine. It's not that hard, if you keep a cool head. I say we do it."

"It's probably a better risk than the chute," Charles said.

"Ray, you have any better ideas?" Hollenbeck said.

I heard myself saying, "We have to do something. It's not getting any easier while we sit around talking."

We stood. Charles said if we didn't mind, he'd like to start, and he walked out onto the sill. This time when he turned in to the rock and began to sidle, I couldn't watch; I kept seeing myself out there.

I looked down at my feet, at Charles's model mountain.

"Some kid," Hollenbeck said. In his words was a strain that I thought was not just from bucking the wind.

"A great kid." As I leveled the mountain with the toe of my boot.

I thought of where I was, what had happened in the last twelve days, what I was about to attempt, and why. Making peace with the reality that all this actually was happening, and to me.

"My turn, I guess," Hollenbeck said. I looked up. Charles was edging out of sight. I decided that I didn't want to wait any longer; didn't want to stand alone and watch Hollenbeck, too, disappear around that curve. If I didn't have him behind me, his expectation pushing me forward, I might never move off the bench.

I touched Hollenbeck on the sleeve and said, "Let me, okay?"

He said, "Sure, go ahead, see you on the other side." And in a tone as soft as wind and tension would allow he said, "Hey Ray, remember. This is the way we get home."

I took three strides, hitched the fourth, and hopped up on the sill.

The wind was out of the northeast, full in my face, grating the skin I had burned two days earlier. It seemed suddenly stronger—an illusion, I'm sure—and when I looked directly ahead my eyes watered.

I wiped them with the back of a mitten, and turned my left shoulder into the wind, to hide my face. Better.

I advanced one step, a second. To my left, when I passed the lip of the bench, the rock seemed to withdraw, a curtain falling away. It revealed sky and clouds, and I was exposed.

The air left my chest but I took a third step, a fourth, and more. Trying to stay fixed on the strip of rock in front of me. Trying to ignore the eternity beyond the brink, roaring like hurricane waves against a jetty.

Charles's boot had left some pancake patches of snow. They were slush and ice now. Most of the sill was clear, but the freezing rain had given bare rock an uncertain slickness.

The sill pinched in. The sky lapped at my left side.

I turned to the wall, raised my hands to shoulder level, and gripped what cracks and protrusions the wall offered. I shuffled to the left, the soles of my boots dragging, my toes and torso and arms and legs scraping the vertical stone.

A gust shoved me, tried to shake me off the rock; I grabbed what I could and held until it passed.

The sill continued to narrow, and now curved perceptibly with the wall. Past my left shoulder I could see it bend to the right, sweeping in front of open sky. My shuffle had become a sideways creep, a couple of inches at a step. Around the curve. Hollenbeck would have lost sight of me by now; maybe he was mounting the sill already.

Under my heels I could feel the edge of the sill. The open space chewed at my ankles.

Still following the curve. Thirty, forty feet away, Charles was standing free on a mantel that was maybe five feet across and nearly as deep. Beyond was the glacier, nearly vertical, beyond that the raked flank of the ridge that slid into the clouds. The whole world was up-and-down, leaning and teetering. I wanted to go back to the bench, where I could stand and sit and jump and lay down to die.

Charles's mouth was moving, and when I stopped and watched his lips I could make out the words.

Careful, he was saying, It gets tricky.

I dipped my left shoulder to see more. Ahead—six, seven feet—the sill receded to the width of a curbstone. After a gap of about ten feet it protruded again. Somehow Charles had crossed that gap to stand where he was now.

"Son of a bitch, Charles." I yelled it into the rock. "You must be crazy."

He had seen this first, after all, had judged it possible. His word had brought us here.

"Easy," he said. "It's not so difficult."

"Oh bullshit. Look at it. Chrissakes."

His presence on the mantle seemed miraculous. I couldn't account for it. Nothing could exist beyond that gap in the shelf.

I pressed my face against the stone.

"Ray. Look at me."

The wind lifted my poncho and teased through my shirt and sweater. I was shaking. The cold, I told myself. A series of muscular spasms ran through my arms, to the tips of my fingers. I tried to make myself part of the wall, use its solidness to stop the jerking.

"Ray. Don't lock up. You can get over here. Really."

There was movement at my right. Hollenbeck, side-stepping toward me. He stopped within arm's length.

"Let's not get in the way of progress," he said. I could hear him trying to make it light, hear the effort it took.

"What are you going to do, George? Kick me off?"

"If I have to. But first we'll try less drastic methods."

The rain was heavier. It ran off the poncho's hood and down into my eyes as I tried to look at him.

"You haven't seen what we've got to cross. There's no place to put your feet. What're we supposed to do?"

"Listen to him. He got over. He says we can do it too."

"He says."

"The little bastard hasn't been wrong yet."

From my left, Charles was calling my name.

"At least look at him, Ray."

I turned my head so that we could see each other, Charles and I.

"Now listen to him."

"A nice hold for your left hand," Charles was saying. "A

couple of steps farther and you can grab that crack. Use it all the way across."

"Tell you how I plan to do it," Hollenbeck said. "I mean after you're over. I'm going to stand where you are now and imagine myself being where Charles is. I'm going to see myself there. It's practically done already. I'm just about there."

It seemed like a good idea, one of those mental tricks that sounds reasonable enough if you're sitting in a chair in a warm room. But I couldn't see myself on the mantel. I had trouble accepting Charles there.

The wind slammed into us. I tried to become stone, blend into the wall.

"All right, this is crazy, this is enough," Hollenbeck said. He was shouting, not to overcome the gust. From sudden rage. "All you have to do is move. Shit. Just move. Charles made it over and I'm going to. You move. That's all. Move that damn leg. You can't even do that. You worthless puke."

It was hatred, pure and uncontrived and real. I had to get away from it. My left leg made an involuntary shuffle that my right leg matched, and I was maybe six inches closer to Charles.

"Shit, go on," Hollenbeck said. "Don't stop now."

I began to shuffle toward Charles again, the sill tapering further, extracting itself from under my heels.

Charles was talking me over. He told me to wait, there's the hand hold, grab it.

I reached. It was icy. My mitten slipped on it. I brought the hand down and pulled the mitten away with my teeth. Then the other, switching grips on the wall, until I had both mittens in my right hand.

I wanted to put them into the pocket of the poncho. But it didn't open right, I missed the slit, and the mittens fell when I let go.

I lifted my right elbow and looked down and watched them fall.

"It doesn't matter," Hollenbeck said.

The hold was still icy, but with a bare palm I had a better

grip. A couple of steps farther along I found the crack, and I was across, stepping onto Charles's mantle. I joined him there. So did Hollenbeck.

————

I suppose the glacier should have frightened me at least as much. It was long and steep, and if any of us had misstepped we'd have been gone.

It wouldn't have been possible without the crampons and the ice axe. The crampons in particular. Charles said they were nonadjustable, so whoever wore the boots that fit them best would have to lead across. I don't believe I was even surprised to find that they went on my boots as if they belonged there.

You're supposed to have a pick in each hand for ice climbing; so Charles told me, several weeks after the fact. We had only the axe, and I needed that for cutting steps. But Charles got out a piton, told me to hold it in my left hand, drive it into the glacier and it would help to hold me. He told me how to use the front points, kick them in, use the crampons as a platform.

Hollenbeck gave me his gloves, and before I stepped out he said, Look at it this way. If we punch out now at least we'll be choosing which way we die—not everybody can do that.

The crampons really do work. They're almost miraculous, the way they drive into ice and hold. I went across without panic, stopping every couple of feet to punch out footwells for the others, swinging the adz end of the axe, bashing out shards of ice that skipped and bounced as they skittered down the side of the mountain.

I felt no panic. Maybe believed. Or maybe we all have an allotment for fear, and I had exhausted mine.

By late morning we were across the high valley, at the head of the long boulderfield. By mid afternoon we had reached the end of the boulders. In between we had taken half a dozen falls apiece. Charles had bashed his face bloody, and I had a bone bruise on my coccyx that would be tender for the next two months.

The meadow, the trailhead, were pulling us down by then. I mean tearing at us. The snowpack thinned as we descended; feeling it ankle deep was like throwing off shackles.

For more than an hour we lurched and stumbled down the trail, fell and picked ourselves up and lurched again.

About a mile from the meadow Charles fell hard, bounced off a tree, and slid down into the stream that ran beside the trail. Hollenbeck and I got him out, but when he tried to stand the ankle gave way.

I caught him when he tried again.

"I don't believe this," he said. "You guys go. Go on, one of you anyway. It's not far. I'll get there."

Hollenbeck didn't argue, but took off his pack and emptied it into mine. All but a folding knife. He opened the blade.

He asked Charles, "How much do you weigh?" As he hacked at the bottom of the pack.

"A hundred ten. Before I left home."

"You must be less than that now."

He made two holes in the bottom. He held the pack and told Charles to step in, one leg into each hole.

Charles refused and Hollenbeck said, "If we're going to walk out together I don't see any other way."

It slowed him some. Some. We got to the meadow just before dusk. I expected that we'd have that one last mile to walk, out to the highway. But during the afternoon the rain had turned to snow, and when we walked into the meadow there were some teenagers with pickups and Jeeps. The kids were drinking beer, throwing snowballs, yelling and squealing.

One of them heaved a snowball our way, and they laughed; we were still some way off, and the evening was dense. We got closer, and they could see our faces, and after that there were no more snowballs and no more laughing.

27

They took us to a hospital. The engine's rumble and the whine of tires on asphalt were unnervingly loud, and in town the lights—street lights and store signs and traffic signals and cars' headlights—slapped my face.

At the emergency room an orderly put us in wheelchairs, and before things began to happen the three of us sat together for a couple of minutes. Under shadowless fluorescence I saw Charles and Hollenbeck as we must have appeared to everyone else. I saw the dirt, the lumps and bruises and dried blood, the gaunt shock of their faces. We could have been human debris. In a way we were.

Hollenbeck glanced at me, and for that moment we were still up there, surviving, existing as we had existed for days: not so much in skin and muscle and sensation as in the mind. Then a doctor was standing over Hollenbeck, trying to talk to him. A nurse began tugging off my jacket so that she could take my blood pressure, and the orderly was wheeling Charles behind a curtain.

The nurse said, "A sweater too—what else are you hiding under there?"

I tried to answer, couldn't speak. When I looked back at him, Hollenbeck was talking to the doctor. He was gone from me; and the mountains were gone, and the snow and the black wind and the desperation were gone.

"I'm full of surprises," I said. "Always something up my sleeve."

The next couple of hours I remember as a disjointed series of episodes separated by periods of creamy oblivion. All I wanted was sleep. I kept passing out and people kept pulling me back. There was a sheriff's deputy asking questions; a doctor holding back my eyelids to shine in a searing white point of light; the orderly stripping my clothes, bathing me, lifting me into bed; the nurse sticking an IV needle into one arm.

And finally Andrea beside the bed, her face inches from mine, speaking words I either didn't hear or didn't retain. But I remember that she put her hand on my cheek, an inexpressible bleakness in her touch. I wanted to tell her about Gary, all the rest. I babbled something, but I could see that it didn't connect—I was exhausted, and there was really nothing to say, after all. Her sad face was the last I saw before I went under again.

And then I slept. I slept.

———

Charles and Hollenbeck were in the room when I woke. Charles wearing a hospital gown, sitting up on the edge of the second bed; George in a chair between us. I stirred and grunted, and they both looked over at me.

I was glad to see them there—it was the first thing I felt, that we belonged together. Then I realized that my throat was parched, and that I was ravenous. Then noticed gray light behind the venetian blinds and tried to place myself in the flux of time.

"How late is it?"

Hollenbeck stood beside my bed.

"Afternoon of the next day," he said. "You've been asleep

about eighteen hours. The doctor let me go this morning. He wants to hold on to you two until tomorrow."

Only then, finally, I remembered unfinished business.

I said, "Eleanor—she okay?"

"She's still there," Charles said.

"Shit. Somebody has to get them down."

Hollenbeck was walking to the window, parting the curtains, raising the blinds. The gray I had seen was the light of late afternoon, diffused through low, deep clouds that seemed to writhe. I realized that the movement was the rocking, unhurried fall of big snowflakes.

"It's been doing that since last night," Hollenbeck said. "Nobody's going up until it stops."

I counted back through sunrises and sunsets, through the sleet and the clinging to rock, through the hours and hours of walking. Three days and two nights since we had left the shelter. I thought of what can happen in three days.

Charles said, "Today's Friday. Friday the nineteenth. This was supposed to be the last day of the trip. We were going to be walking out right about now."

The idea of supposed-to-be, the image of us intact, tramping together to the end of trail, made me think of Poague. I asked about him.

"Poague split a week ago," Hollenbeck said. "He's been back at work since Monday."

I imagined him in his office, in the existence that from Beartooth Plateau had seemed so distant as to be fantastic. Having leaped so easily that chasm between worlds.

I said, "I guess that surprises me."

"It surprised me too," Hollenbeck said.

"I mean, I don't know what I expected. But I sort of assumed that he was hanging in there with us, you know? It's like he ran out on us."

"That's how it hit me."

From over on his bed Charles said, "He didn't know what was happening."

I said I understood that. But I told him it still didn't feel right—it felt like a shitty thing for him to have done.

"You don't know what's in somebody," Charles said. His voice seemed stressed, almost overloaded. "People have their reasons, that's all I'm saying. You can't ever tell."

———

All through the next day the snow continued. The day after that, a Sunday, the snow turned to rain down in Red Lodge. But the sky was still too low for mountain flying.

By then Charles and I were out of the hospital. The three of us had taken rooms in a motel at the southern edge of town. Andrea had been there all week. The lobby had a big picture window, a view of the mountains, and we spent hours there together watching clouds mill and roil around the peaks.

Nothing we had done in the past two weeks was more difficult, more excruciating, than that wait. We had felt the lash of wind and sleet under those clouds, had felt the cold as it chased us into the burrow of our bags. We knew. Even worse, we could imagine.

On Sunday evening we went out to dinner. On the way back I stopped at the front desk to check for messages; the sheriff had said he would tell us when he planned to call for a chopper.

At the desk, the clerk said to someone over my shoulder, "This is Mister Furlow."

I had glanced at him when I came in. A man about my age, my height—but not at all like me. Flawless teeth set off a uniform tan on a seamless face. A crew-neck sweater with a snowflake design across the chest, stretch ski pants, après-ski boots of furred cowhide. Perfectly arranged.

"I'm Coleman Farris," he said; but I think I guessed it before the words were out. "I'd have been here sooner. But I was out of town, and the sheriff had trouble getting in touch with me."

He seemed uncertain about whether to offer his hand. Or maybe he was sensing my own indecision. After a few seconds he settled it by sticking both hands behind his back, and he said, "I wanted to see someone who has seen Eleanor."

"Well. I saw her. That was Wednesday. I guess you know that. She was okay then. I don't know what else to say."

I looked at him and tried to remember the last time I had beheld someone so wonderfully put together, both by birth and conscious effort. And I realized: Travis.

"This isn't an accusation," he said. "But I keep asking myself. How is it that you and the other two are here? And she's still there? How does that happen?"

At first I didn't answer. I knew I ought to be angry. But I didn't feel it. I kept looking at his outfit. The clothes looked new, and it occurred to me that he might have bought them within the last couple of hours, after he arrived in Billings, so that he'd be acceptably dressed. His idea of mountain wear.

He looked so prim. So damn innocent.

He said, "I guess you were afraid she might slow you down, and none of you get through."

"No. She'd have done as well as anyone else. We wanted her to leave with us. She wanted to stay."

"Why didn't you make her come?"

"She wanted to stay. So she stayed. Nobody could make her leave."

I could see him try to work through that one, then put it aside.

"Because of this boy?"

"Donnie."

"What's so special about him, that she would do this?"

"He's just a boy. She thought he needed her. I don't know what to tell you."

He didn't understand: this wasn't about Donnie, or about her. All that counted was the place, what the place had done to us, what we had been through.

Something nagged at me. Something I needed to know. I remembered: left hand, ring finger.

"This is a nightmare," he said. His arms were folded. I could see the finger—he wore a wedding band. I wondered whether he had replaced it at the same time he bought the outfit. To complete his suitable attire. "I can't believe this is happening. My wife stranded in a place like that."

"They've got a good shelter," I said. "Their sleeping bags were dry—that's important. And she has a lot of strength. You probably don't believe that, but it's true."

"I hope to hell you're right," he said. He left me standing there.

I was in my room, ten minutes later, when Andrea called. The sheriff had told her the front was clearing, the National Guard would have a helicopter ready at first light.

28

Early dawn, we stood at the air strip outside town. Andrea and Charles and Hollenbeck and me. Cole Farris. A sheriff's deputy. A paramedic. Two search dogs—German Shepherds—with their handlers, down from Billings.

The chopper came out of the southeast, and landed in front of us at almost the exact moment of sunrise. It was a Huey. There was room for the searchers and their dogs, for the deputy and the paramedic and for one of us, someone who knew where the shelter was.

The deputy had already chosen Charles, to save weight.

Two dogs, five people. The chopper swallowed them up, lifted off, dipped its nose and clattered west toward the peaks.

Charles never went into much detail about the next few hours. I never pressed him, either. All that really matters is the outcome, and that had been decided hours, maybe days, earlier, while the snow still fell up there.

Finding the ridge was no problem. Charles had the pilot hold three hundred degrees from the pass above Exile Lake. It was all so easy, Charles told me later; everything laid out below so plainly.

He could see that there had been much more snow. Where we had bivouacked in the trees, only the tops of the highest pines showed through.

They found the ridge, but no sign of the cleft rock or the shelter. They swept back and forth, dropped lower, until Charles saw a dimple in one of the white swells. They dropped to within eight, ten feet above it. The surface was crusted, so it didn't blow. He could see that the dimple was the shelter's passageway, clotted with snow.

Charles kept waiting for Eleanor to emerge, come clawing toward the noise. But nothing happened. The pilot let the chopper down until its skids were almost touching the surface, and they all jumped out. The deptuy and the searchers with their dogs, the paramedic, and then Charles last, all leaping into chest-high snow.

The deputy and the paramedic crawled into the shelter. A couple of minutes later the snow above it began to quake, and then it burst. The deputy stood up. He was pushing away the tarp and the snow, laying open the pocket within the cleft.

Charles tried to get closer. He saw the paramedic bending over someone. Over Donnie. There was nobody else.

They called the chopper close again, got a litter off one of the skids, strapped Donnie into it. He looked dead, but Charles thought that the paramedic wouldn't be bothering with a cadaver. They lifted the litter, the paramedic jumped up with it, and the chopper was gone.

Charles fought through the snow until he was standing where the shelter had been. It was the only bare spot for as far as he could see. There were two sleeping bags. One of them had been cut open—he thought the paramedic must have done that, to get at Donnie. The other one had to belong to Eleanor. He saw the stove, two empty fuel bottles, a pack that lay almost flat.

The deputy was asking him where she could have walked. Charles told him there was no place to go. Then he remembered that when the trickle nearby had frozen, I had hiked down to the stream. He saw that there were no water bottles, and he knew where she had gone.

————

I can't see belaboring this. I don't have the heart.

Travis's body stayed buried until the snow melted in the chute. Some hikers found it. That was June.

Within an hour after the chopper had taken him off the ridge, Donnie was at a hospital in Billings; two hours more, on an operating table for neurosurgery. For months all I learned of him was from Charles, who had been told by Andrea that he had survived, would never walk or talk. It was more than I wanted to know.

After three days of searching, one of the dogs found Eleanor—dead—about a mile south of what would have been the direct path between the shelter and the stream. She wore a backpack, and the water bottles inside it were full, frozen. The sheriff supposed that she had gone to get water, had become lost in the storm, and died before she could find her way back.

Some images I refuse to assimilate. That's one: Eleanor lifeless. I won't let myself see it.

Not that I'm denying the fact of her death. I can tell you exactly the time and place when I realized it: the afternoon of the third day of the search, before the dog turned up her body, but long past any real hope that she survived. The lobby of the motel.

Andrea was driving Charles and Hollenbeck to the airport. Only Cole Farris and I were left, the two of us waiting in the lobby, standing a few feet apart, alone. Even the desk clerk had stepped away for a few minutes.

A sheriff's deputy came in from outside. Cole saw him first, and went over to him. But the deputy would have spoken to Cole first, anyway. Her husband.

I didn't have to hear the words. I could see Cole shriveling where he stood, crumbling from the inside out until there was nothing to support the stupid snowflake sweater and ski pants, nothing to fill those ridiculous furry boots. And I knew that she was gone.

29

Hollenbeck got home on a Wednesday evening, and was back at work Friday morning. I returned to D.C. six hours after he did, and I stayed away from the office for two and a half weeks. I slept late, read, went to the zoo, took the Metro downtown, browsed in the National Gallery. One afternoon my daughter cut class and we went to a matinee at a shopping mall.

I didn't once call in, didn't make excuses. I suppose I was daring Poague to fire me, but it didn't happen. Nothing happened. To my immense disappointment.

On a Monday morning, the second week in October, I drove into Bethesda, went to my cubicle, and logged in at 8:48 A.M. Maybe an hour later I looked up from my screen and caught Poague standing across the floor, positioned in such a way that he had clear sight of me through the opening in my cubicle. His face showed nothing. Nothing. After a few seconds he walked away.

My return attracted little more notice than if I had been absent for a long weekend. After two weeks, all curiosity about the ordeal had been expended on Hollenbeck; to have survived a Real Life Wilderness Adventure was no longer a novelty.

Anyway there was more substantial gristle to be chewed over. A few days after Poague came back to work, he ordered furnishings and equipment for a spare room in the office suite. The next day Noreen Poague walked in with him, and occupied the office. She came to work every day afterward.

Her duties were undefined, at least as far as we in the outer office were concerned. But she sat in on meetings in Poague's office, and like Poague patrolled the aisles and policed the workspaces. Not as aggressively as her husband, perhaps; not so abrupt and grating a presence. But she was there. No more seersucker shirtwaists, either. I'm a rube in such matters, but on three successive days I spotted her in a Nipon, a Blass, another Nipon. She wore her hair long, wore heels maybe a quarter of an inch higher than the manuals prescribe for female executives, and one morning when she walked past my cubicle I caught the scent of perfume, the hiss of silk, a flash of trim legs and emerald green fabric—and I could almost believe that Travis had wanted her before he ever knew there was the new job.

The job. Hollenbeck got it a couple of weeks before Christmas. But by then there was no more speculation about Poague's successor. That was clearly going to be Noreen. In October some office memoranda showed her initials beside his. By November, most bore hers alone. That included the one announcing Hollenbeck's promotion. Poague had always worked days as long as any of us, but that fall his hours became irregular. Sometimes he left for lunch and didn't return for the rest of the day. Sometimes he didn't come in at all. But there was no void of responsibility. When there was a decision to be made, we assumed that Noreen would make it, and she always did.

So Hollenbeck had no grand illusions about ascending to the throne. He did get a good raise, and an impressive office behind the double walnut doors. I was happy for him. In Montana he had lost thirty-seven pounds. He promptly gained back nine, enough that he didn't look gaunt, and he stopped there. What's surely more important, he took the new job as if he deserved it. Which he did.

I left MDC within three weeks after I returned to work. I went in one morning and knew I couldn't last to the end of the afternoon. I typed a letter of resignation on the computer, filed it with Poague's secretary, and left. When I returned a couple of hours later an envelope with my name sat on the desk at my work station.

It held a check for just under fifty thousand dollars, a year's salary less deductions and withholding.

I wanted to go to Poague and tell him that if this was severance pay it was too much, and if it was compensation for the Beartooths it could never be enough. But I didn't want to talk about the trip, least of all with Poague. And I had never before quibbled with the size of his checks. So I just took it and walked out and never went back.

After that I didn't see Hollenbeck as often. Even when we were still together in the office some awkwardness had inserted itself between us. Not that we were distant—just the opposite. We knew each other too well now; cordiality was no longer an option. But what had brought us close was gone, and nothing else felt right.

We didn't play racquetball any more.

———

I resumed the routine of books, museums, movies. It was my year to have Franny for Christmas, and we had a great week.

I didn't even think about another job. I tried not to think about Beartooth Plateau.

In January Poague died. Hollenbeck passed on the rumor of an inoperable malignancy in his brain, but all anyone in the office knew for certain was that he was dead and that there would be a memorial observance the following Tuesday.

It was a non-sectarian service at a mortuary chapel, annoyingly trite. At first I thought that somebody like Poague should have had better than a one-size-fits-all funeral. But I realized that Poague must have wanted it this way; he always knew what he wanted, and always got his way.

I called Charles in North Carolina; in Red Lodge we had exchanged phone numbers.

After we had chatted for a few seconds I said, "Charles, I have some bad news you ought to know."

He said, "Jonas, right?"

"Somebody called you already."

"No. He told me when we were in the mountains."

"He told you?" More than anything else I was shocked that Poague had confided in a boy, but not in Hollenbeck or me. "Why did he tell you?"

"I think he wanted to tell somebody."

"But why you?"

I let my bewilderment show through, I guess, because he snapped back, "I wasn't after any job." More softly he said, "I wasn't supposed to tell anybody else. I wanted to a couple of times, but I didn't. He really wanted to finish the trip. He said he was going to cancel it at first when he found out, but he decided to try it. He really loved the mountains."

"I know."

"He was a good guy, Ray. No kidding."

We talked for a couple more minutes, and the conversation wound down. I was ready to hang up. Before I could tell him good-bye he said, "I think about you. You doing okay up there?"

"I'm fine."

"We all did our best. We couldn't make it come out the way we wanted. You just go on, that's the way I feel about it."

30

In November I met a woman. A tall blonde named Karen, thirty, a commercial loan officer. We dated several times before Christmas, and decided that before spring we would take a vacation together. We made reservations for seven days on Kauai, end of February.

We rented a condominium near the beach. For six days we sat in the sun and made love in the afternoon, and drank, ate, indulged.

Our bedroom had a sliding glass door that faced the ocean. We kept it open after dark, to let in the warm breeze that blew off the water.

The last night, we lay naked above the sheets, sweaty with sex. She lightly held my hand. The breeze seemed cooler than before. I could feel it drying the perspiration from my bare skin, chilling me.

I got up to close the door. A window was open and I closed that, too. She looked curiously at me but didn't say anything. I got into bed, pulled the sheet around me, but it didn't help; I kept getting colder.

I began to shiver. She got up—still naked; I didn't see

how she could take the chill—and found a blanket. That didn't help, either. I shivered and shook. My feet ached. The last time they had hurt that way I was standing in snow, wear-wet boots.

She was asking me, "Are you all right? Ray? Honey? Say something."

Her voice was distant. I held the blanket around me; it had the feel of nylon, the bulk of a sleeping bag. The cold was looking for a way into my skin; I could feel it nibbling at the fabric. I shook and shuddered.

It passed after a few minutes. But by then she was in a chair across the room, looking at me as if she were afraid I would come too close.

––––––

The next morning we left. The connection was through Los Angeles, with a layover of about two hours.

A few minutes before we were supposed to board the flight to Dulles I told her to go without me. She didn't argue.

From L.A. there's at least one flight to San Francisco every half hour. I caught the first one I could. The cab ride to Tiburon was more than forty dollars. At the door the maid told me the Langs were out of town, but if I wanted to see Donnie, that was okay. She showed me into the living room, and left. One wall of the room was glass. It looked south, toward San Francisco, and I stood at the window and looked at the city across the bay, breakwaters and docks and harbors that nibbled at the water, stacks of offices and apartments that ate into the sky.

I heard feet on the carpet, and a soft mechanical squeak.

He was in a wheelchair. I had prepared myself for that. But I wasn't ready for Donnie. He had lost at least twenty pounds. Flaccid skin sagged over shrunken muscles in his face and his forearms. He sat in the chair as if he had been dropped there, arms and legs and spine carelessly, randomly, arranged by someone other than himself.

Behind him was a tall man—a kid, actually; he had acne,

couldn't have been more than a few years older than Donnie—
who was pushing the chair into the room.

He said his name was Ricky, and he was Donnie's nurse.

"I'm a friend of his," I said. "I'd like to be with him for
a few minutes."

"Sure. Whatever. He's all yours. He has trouble holding
his water. He wets himself, you let me know."

He pushed the chair to face the sofa, and left. I was alone
with Donnie.

He might have been dead, he was so still. All but his eyes.
They followed me when I went over to the sofa. I sat in front
of him. They were as vivid as ever, the eyes. He was alive inside them.

"I hope you don't mind," I said. "I had to see you. It
seemed important. I don't know why."

He might have been angry, or joyous, or just bored. The
eyes didn't change, only bubbled and flashed. They were surrounded by deadness, and alone they were inarticulate.

"It seems like a stupid idea now. Maybe you don't even
want me here. I never thought of that. I won't be long, I
promise."

Nothing moved on him. Nothing around him. His eyes
were fixed on me, and I wondered what the world and I
looked like from in there.

I began to tell him about the others, about Eleanor and
Poague and the rest. For the first couple of minutes I felt as
awkward as if I were talking aloud to myself. I made myself
remember the boy I had known in the Beartooths, and told
myself that he was still in there, somewhere. That made it
easier.

"George is doing great," I said. I told him about the job.
"I talked to Charles a while back, and he sounded good. He's
going to end up doing something terrific. I know it."

I stopped and let him watch me.

"I've been so-so. Things have sort of fallen apart in my
life. I don't mean to sound sorry for myself. I'm not blaming
it on the trip. I mean, things have been pointing in that direc-

tion. It's not like this is something that happened in the last few months."

For a while I didn't say anything. We just looked at each other; during those moments I may have been as motionless as he.

Softly I said, "Do you do anything? At all?"

His arms lay on the side rail of the chair. At first nothing happened. Then I noticed movement below the left wrist, a minute contraction of the fingers, the joints bending, fingertips curling inward toward the palm. They halted in an open clench, then slowly relaxed.

I got off the couch and stood in front of the chair. I knelt in front of the chair.

"I've been thinking about you a lot. I've been thinking about what happened. I can't talk to anybody else about it. With Charles and Andrea, the telephone, it doesn't work. I see George every now and then, but I know it's over as far as he's concerned. He kept what he wanted out of it and got rid of the rest.

"I'm not knocking him. I think it's great. I wish I could do that. I have to do that."

I found my right hand holding the fingers of his left. They were limp.

"The ones that are dead are gone. All the others are leaving. I feel like it's you and me, still up there."

Now the fingers were tightening. His eyes snapped and burned. I looked into them, spoke directly at them.

"Here's the thing about it. I've got to get down. That's all. I feel bad about it. I feel like you're going to be alone up there again, and I'm sorry. I really am. That's the only place it made any sense, but I can't stay there any more."

His fingers held me. I know his arm didn't move, but all the same I felt those fingers drawing me toward him.

I held him with my free arm. I told him, I'm sorry, I've got to get off the hill, It's just too real. His cheek was on my cheek. They were wet where they touched. Wet at first with my tears, then with ours.

———

A warm afternoon, spring on the verge of summer. I rock in the front porch swing. Wind blows the leaves, dogs bark, kids shout in the street.

I can remember being sure about life and people during those few days in the Beartooths. It was all so sharp-edged and defined. But down here the edges got dulled, the definite became ambiguous, imponderable. There's truth in the mountains, but it doesn't travel well. You can't spend that currency anyplace else.

But I can live with ambiguity; it's the one change I see in myself since I left the Beartooths. I might have wished that I had walked out stronger, or smarter, or more resolute. But I don't believe I did. The only difference in me is this: in human affairs, I no longer ask why.

Lately, without trying, I have thought a lot about my father. About his conviction that I had betrayed our station.

In truth, I have accomplished far less than I might have. For a long while I blamed his stifling expectations. I used to tell him that if he had asked less, I might have been free to deliver more.

It seemed a good argument and I used it often. He would absorb it with a slow shake of the head and an infuriating smile. Now I know that he understood what I have only begun to grasp: that nothing is more ephemeral than intentions and motives, and that when those are gone there remains the stark enduring evidence of deeds done or left undone.